YARA'S
SPRING

YARA'S SPRING

JAMAL SAEED
&
SHARON E. McKAY

annick press
toronto + berkeley

To my sons, Ghamr and Taim, and their peers. —J.S.

To my sons, Sam and Joe. —S.E.M.

We acknowledge the support of the Canada Council for the Arts and the Ontario Arts Council,
and the participation of the Government of Canada/la participation du gouvernement du Canada
for our publishing activities.

ONTARIO ARTS COUNCIL
CONSEIL DES ARTS DE L'ONTARIO
an Ontario government agency
un organisme du gouvernement de l'Ontario

Library and Archives Canada Cataloguing in Publication

Title: Yara's spring / Jamal Saeed & Sharon E. McKay.
Names: Saeed, Jamal, 1959- author. | McKay, Sharon E., author.
Identifiers: Canadiana (print) 20200194127 | Canadiana (ebook) 20200200798 | ISBN 9781773214399
(softcover) | ISBN 9781773214405 (hardcover) | ISBN 9781773214436 (PDF) | ISBN 9781773214412
(HTML) | ISBN 9781773214429 (Kindle)
Classification: LCC PS8637.A34 Y37 2020 | DDC jC813/.6—dc23

Published in the U.S.A. by Annick Press (U.S.) Ltd.
Distributed in Canada by University of Toronto Press.
Distributed in the U.S.A. by Publishers Group West.

Printed in Canada

annickpress.com
sharonmckay.ca
nahidkazemi.com

Also available as an e-book. Please visit annickpress.com/ebooks for more details.

MIX
Paper from
responsible sources
FSC® C103567

There is hope after despair and
many suns after darkness.

—Rumi

THE END

AZRAQ REFUGEE CAMP, JORDAN
2016

T he morning sun was a thin, orange strip on the horizon. Spinning golden sand blurred the rows and rows of the camp's rectangular tin shelters. Around Yara, women charged the wind, their eyes blinking under sand-encrusted scarves, their long black gowns slapping against their ankles like the beating wings of crows.

She felt the scribbled note in the pocket of her jeans. It read:

> *Stop by the office tomorrow. Mr. Matthew wants*
> *to see you.*
>
> —*Lina*

The note had been delivered to her shelter last night. She hadn't slept since. What did he want? Had her application to go to a foreign country been rejected? Had they discovered that she had lied? That she had killed a man?

The rules are clear: if a lie is discovered on your immigration application, it will be terminated immediately, Mr. Matthew had said.

Yara moved through the camp, a long-limbed, sixteen-year-old girl who walked with purpose. From afar, she had the body of a long-distance runner. Up close she looked like a girl who had been half-starved for a long, long time.

It wasn't Yara's beauty that made her unforgettable. Her arched eyebrows and razor-sharp cheekbones were intimidating. Her brown eyes shot through with bolts of gold gave her the look of a tiger. She held her head high on thin shoulders that were as straight as arrows. But the set of her mouth, her clenched jaw, and a chewed lower lip told the real story. She had seen things, done things. She might have looked sixteen but inside she was old. Fifty? A hundred? How, in a war, could it be otherwise?

The office was ahead. It was a long, temporary shelter made of tin. Squinting, she could make out the blue letters "UN" on the office door, and beneath the letters, the name:

MATTHEW MCGONAGALL
Counselor

Yara climbed three shaky wooden steps and knocked. "*Marhaba!*" she called out, offering hello in Arabic. She pressed her ear to the door. "*Marhaba, Lina!*" Lina was

Mr. Matthew's Jordanian assistant. She was kind and soft-spoken, with dark eyes rimmed in charcoal-black. She was not much older than Yara, maybe eighteen or nineteen?

"Hello? Mr. Matthew, hello!" Yara tried English this time and again hammered the door. Still nothing. But Mr. Matthew often worked in the early morning, before the heat of the day set in. He used to call himself "Matt," but his Jordanian co-workers had laughed. "Matt" in Arabic meant "died."

And his last name was unpronounceable. *Mick-gooo-naa*? No. *Mack-gone-gal*? They had agreed that "Mr. Matthew" would do.

He was from Canada. Or maybe Scotland. But the Scots talked differently, didn't they? He had red hair that lit up his head like he was on fire. His eyes were pale blue, like water. And he was big—not fat, but when he stood up from his desk it seemed as if the tin walls of his office might burst apart.

"Hello?" Yara called out again. Still nothing. "Damn," she mumbled. It was her favorite English word. She gave up and thumped back down the steps. If she returned to her shelter she would be put to work changing, washing, and feeding babies. And she was so tired.

There was only one place she could hide and wait for Mr. Matthew or Lina to open the office.

Head bowed, Yara covered her mouth with the end of her headscarf and trudged on.

The hospital with the new maternity wing was to her right; the community hall was to her left, and there was a basketball court beside it. The main gate was ahead. Even this early there were boys clustered around the gate like bees. Likely they had not been to bed. This was the place where recruiters for ISIS, al-Nusra, and other gangs chanted into young boys' ears: *Make your life worthy of Allah and join us in the fight against the infidels.*

The United Nations guards chased the recruiters away, but they came back and back and back—waves of black-toothed, evil men with sneers on their lips and dull, empty eyes.

This was also the place where rich men from other countries came to buy girls. They wanted wives, or so they said. Yara pursed her lips so tight they went white. She knew the English words for it: human trafficking. She knew better words: *tijarato ar-raqeeq,* slave trading.

They were told that they were safe in the camp but only if they were not stupid, another good English word.

A boy spotted her. "Where are you going?" he called out. "Come and talk with us. We can make you rich."

Yara hunched her shoulders and pulled her headscarf down over her forehead. She wished the UN guards would chase the boys away, too. But where would they go? Back to crowded shelters that stank of dirty diapers.

"Hey, *sharmouta!*" The boys came closer.

Yara spun around, fists clenched. There were three of them. How old were they? Ten? Eleven? In the early light she could make out their shapes but not their features. They stood with their feet rooted like trees.

"*Sharmouta! Sharmouta! Sharmouta!*" they chanted. Prostitute? Were they calling her a prostitute? Did they think she would take their dirty talk?

"You are old. You need a husband," one yelled again while the other two laughed. "We can get you a husband," the second boy shouted. Rage surged through her as fast and hot as a bullet. "Fifty American dollars—that is what we can get for you. Maybe a hundred!" All three boys stomped about and cheered.

On the ground in front of her was a round gray rock. It fit perfectly into the palm of her hand. As her arm crested into an arc above her head, the rock sailed gracefully up into the air and disappeared into the grainy mist. *Thud*. A scream. Her eyebrows arched and her mouth twitched into a smile. She had hit her mark.

"Come and get me, dirty donkeys," she growled through clenched teeth. One boy was making mewing sounds, likely the one who got hit. Good. The others had stopped dead in their tracks.

"YOU ARE DONKEYS!" she yelled. She had called them idiots. They reared back like pack animals.

A man, likely a guard, called out, "What's going on?"

Yara waited. She heard the stupid boys' retreating footsteps. "Cowards," she muttered. "COWARDS!" she shrieked.

The guard called out something else. His voice was only an echo now. He was following the boys.

The tip of her shoe stubbed against another rock. The donkeys might return. She crouched. Her fingers curled around another lucky find. It was a hunk of concrete. It would do.

The wind blew stronger and faster. Nearly blind from the sand, Yara stumbled into the school area that was tucked behind the basketball court. Nine tin shelters used as classrooms were boxed in a large square play space. There was a nook, a small opening between two buildings that shielded her from the wind and prying eyes. It was a good place to hide. Privacy was a precious thing in the camp.

Slipping between the buildings, with her back pressed against a wall, Yara slid down until she sat on her heels. Cradling the small chunk of concrete against her chest, she pulled out the tobacco pouch from the pocket of her jeans and sniffed it, getting whiffs of apple spiced tobacco. "Oh, Baba," she whispered. She rested her chin on her knees, hugged her legs, and closed her eyes. She was so tired.

There were five people she truly loved left in the world. Of the five, three were in great danger. As for the others who had died, she knew now that it was possible to love the dead as much as the living.

"Uncle Sami, I remember. I remember. I remember that I am loved," she whispered. Tears caught in her eyelashes. "Remember the good times. Remember how it was. Remember the days before it all changed. Don't cry. Don't cry. It doesn't help. Don't cry."

PART 1
Life in Aleppo

CHAPTER 1

ALEPPO, SYRIA
March 11, 2011

Yara slept in. She wouldn't have if she'd had her own phone. Cellphones came with alarms. But Mama said that a ten-year-old girl did not need a cellphone. *Wait, wait, wait.* She forgot. It was Friday. No school today!

Kicking off the sheets, Yara leapt out of bed and stood on her tiptoes. Friday was *Samah* dance class at the cultural center. Nana would take her. Arms up, she pinched pretend veils in her fingers. "Twirl. Lower arms. Softly! Softly, girls! Raise arms. Twirl," Yara said, in her dance teacher's crisp voice. *Pay attention, girls,* the teacher would repeat. *Twirl.*

And then she had a brilliant idea! Mama would make her those balloon pants, like a genie in a bottle. "Lift arms. Twirl again, girls, and again, and again." Yara loved dance class. She loved swimming more but it was March, and the pool didn't open until May. Women and girls swam on Fridays from 10:00 a.m. to 4:00 p.m. Mama had promised her a new swimsuit, a two-piece with a little skirt. "Twirl. Twirl."

"Yara, come and eat," Nana called up the stairs.

No genie pants today! She pulled a dress over her leggings and padded down the stairs to the kitchen, skipping over the last two steps, the ones that squeaked like a trapped mouse. The diesel generator hummed in the distance. Mama and Baba were already at work in the bakery. The smell of baked almonds and buttery-crisp sugar cookies with nutmeg and cinnamon filled the air! There was a faint, sour smell of diesel oil, too.

"You must get your deliveries done before dance class," said Nana as Yara plopped down at the table. Yara rolled her eyes. Of course. Folding a small piece of bread between her thumb and fingers, Yara scooped up the creamy yogurt and topped her creation with a slice of fried eggplant.

"Will Shireen come with us, too?" Yara mumbled.

"Do not talk with your mouth full. I will call her mother," said Nana.

Mama and Shireen's mother were best friends, so even though Shireen was eleven years old, almost twelve, and Yara a pitiful, miserable ten, they played together. Maybe "play" was the wrong word. It wasn't like they played dolls. Mostly they talked, although Yara couldn't say exactly what they talked about.

Yara swallowed. "Can we pick up Kasandra on the way?" Kasandra was her other best friend. It was supposed to be a big secret, but Kasandra's family was planning on moving to Germany or Australia or someplace far, far away. Imagine petting a kangaroo! Could you pet a kangaroo? Would they bite? She'd seen a cartoon of a kangaroo boxing once. Was that for real or made up?

"Yara! *Yara.*" Nana lowered her voice. Other people's voices went up when they were cross. Nana's voice went down. Nana was not a normal grandmother. "Did you hear me?" she asked, hands on hips. Yara shook her head. "I said Kasandra can meet us there. Now, go see your parents." Nana rolled up the sleeves of her deep-purple gown, her *abaya*, and plunged her hands into soapy water.

Nana did not especially like Shireen or her parents, despite the fact that her father was a professor. Roja, Shireen's mother, taught classes at the university, too. It wasn't that there was anything wrong with Shireen's parents—Yara thought they were wonderful—it was just that Nana believed one could only trust family. And then it might also have had something to do with the fact that Nana did not like Yara visiting Shireen's house when Shireen's twin brother, Ali, was around. *I don't care how modern our country has become, a girl should not be alone with a boy without a family member present,* Nana repeated over and over and over and over and over until Yara wanted to put her hands over her ears and scream, "STOP!"

Nana was always talking about "family." But they hardly had any family! Baba's brothers and sisters had left Syria years ago, and Mama had only one brother, Uncle Sami.

Yara shoved the last bit of food in her mouth. "Finished," she announced.

"Go." Nana waved Yara away as though she were an irritating fly.

Barefoot and flying, Yara raced down the path that connected the bakery to the house. Purple and red bougainvillea climbed wooden arches and trellises on either side of the path, and small lemon trees in giant pots gave the air a tangy, sweet smell.

It was twelve long, leaping jumps from the house to the bakery. Three, four, five . . . "Ahhh!" she cried, hopping on one foot.

"Yara, YARA!" Mama came running out of the bakery, wisps of flour floating around her like tiny clouds. "What's happened?"

"I stubbed my toe." Yara, near tears, glared at the potted lemon tree, half expecting it to apologize.

Nana, standing in the doorway, clucked her tongue against her teeth. "Such noise!"

"Hush now, sweet girl." Mama wrapped her arms around her daughter.

The pain, at first as sharp as a hammer blow, turned into a pulsing throb. Yara looked over Mama's shoulder. Nana was gone. She bit down on her lip. She could break a leg and Nana would still tell her not to make a fuss.

Mama rubbed Yara's sore toe. "Are you all right now?" She planted a kiss on her daughter's forehead. Yara nodded. Mama was as kind and soft as the dough she turned into bread. Her hair was covered with a ruby-red headscarf, making her coal-black eyes stand out like black pearls. (*Black pearls!* Those were Baba's words. They made Yara laugh and Mama's face glow like she was standing in front of a hot oven.) Even wearing baggy pants and a loose tunic tied with a brown leather belt, her mother was, in Yara's eyes, the most beautiful mother in all of Aleppo.

"Where are my helpers?" Baba hollered from the bakery.

"Coming!" Mama laughed, and Yara managed a weak smile.

Baba, dusted in flour and wearing his black baker's hat, opened the oven and poked at the contents. "What happened out there? It sounded like a tiger attack."

"The pot of a lemon tree assaulted a toe," said Mama.

Baba pulled a tray of cookies out of the oven. The blast of warm air was honeyed and spicy and powerful enough to instantly cure a stubbed toe.

"Ahh, those vicious pots. I will make extra *barazek* cookies today just for my sweet girl," he added.

Yara grinned. Nana said that Baba spoiled her. Baba would reply to his mother-in-law, *Meat spoils, not children!* And Nana would respond with *Phah!* and a dismissive wave of her hand. It was always the same.

"How is your toe now?" Mama whispered as she hugged her daughter.

Yara rocked her head from side to side. It was fine.

"Look at my women," said Baba, who was not actually looking at either Mama or Yara but fiddling with the dials on the new stove. "You are as close . . . as . . . a rind on a lemon." He laughed. It was a game they played.

It was Mama's turn. She said, "We are all as close as . . ." She paused. "The skin on an olive!"

Yara giggled. Now it was her turn. *Think, think.* Yara squeezed her eyes shut. "We are as close . . ." She opened her eyes and saw a discarded piece of bread. "As close as crust on bread!" she cried, fist in the air. Baba and Mama cheered.

"Time for you to go," said Mama as she stood and adjusted her headscarf.

"What is our rule for today?" asked Baba as he examined the tray of cookies.

"I shall not tell a lie," replied Yara, feeling perfectly brilliant.

"Good," said Baba.

"I hope you obey that rule every day," Mama added dryly.

"My daughter will never lie." Baba's eyes twinkled. "Except"—he held up a hand—"to tell your grandmother that her sheets are the whitest sheets in the neighborhood."

"But what if they are not?" Yara grinned.

"You know what I mean." Baba pulled a second tray of cookies from the oven. Yara *did* know exactly what he meant. She reached for a sugar cookie.

"Careful, now, they are hot, and one injury is enough for today. The cookies will be here when you return from your deliveries." Mama spoke while stacking the bread on a length of cotton. "Give extra bread to Mr. Khalid. Your father passed him in the street yesterday and said that he did not look well. And the order for Khalto Beitar has doubled. She has had another baby—her tenth! Here, take cookies for her children." Mama rhymed off three more names before plopping the cotton-wrapped bread, and a small stack of warm cookies, in Yara's arms.

Their customers came to the shop, but Mama always made exceptions for regulars who were old or sick. Delivering bread to those in need was a "good deed." Mama planted a kiss on her forehead. "Give what you can, my daughter, even if it is only a smile. Off you go."

Yara slipped on the sandals she kept tucked under Baba's worktable and skipped out the front door of the bakery. The door banged behind her as Yara ran out onto the road, her long, dark hair flying behind her.

They lived in Bustan al-Qasr, in the middle of Aleppo. Their bakery was on a corner, and their two-story home was tucked behind it. The road in front of their bakery was wide enough for two cars to pass, but only if the cars were small. Big cars sometimes lost their side-view mirrors. A seven-story apartment building loomed behind their house and bakery. Shireen lived right across from the bakery in one of the most beautiful two-story houses on the street. It was a pity that Shireen's little house was squashed between two ugly concrete buildings.

Yara bolted down the cobblestone road and then turned into an alley. The air smelled of car fumes, dog dung, frying meat, and whiffs of coffee. Above, laundry strung from balcony to balcony created a multicolored cloth sky. Sheets crackled and flapped like sails.

"Yara. YARA!"

Yara turned at the sound of her name.

"Up here!" Kasandra waved from her apartment window three stories up. Horns honking, motors roaring and coughing, the shouting of street vendors, and the noon call to prayer all threatened to drown out her voice, but still she bellowed.

"Are you going to dance class?" Yara called.

Kasandra shook her head. "Baba is taking us to Darat Izza for a few weeks to stay with my grandparents." One of her little brothers poked his head out the window, too. Kasandra gave him a good swat.

"Weeks? What about school?" Yara cried, but all Kasandra did was wave. "Have a good time!" Yara sighed. She would have loved to go to the countryside.

The street underfoot was uneven but Yara was as sure-footed as a goat. She weaved and dodged around bicycles, cars, a mule and cart, and a boy roasting corn on the sidewalk. All around her the city was waking up. She loved her neighborhood. When she was small, Baba had carried her on his shoulders through the streets of Aleppo. The way he waved to friends, the way she bounced on his shoulders, it was as if he was telling the entire world, "Look at my daughter. Is she not the most beautiful child in the world?"

"Ammo Khalid, your bread!" Yara called to an old man. He wasn't really her uncle, but she called him "Ammo" out of respect. He sat on an overturned pail near the kabab seller.

"May God protect you." Ammo Khalid touched his hand to his heart in thanks and gave her a toothless, lopsided grin. Yara smiled back. It was curious. Why had he ended up here, alone, without family to care for him?

"Yara, come, come." The kabab-seller, standing a few feet away, motioned toward his smoking grill. "For you, *kabab halabi*, the best kabab in all of Aleppo!" He skewered a tasty, meaty morsel and passed it to her.

"Thank you." Yara beamed.

"You tell your father that he is the best baker in all of Aleppo." He laughed so hard his cheeks wobbled and his big belly bobbed up and down.

Yara's next stop was the home of Khalto Beitar. She and her ten children lived three floors above a shop in an ancient building. Yara trudged up the uneven stone stairs, clinging to a rope railing that went round and round, up and up, until at last she landed at a wooden door that stood wide open.

"For you," huffed Yara as she handed the bread to Khalto Beitar's oldest daughter. "And these are for the children." She drew in a deep breath as she handed over the cookies. "Is the new baby a boy or a girl?" she asked.

"A girl, thank goodness," the daughter replied as she wiped sweat from her forehead with the heel of her hand. Seven snot-faced, damp, and mostly hysterical little boys raced around the small apartment behind their exhausted sister. Two babies were in cribs by a window.

Yara pursed her lips. It would be awful to be so young and take care of so many children. "I'll come back on Monday with more bread. I promise." Yara smiled.

The grateful girl nodded and, to Yara's surprise, smiled back.

After three more deliveries Yara headed for home.

A neighbor, trailing her grandchildren, spoke as she hurried past. "Yara, I just passed someone you know in the street! A surprise awaits you at your house."

"Who is it?" Yara called back.

"Run home and you will see." The smiling woman went on her way.

Yara flew into the house. "Nana, Nana, is there a surprise?" She stopped and stood still, her words hanging in the air. The hallway was dark, with just a faint stream of light coming from a small window at the end. In the shadows stood a tall, muscular man with a bag at his feet. It took a moment for Yara's eyes to adjust, and then . . . "Uncle Sami," she screamed as she raced down the hall and flung herself into her uncle's open arms.

He swung her high in the air, then hugged her close. There were only moments to feel the warmth of him, feel his big bear arms holding her, before Nana came running down the stairs from the roof.

"What is it? What . . . Oh, Sami, my son, my son." Nana's voice warbled like a bird's as she hurled herself at Uncle Sami. Yara was squished between the two.

"Sami!" Yara heard her mother's voice now. Still cradled in her uncle's arms, Yara looked over his shoulder. Baba and Mama rushed towards them, leaving a trail of flour dust that winked in the fractured light. Uncle Sami's big arms reached out to his sister, and now they were all hugging and laughing while Baba stood back, rubbed his hands in a kitchen towel, and beamed.

Uncle Sami lived four hours away by car, in Damascus, where he was a high school teacher. He hadn't been home in months, and if you missed someone very much, months could feel like years.

"You are getting big, niece," said Uncle Sami as he set Yara down. The tips of her ears grew hot. She was the tallest girl in her class, and she hated it!

Nana, not ready to let go of her son, hung on to his huge frame moments longer. Mama, her eyes glistening, whispered to Yara, "The monkey in his mother's eye is a gazelle." What did that mean? Yara gave her mother a quizzical look. "It means that a mother thinks her son is the best of men." Mama nudged Yara and the two giggled. Uncle Sami was Nana's oldest child, her only son, and she loved him fiercely. Anyway, Uncle Sami *was* a gazelle, and so was Baba. Uncle Sami was tall, built like a soccer player, with flecks of silver in his hair. Baba was a little younger than Uncle Sami but quick and smaller, and his hair was jet-black. The white that dusted his head was flour!

"Come, sit. I will close the shop for an hour," said Baba.

"Fetch some cookies," Mama called out as she walked to the kitchen to make tea.

Nana, Uncle Sami, and Yara ignored the Western-style sofa in the middle of the room and sat on a soft mat against the wall. They fell gently into big, plump pillows. Yara cuddled in close to her uncle. Baba smelled of cinnamon, laurel soap, and sometimes of apple spiced tobacco, but Uncle Sami smelled of coffee and musk and the kind of smell men have when they work hard.

"How is your schoolwork, Yara?" Uncle Sami asked, his eyes crinkling in the corners. "If you are to be a doctor one day you will need good marks."

"A good marriage and many children is all a woman requires." Nana sniffed.

Uncle Sami laughed again. "Mama, you did not always believe that. And anyway, a woman can do many things at once."

"There is no sense putting ideas in her head," she added, her mouth pulled into a hard, thin line.

Mama returned with tea and Baba with cookies as Yara pulled her school notebooks out of her pink schoolbag. The room went quiet while Uncle Sami flipped through the pages, stopping to read an essay or the teacher's comments at the top of a test. She could see Mama's and Baba's smiling eyes over the rims of their teacups.

At last Uncle Sami patted the notebooks and said, "Such good work deserves a reward." From his own bag he took out two new notebooks, a book of stories and poetry, and a set of colored pencils.

"Thank you, thank you!" squealed Yara.

"Wait." Uncle Sami opened the book of poetry and read a line. "'I'm already drowning so why should I be afraid of getting wet?' You see, it is written by al-Mutanabbi." He tapped the page.

"What does that mean?" Yara tilted her head to one side.

"It means worry about the big things. Let little problems go," he replied, eyes twinkling, mouth curved in that familiar grin.

"I won't drown. I am a good swimmer!" Yara giggled, and Uncle Sami laughed, too, as he kissed the top of her head.

"Of all things, niece, know you are loved." He laughed again.

"Yara, fill your uncle's cup." Nana pursed her lips. "*Now*, Yara." She motioned to Uncle Sami's empty teacup. Uncle Sami winked at Yara. Head bowed so Nana could not see her smile, Yara poured out the tea.

"Have you met anyone yet, my son? A nice girl? Someone to marry?" Nana asked.

Yara's head snapped up. This was interesting. Had her uncle met someone? Nana believed that a man needed a woman to take care of him. *How else can a man eat a good meal?* she would say. Or, *Who will do a man's laundry and keep his house if not a wife?*

The lines between her uncle's eyes furrowed as deep as ruts in an old road. "Mama, this is not the time to marry. There is a revolution coming." His voice deepened.

Nana's eyes grew round. She looked over her shoulder as if someone, one of President al-Assad's soldiers, perhaps, was listening at the door! "Walls have ears," she hissed.

Uncle Sami reached for his mother's hand and, in a quiet voice, said, "This is why I came, to talk to you, Mama. I want you to understand. We can no longer live with oppression. We—"

"I do not understand. Why do you talk about politics? Do you need a reason to visit your family?" Nana sounded indignant but looked frightened. What had just happened?

"Mama, I wanted to talk to you face to face. I could not explain it on a cellphone. The Mukhabarat . . ." he whispered. They all knew that the secret police listened in on phone conversations.

"Explain what?" Nana eyes widened as she leaned forward.

"We want democracy." Uncle Sami reached for his mother's hand. "We *need* democracy."

"'We'? Who is 'we'?" Nana pulled her hand back.

"Mama, there are many of us who believe—"

"Believe? We believe in God, Glory be to Him. Democracy is nothing but a shiny new toy. You are not a revolutionary. You are a teacher, not a rebel." Her voice trembled as she clutched her hands, rubbing them over and over.

"There are changes coming, Mama. It's happening all over the Arab world. It's the Arab Spring."

Yara looked from face to face. Baba's jaw tightened and Mama's mouth twitched. Their eyes spoke to each other, but what were they saying? Democracy? Revolution? Why was Uncle Sami speaking like those protesters on television?

"Hush, Sami. You think we have not heard about this? Phah! Spring? More like an Arab Winter." Nana's voice was harsh. Nana never, ever talked harshly to Uncle Sami.

"Mama, watch Al Jazeera. Go on Facebook. Democracy is the chance to choose our own leaders. Think, Mama, no more secret police running around in their Range Rovers arresting people. No more spies in our midst. No more torture in prisons. The Americans will help. They want us to have democracy."

"Stop, Sami." Nana lifted her hand as if trying to halt traffic. "This . . . this Arab Spring, it started in Egypt, no? Well, it can stay in Egypt." She slapped her hand down hard on her knee.

"No, Mama, it began in Tunisia and then it moved to Egypt," said Uncle Sami, softly.

"Moved? Is democracy a piece of furniture that can be moved? Is it a disease? Can I catch it? Phah!" Nana's voice rose up in exasperation just as her hands lifted into the air as though pleading with God Himself. "And what has Tunisia or Egypt to do with us? How did this even begin?"

"Mama, listen . . . please. Here, in Syria, it began with boys in a school. They were arrested." His voice cracked.

"Boys? Boys were arrested?" Nana, eyes wide, shook her head in disbelief.

"Mama, you must have heard about it." Yara could hear the strain in her uncle's voice. He didn't want to hurt his mother.

"No! I don't want to hear any more." Nana clamped her hands over her ears. Yara looked on in astonishment! Why was Nana behaving like a child?

"You must listen, Mama. You must understand," Uncle Sami implored, but Nana had turned her face to the wall.

"There was graffiti on the wall of the school in Dara'a. You know the city Dara'a, Mama? It's near the Jordanian border," said Uncle Sami.

Nana flicked her hand as if to shoo away a fly. Of course she knew where Dara'a was.

"The boys in that school wrote stupid things on the walls about President al-Assad, like, 'Down with the regime' and, 'Your turn, Doctor.' Words that in another time and place would have meant nothing!" Uncle Sami ran a hand through his hair, took a breath, and continued. "The principal called the police."

Nana stared into the face of her son. Her lovely face, normally the shade of a copper coin rubbed to a brilliant shine, was ashen. Tears circled her eyes. Nana, who never faltered, who would not allow herself to show weakness, was holding her breath.

Yara suddenly felt like crying out. She wanted Uncle Sami to stop talking, but he kept on.

"The police wanted to make someone responsible. They arrested the students." His voice caught. "They went to their homes in the middle of the night. Imagine, Mama, the pounding on the door, the screams of their parents, babies and children crying, the fear in the boys . . . I know that fear." Uncle Sami took a deep breath.

What fear? Yara's heart began to pound in her chest. Something was very wrong. Mama, her lips tight, took Yara's hand and squeezed it.

"It was like before, Mama." Uncle Sami put his head in his hands.

Nana moaned, "Like before? What do you mean? What are you talking about? You are not speaking about . . ." She gasped. Her hand flew to her mouth. Her eyes grew wide. The room became very still.

Yara looked from person to person. What was happening?

Uncle Sami leaned in and whispered into his mother's ear, "I remember. I remember everything."

Mama touched her brother's arm. "Stop, Sami, please." Two streams of silver tears ran down her face.

Baba stood up abruptly. "Come with me, Yara."

"But . . ." Yara looked at her grandmother, at Mama, and then back at Uncle Sami. What did he remember?

"Come, Yara," Baba said, more forcefully now. Without another word Yara followed her father out of the room, out of the house, and into the bakery.

"Baba, what does Uncle Sami remember?" Yara stood between the long baker's table and the two ovens.

Baba crossed the tile floor, unlocked the bakery door that led to the street, and turned the sign in the window to "OPEN." He shook his head. "When you are older, Uncle Sami and Nana will tell you." He covered his hair with his black baker's hat, put on his great big oven mitts, and pulled a pan from the oven.

"Please, Baba, I am not a little girl." She stood as straight and tall as possible, hoping to make herself look older, more mature.

Baba, holding the hot pan in his gloved hands, looked confused, angry, and frustrated, all at the same time. "It was before your mother was born. Uncle Sami was very young, just five years old, I think . . ." Baba shook his head as he set the pan down and threw his gloves on the table. "No, I cannot. It is not my story to tell."

Baba looked as sad as Yara had ever seen him. She peered back down the path and into their house. She could see Nana, Uncle Sami, and Mama sitting together on the mat, holding each other.

"Baba?" Yara watched her father place cookies in the window display.

"Yes, daughter?" He sounded like Baba again, steady and sure.

"What is a revolution?"

Baba hung his head. "It is another name for war," he said softly.

War? War was something that happened far away, not here, not in her country.

She shivered. "Are you afraid, Baba?" she whispered.

"Afraid? No one can *make* me be afraid. Only I can make myself afraid," Baba said. Then, for the second time that day, Yara, who was really too old to be picked up, was picked up. Baba held her tight. She could feel his heart pounding and the intake of his breath.

"Baba, what's wrong?" she whispered.

"I will keep you safe, daughter. You and your mother are my heart."

CHAPTER 2

S hireen burst into the bakery, her dance bag dangling from her shoulder, her long red hair in braids drifting down her back. "Are you ready?" she asked with a big smile. Her face was heart-shaped, and her emerald-green eyes sparkled with intelligence. For Yara, everything else fell away—Nana's tears, Mama's sad face, Uncle Sami's worried expression. Shireen could do that—light up a room.

"What's wrong?" Shireen asked. She must have seen something in Yara's expression.

"Nothing," Yara replied, too quickly.

Shireen tipped her head to one side. They'd grown up together, and Shireen knew Yara well enough to know something wasn't right.

"Really, nothing is wrong," Yara insisted. "It's just that Uncle Sami is here." Yara looked from Shireen to Baba. Should she leave?

"Go, go. But say goodbye to your uncle first," said Baba as he handed Shireen a choice cookie. Shireen bit into the cookie, then mumbled a thank-you through a mouthful of crumbs.

"Won't Uncle Sami be staying with us for a few days?" asked Yara. When Uncle Sami stayed overnight, or even longer, they ate like kings the whole time!

Baba shook his head. "Just say goodbye." He turned back to his oven.

"I'll be quick." Yara spun on her heels.

Back at the house, the room went silent when Yara re-entered. Nana's face was unmoving, but her eyes were full of sadness. Mama and Uncle Sami looked stone-faced.

"I am going to dance class," Yara announced quietly.

"Your dance bag is in the hall," said Mama, without moving.

"Excellent. You are a beautiful dancer." Uncle Sami beamed. At least he looked happier than he had a moment ago. Yara peered into his brown eyes. Next to Baba, he was the man she loved most in the world. Why did he have to live in Damascus? He was a teacher. There were schools in Aleppo.

"Will you come and watch me dance?" Yara asked her uncle, and in the next instant she felt suddenly shy.

"Not today, but one day soon. Come." He opened his arms. "You are my heart," he whispered as he hugged her. That was what Baba had just said.

Yara went back to the bakery to get Shireen and together they left through the door to the street. Across the road, Yara saw Shireen's father climbing into a car.

"Where is your father going?" Ali, Shireen's twin brother, and her mother, Roja, were standing at the fence of their small house waving him off.

"He is off to a funeral. One of Father's colleagues at the university fell down the stairs," said Shireen.

Yara was astonished. "Just like that? Fell down the stairs?" Shireen nodded. "Was he very old?"

Shireen shook her head. "I think he was younger than my father. Come on." Shireen walked on. They'd need to hurry if they were going to be on time.

Despite their almost two-year difference in age, Yara was taller, and with her long legs she was faster, the fastest girl in her class. "Wait for me!" Shireen laughed as she caught Yara's hand. Her touch was electric. Everything about Shireen was perfect—a perfect nose, full lips, long, thick red hair. Yara, in her own opinion, was decidedly imperfect—all bony limbs and knobby knees.

The streets were almost empty. It was Friday, and except for the bakery, the shops were closed until after noon prayers. In the afternoon, ice cream parlors, sandwich shops, and juice shops would open, and there would be street vendors hawking falafel and bright-yellow cobs of corn bubbling in huge copper pots.

"We'll get corn on the way home," Shireen said.

Grinning, Yara's head bobbed like a bobblehead in a car window. Thoughts of Uncle Sami lingered in her mind, but when she was with Shireen it was like having an older sister and a best friend at the same time. Just being with Shireen made everything better.

The only problem about Shireen and Yara's friendship was Nana. Nana didn't much like Mama's friendship with Roja, Shireen's mother, either. *You can only trust family,* Nana repeated, over and over and over. *Neighbors betray neighbors.*

That's a terrible thing to say, Mama told Nana, but there was no talking Nana out of her way of thinking.

Dance class was on the second floor of the cultural center. The place was packed when they arrived.

"What's happening?" Shireen whispered to a girl beside her.

"The older girls are putting on a show tonight. This is their final rehearsal."

Yara and Shireen sat cross-legged on the floor and watched the senior girls rehearse in full costumes. The lights in the room dimmed. Ten young woman, trim, elegant, wearing long skirts that flowed around them like pink and blue clouds, held up matching veils. They whirled and twirled to the beat of the soft and rhythmic music. Yara held her breath. It was like moving poetry. Would she be able to dance like that one day?

Spellbound, they watched for an hour. Only when the lights came up did Yara see Nana standing by the door.

Shireen nudged her. "I think your grandmother wants you." But Nana was pointing to Shireen, not Yara. Puzzled, Shireen inched her way past the girls sitting on the floor.

Nana whispered in Shireen's ear. There was a sudden pained look on Shireen's face. Without glancing back, she bolted out of the room.

"Shireen!" Yara called out softly. Where had she gone? She collected both dance bags and made her way over to Nana, apologizing to a long line of girls as she stepped on toes and the fringes of clothes. "What's wrong?"

Nana pressed a finger to her lips. "Come." She led the way down the stairs and out of the cultural center. They stood on the road, and Nana checked to see if anyone was close enough to hear.

"Shireen's father was arrested at a funeral. The man who died was said to be an organizer of the Kurdish Future Movement Party." She spoke slowly, quietly, her lips close to Yara's ear.

A party? Like a birthday party? No, that wasn't right. "What, who is . . . are . . . they?" Yara was so mixed up.

"They are rebels. Many are students, I think. Shireen's father is a professor. He may have been reported for saying something against the President or the regime." Nana scowled. "Fool! Does he think he can topple President al-Assad?"

The Kurdish Future Movement Party. Yara repeated the name in her head. She knew so little about the Kurds. They were a minority group that had been in Syria for hundreds of years, but still many people thought of them as foreigners. She knew that, at least. And they wanted their own land, their own country, even! But what did any of that have to do with Shireen's family?

"He has been taken to prison," Nana said quietly.

Prison? Yara felt goose bumps rise on her arms. Shireen's father was a mathematics professor. He was a kind man, a nice man. Yara inched closer to Nana. "Is Shireen's father a rebel?" She wasn't sure what a rebel was, not exactly. But she did know that to even speak about toppling the government could get a person arrested. As for prison, it was a mythical place, like hell.

"I do not know, but I have heard that he supports the Kurds," Nana whispered.

A group of girls filed past. Nana and Yara stepped to one side, their backs against the wall, and waited until the girls were out of earshot.

"Where is he?" whispered Yara.

"In the prison at the corner of the al-Shuhadaa neighborhood, near Omar Bin al-Khattab Street," Nana whispered back.

Yara stared at her grandmother. So, prison was a real place with an actual address. "We could go there. We could explain," she said.

Nana shook her head. "The prison of the Mukhabarat does not allow visitors. We must get home." Nana began to walk, head high as though she were leading a band. Every few steps she looked over her shoulder. If anyone looked guilty of something, it was Nana!

"Wait." Yara, running up from behind, tugged at Nana's *abaya*.

Her grandmother stopped, pulled Yara in close, and whispered, "He is a *political* prisoner. It's better to be a thief or a murderer. It does not matter if he is or is not a rebel. There will be no trial, no lawyers, and no judge. The charge is enough to keep him in prison for years." And then she added, "Or for life."

Life in prison? Yara felt sick. "I must see Shireen."

Nana put a hand on Yara's arm. "There will be time to comfort your friends, there will be years. And they, too will suffer."

Yara's heart was pounding. "What do you mean? Shireen and Ali did nothing wrong!"

Nana sighed deeply. "The families of political prisoners are punished, too. Likely their mother will not be able to continue to work at the university."

"Roja not work? But if her husband is in prison, how will they live?" Yara's eyes were as round as coins.

"There is more. They will be lucky if they can provide his food. Generally it is forbidden, but she will try." Nana stopped talking and waited for two women carrying baskets to pass. "The government gives them moldy bread and thin soup not fit for animals. But without work it will be hard enough for Roja just to feed herself and her children."

CHAPTER 3

One year later

Mama's moan was long and deep, and it ripped through
Yara's own body like a blunt knife. Mama, the midwife, and Nana, too, were in the bedroom below her.
Sitting with her back against the empty water tank, her toes
brushing Nana's dusty roof garden, Yara looked up into a
pale-blue sky and mumbled a prayer: "Please let the baby
come quickly. Please let Mama be all right. Please. Please.
Please."

Mama needed a doctor and a hospital, but because of this
revolution, this *war*, hospitals were dangerous places now.
President al-Assad and his soldiers were bombing hospitals—
deliberately! Monsters bombed hospitals.

Yara brushed the dust off her feet. Nana and Yara swept
the roof often, sometimes twice a day. But no matter where
in the city the bombs landed, dust sprang up into the air

and then sprinkled down from the sky like flour shaken from a tin.

She pushed back her limp, sweaty hair. The sun had streaked it, turning some of the strands of brown a coppery red. She wore skinny jeans and a long-sleeved T-shirt. The day was hot and hazy and the sky was clear of bomb-carrying helicopters. She looked out over the eastern part of the city. Her city was cut in half now. The east was held by the rebels, and the west was under government control. A year ago, big city buses—gutted, stripped, and upended—had blocked the road. They were as tall as a three-story building. The bus-blockade was supposed to prevent snipers from firing at people. It mostly worked.

Mama cried out again. Yara leapt up as if she had been stuck with a needle. She stood at the top of the stairs and listened.

"Breathe in . . . slower . . . now push . . . not too hard." The midwife's voice was soothing and calm. And then came Mama's cry. Yara closed her eyes. Twice she had gone downstairs and asked to be let into Mama's room. Both times Nana had waved her away.

"Deep breath . . . You are doing well." The midwife's words, the dust, and the smell of baked bread and smoke from *shisha* pipes wafting from surroundings rooftops mingled and floated up on the hot air.

Again Mama cried, and again, and again, each one piercing the air. And then came another. Enough! Yara ran down the stairs.

She cracked open the door. "Nana, let me in."

There was a sour smell in the air that she didn't recognize. The curtains were closed and a lamp was lit. The room was filled with shadows as the ceiling fan chattered overhead. She could see Nana bent over Mama, wiping her forehead, whispering something into her ear. Yara braced herself for a look from her grandmother that would nail her to the far wall. Instead, Nana came to the door and spoke softly.

"Go and visit Shireen. Your father or I will come and get you when the baby arrives."

Yara looked up into Nana's liquid brown eyes. "Is something wrong with Mama?" She tried to keep her voice level but inside she was screaming.

"Your mother is fine. Tell your father that you will be at Shireen's house. Go," Nana whispered. Yara hesitated. It would have been more reassuring if Nana had been her usual cranky self.

The cellphone rang as Yara walked down the hall towards the bakery. Mama kept the phone caged in a little box, ever since Baba had accidentally baked it into a cake. She answered it. "Yes?" She heard Uncle Sami's voice and instantly felt relief. "No, not yet," was her answer to the predictable question. Yara dithered. She wanted to say something positive and reassuring. "Soon," she added. "The baby will be here soon," as if the infant would arrive by bus at a scheduled hour.

Uncle Sami had called five, six times already today. And when she had said that the baby was not here yet, Uncle Sami had asked other questions that seemed almost silly. Yes, she was still going to school, but it was getting more dangerous to walk even the five blocks. Yes, they had electrical power now, but it came and went.

"You said that the United States and the other nations would help us get that *democracy*. Are they coming soon?" Yara asked.

Uncle Sami whispered, "Soon." What Yara really wanted to say was, "What is taking them so long?"

"I miss you," she whispered. The line went dead. What if there was someone bad listening in on their phone calls? She placed the phone back in its box. But who would bother? They were bakers, and Uncle Sami was a teacher. They weren't important. It was so confusing.

Dragging her feet, Yara walked down the short path and into the bakery. Baba was pounding the dough as if it were his enemy.

"Nana says I should go to Shireen's." She hesitated, the tips of her shoes making circles in the loose flour on the floor. She wanted him to say, "Stay, I need you."

Instead he said, "Yes, yes, go, and take some bread for Roja with you."

With warm bread in her arms, Yara opened the door and stepped out. She stopped. She had the overwhelming feeling that she should stay, that something was going to go wrong. Mama had lost many babies. *Lost*, as if a baby could be misplaced somehow, forgotten while shopping in the *souk* or left in a coffee shop. They were not lost, they had died, and most before they had taken a breath. What if this baby died, too? What if Mama died? The thought paralyzed her. She stepped off the curb and she didn't see the car, didn't hear the honking or the voice screaming her name. Before the screaming stopped she felt two strong hands grip her shoulders and her feet lift off the ground. She was being held so tightly she could hardly breathe.

"What are you doing? Are you blind?" yelled a driver.

"Can you not see a girl in the street? Who was the foolish person who gave you a driving license?" It was Roja, Shireen's mother, who was yelling at the driver. The car swerved around the two, kicking up small pebbles that nicked their legs.

"Why did you stop in the middle of the street, Yara? You could have been killed!"

Yara, startled, peered up into a beautiful, strong face that might have been carved out of stone.

"Come into the house, hurry." Roja pushed Yara onto the narrow stone sidewalk, into her little fenced yard, and closed the squeaky gate behind them. The door to the house gaped open.

"Is everything all right?" Shireen dropped her book and ran across the room. "What happened?" She hugged Yara, then looked into her friend's pale face. Yara's legs wobbled under her.

"Everything is fine now," said Roja. The near-miss was eclipsed by the bigger subject. "Tell me about your mother," she said, as Shireen dragged Yara down onto cushions.

"The baby is not coming." The car, the honking, Mama's cries, Baba's ashen face—the tears that had threatened to fall all day suddenly filled Yara's eyes and trailed down her cheeks.

"Here, drink." Shireen gave Yara a sip of tea.

"What does your grandmother say?" asked Roja.

"She says that Mama is fine." Yara wiped her face with the back of her hand.

"Then we must believe your grandmother and trust in Allah, His name is glorified," said Roja as she took the bread from Yara's folded arms. It had been squished into a lump.

Yara nodded while sipping tea. What right had she to cry when Shireen's family had suffered so much?

There had been only one message from Shireen's father since his arrest more than a year ago. Shireen told her everything. A man, just released from prison, had come to their home. Roja, crying with joy, had ushered him into the house. *Your husband is . . .* The released prisoner paused as if to carefully consider each word. *He is a good man and much respected by his fellow prisoners.* He spoke slowly, his voice wavering as he sipped tea and nibbled on bread. *He worries about you and the children. He said that you must follow the plan. He said, "Tell my wife that she is my heart and I love them all."* The man offered no hope for the release of her husband. When he left, Roja collapsed. That was a month ago.

Yara took a breath, pushed back her hair, and caught Ali's eye. He was standing between the sitting room and the kitchen. Despite being twins, Shireen and Ali did not look at all alike. Shireen was small, tiny really, while Ali was already as tall as his mother, with broad shoulders and thick black hair that fell over his eyes. Was she staring at him? Did he notice? Embarrassed, Yara looked down into her teacup. She was eleven years old and couldn't even cross a street without almost getting killed. When she looked up, Ali was gone.

Shireen chatted about babies and baby names and Roja talked about her sewing business. Nana had been right. After her husband's arrest Roja had been asked to leave her job at the university, and both Shireen and Ali now studied at home.

"Do you want a brother, or a sister?" Shireen asked.

Yara had thought of very little else since Mama had said that a baby was coming. "A sister," she said, but then she looked at Shireen and thought that she already had a sister. And then came the knock. Roja flung open the door.

"Nana!" Yara leapt to her feet.

"Come, Yara," said Nana. She looked serious, not at all the way a grandmother should look at the birth of a new grandchild. Had something happened to Mama? Yara darted past her grandmother and again bolted out onto the street.

"Look both ways," Roja called out.

Moments later, Yara was crouched beside her mother's bed.

"I am here, Mama." Yara seized her mother's hand and held it against her cheek. Was she sleeping? Yara hadn't even looked at the bundle in the midwife's arms. "Mama, MAMA. What's wrong with my mama?"

Just as the words came out of Yara's mouth, her mother's eyes opened. "I am fine, daughter," she whispered. The room spun around Yara. She hadn't realized that she had been holding her breath.

Nana closed the bedroom door and took the tiny bundle from the midwife's arms. "Here, Yara, hold your baby brother."

"A boy!" Yara cried. She had a brother. A real brother, someone she would love forever, someone who would love her. She climbed on the bed, tucked her legs under her, and reached for him. He was so small, so light! "Look at his tiny fingers! And his hair, Mama." Yara brushed her face against his feathery head. And then he gave a smile of such sweetness that Yara almost lost her breath. "He smiled at me!" Laughter bubbled up and burst into the air. "Oh, Mama, he is beautiful." Yara gazed into his black eyes and he looked back intensely; it was as if she could hear him speak to her somewhere deep inside. He knew her and she knew him.

"He loves you already. We will call him Saad. His name means 'good fortune,'" Mama said quietly.

"I love you, too," she whispered while kissing his fuzzy head again and again.

Yara tore her eyes away from her brother's face and watched as her grandmother left the room. Her shoulders were hunched and she dragged her feet as though she was more than tired, as though she was someone who carried a great burden. The birth of a new baby was the happiest thing in the world—next to a wedding, of course—and yet Nana seemed so sad.

CHAPTER 4

2014

Yara wasn't supposed to be on the roof anymore. Though a teenager, she was hardly allowed outside of the house. She might as well have been living in a prison, she thought. But then she winced. That wasn't fair. Shireen's father was still in prison. Compared to his life, or at least the one she imagined, she had lots of freedom.

With a pastry in one hand, Yara sipped apple cider, except it was more water than cider. She balanced the glass on the edge of the roof, dropped her chin onto two cupped hands, and looked up into a dull, gray sky. The air smelled of metal and chemicals and left an oily taste on her tongue. It was quiet. Even the birds were silent. Likely it would not stay that way for long.

Looking east from her rooftop, Yara could see that almost all of the city's pencil-thin minarets had been knocked down by bombs.

Minarets, Nana said, were the hands and arms of Aleppo reaching for Allah, Glory be to Him. Now they were like shattered limbs lying on the ground. As for the creamy-white buildings of the city, most were bullet-scarred or scorched tar-black. Even the main pipes for drinking water had been destroyed. How could a city survive without water? West Aleppo was still controlled by the government, but bit by bit East Aleppo was being demolished by President al-Assad and his bombs.

We should move. The rebels may control East Aleppo completely again but they can't protect us, Mama said more than once.

And what about the bakery? How would we live? Your father and I started this business, Nana added.

And what about our customers? Look at the big bakeries—all bombed out of existence, said Baba.

But think of the children. Mama's voice was always soulful.

They talked endlessly, and when it all got to be too much, when they were all talking in circles, Nana would say, *Quiet! The walls have ears.* She repeated it so often Yara thought she might clap her hands over her own ears.

How could they move? To leave Aleppo seemed like a kind of betrayal. And as for leaving Syria, that felt like treason.

Yara looked up at the blue sky. If only she could go back to school. She hadn't been to a real school since Saad was born, and Saad was already two years old. There were some classes in people's homes but they never lasted long. Some religious schools were still open but Baba said that they only prepared boys and girls to fight. "Allah, glory be to Him, does not need fighters," Baba would say. "He wants believers. Your grandmother knows more than all the teachers in Aleppo!" It was true. Nana spoke French and even English, and she liked mathematics and science, but literature more, of course. How was it that a baker's wife knew such things?

"Nana, where did you learn French?" It was a simple question, but every time Yara asked, Nana turned her back and refused to answer. Well, at least there was one good thing about being taught at home. Shireen came over most days and she and Yara studied together.

Yara looked over her shoulder at the apartment building behind their house, and her eyes skipped from window to window. Snipers, hiding on rooftops or in windows, would take aim and shoot. Imagine sipping apple cider and then, *bang*, you're dead!

Nana clomped up the stairs and rested a basket of damp laundry against the empty water tank. Her breathing was labored because of all the dust.

"Yara, stop your daydreaming and help."

"Yes, Nana." Yara rubbed a bit of dirt off the ledge with her elbow, put her pastry down, and carried Nana's laundry basket under the clothesline. What was the point in hanging laundry? Nana's white sheets would be covered in dust in minutes.

Saad ran past Nana towards her. "Can't catch me!" he squealed in triumph.

"Oh yes, I can!" Yara snatched him up, heaved him into the air, and plopped him into a small play yard that Baba had built for him. *Oof!* He was almost too heavy to lift now.

"No, Yara, noooooo. I don't like it." Saad gave the fence a good shake.

"Here." Yara held out her pastry, and he lifted his pudgy arm for the treat.

"Yara, come here!" Nana gave Yara an exasperated look. It was her fourteenth birthday, couldn't Nana be nice to her for one day? But then her grandmother reached under the laundry and handed her a small paper bag. Yara peeked in the bag and squealed, "*Qabaqeeb*! Thank you, oh, thank you." She wrapped her arms around Nana's tiny waist. Where had Nana found her favorite candies?

Nana gave her granddaughter a rare smile. "Happy birthday. Now share them with your brother," she snapped, and went back to pegging the laundry, being careful to pin their underwear between the rows of sheets and out of sight.

"Here, Saad." Yara plucked a tiny, round yellow meringue out of the bag for him and took a green one for herself. "I love you." She patted her brother's head.

"I love, love you!" he echoed.

She kissed him, fished out another candy, and popped it neatly into his mouth. He pursed his lips until they looked like kisses. "You are like a fish," she said.

"Fish don't talk," he said, licking his lips.

"Yara!" Shireen, waving madly, appeared on the opposite rooftop.

"Shireen!" Yara waved back, laughing. Ali appeared, one hand in the air, the other casually tucked in his pants pocket. Ali, nearly fifteen, had almost a man's body. He wasn't stringy like most boys, with bones that poked out of their skin like sticks in a woodpile, and he was tall, six inches taller than Shireen. But the brother and sister shared the same smile, the same green eyes. And just like Shireen, Ali's whole face lit up when he laughed; his eyes crinkled and his cheeks rounded, revealing teeth as white as Mama's icing sugar. Yara could hear him laugh from clear across the street!

Shireen bent down and was out of sight for a moment. When she leapt up again she yanked a sheet off an old, broken satellite dish. A great big smiley face had been painted on the dish! Yara let out a whoop. It was amazing.

"Happy birthday!" Shireen cried as she waved the sheet like a huge flag.

"See, Nana? It's wonderful! Can you see it, Saad?"

Nana scoffed. "That smile-on-the-face could make their house a target."

Target? Yara looked up into the sky. Could bomb-carrying helicopters see the smiley face from the air?

Shireen waved again. "I will see you later," she shouted as she followed Ali into the stairwell of their house.

"Wait! Don't go!" Too late, they had disappeared through the door.

Yara, feeling suddenly alone, wrote Ali's name in the dust with her foot. It was a lovely name. Though she had never really had a conversation with him, he was always nearby. She collected crumbs of information about him as though each was a bit of gold. One time, when Nana had allowed her to visit Shireen, Yara had heard the hisses and whispers that went on between Ali and his mother. He wanted to join the rebels, and who could blame him?

"Do you want to join your father in prison?" Roja had asked.

"It's better to fight like a rebel than to die in the President's prison!" he had answered.

"Your father fights for others peacefully. He is a hero!" Yara had never heard Roja raise her voice before. It was a shock to them all. After that, there was only silence.

"Yara, what's the matter with you?" Nana's stare was like a poke in the arm. Yara felt her face redden as she wiped away Ali's name. Nana gave her a sharp look before turning back to pegging up the laundry.

Sighing, Yara leaned over the lip of the roof and peered down to the street through the branches of a gnarled olive tree. She could almost, almost, pick an olive off the top branch.

"I see Mr. Baggy Pants," said Yara. The man on the street below hurried away with a loaf of Baba's bread wrapped in paper. What was the rush? Everyone dashed about as if they were running away from bombs. But who could tell if one was running to, or from, a bomb?

"His name is Mr. Kadan, and he is talking important business with your father." Nana swished a clothes peg in her mouth from side to side.

"What business?" asked Yara.

"Money business." Nana was clearly irritated.

"What money business?" Yara tilted her head.

"None of your business." Nana plucked the peg out of her mouth and fixed another sheet firmly on the line. "Yara! Step back from the edge. Isn't it enough that bombs drop on our heads and gunmen shoot us from far away? Do we need to take a child to the hospital because she falls off a roof?" Nana pulled the last sheet from her basket.

Hospital? What hospital? There were hardly any left.

"Look at the moon, the moon, the moon," Saad cried.

Yara shaded her eyes and looked up. "There's no moon. It's daytime!"

There was a sound; it was sharp, like ripping silk. Something dark and round was coming out of the sun. The sun's rays pierced her eyes. She willed them open. First one dark, menacing dot, then another and another. Helicopters. How many? Six? Seven? Usually they came two by two, not like this. Not a fleet! She didn't breathe, couldn't move, as if she were nailed to the spot.

"YARA!" Nana screamed. "GO!" Nana lunged for Saad.

Yara could see silver tubes drop out of the helicopter as calmly as summer rain might fall from a cloud. The air cracked. There was a flash of light, a whistling sound traveling on a wave, followed by an echo that rumbled like thunder. The horizon was filled with vertical lines of dark gray smoke. It was mesmerizing. She couldn't pull her eyes away. And suddenly, it happened in seconds, the helicopters were upon her—right above her! She could see their silver underbellies and the black whirl of the blades against the sky. Her mouth opened, but if she screamed she didn't hear it. Cries were lost in rolls of shock waves as the floor she was standing on jumped and fell away. Her arms went up as if she were trying to fly. Saad sailed past her, his mouth open and cheeks fluttering. "SAAD!" Yara thrashed the air. He was gone. He'd vanished into a storm of white fog. The dirt choked and the dust blinded as she twisted and tumbled in the air, her arms and legs as stiff as tent poles. A searing pain followed, as if she were being ripped apart, limb from limb. And then the ground rose up to meet her.

In the stillness, before she felt fear or pain, she felt peace. Had angels come? She lay on her back. Blinking madly, she watched as a giant stone rolled across the sun, and then she closed her eyes.

CHAPTER 5

I n the dark, it is hard to tell if eyes are open or closed, but
what does it matter? Blind is blind. Yara lifted her hands
and felt—felt what? Stone? Plaster? What was this place?
She wasn't panicked, not yet. The realization of where she
actually was came to her slowly, like a cup filling up drip by drip
and suddenly overflowing. And then she knew. She was alive
and buried. Buried alive.

Breathe. Inhale. Exhale. She gulped air in snatches, barely
enough to fill her lungs. Had a minute gone by? An hour? A day?
"Mama, Mama, Mama." She scratched at the concrete slabs
on either side of her, put a finger in her mouth, and tasted
blood. She stretched her toes and felt jagged stone. Stone—
everywhere, above her, all around her. "Baba, Baba, Baba."
A shooting pain reverberated up and down her spine. Tears
bubbled up and slid down the sides of her face into her ears

and hair. The tears carried away the sand under her eyelids. And then she took a deep breath and with all her power she cried out, "NANA, Nana?" Nana had been right there on the roof with her, hanging laundry. She had to be near. The effort scratched her throat like sandpaper. It hurt to swallow. Her ears were ringing with great clangs that distorted sound.

Then she heard something. It was hard to distinguish from the banging in her head but it had a slightly different tone. It was grating, like nails on a chalkboard or a shovel being dragged across concrete. "*Marhaba! Marhaba!* Hello!" she cried out. "Please, Allah, let me out. Oh, please. Help. Help." Was she screaming? Could anyone hear? She took a breath, and then another. Was there enough air? Would she suffocate? "Get me out. I am here. Get me out!" The words bounced off the concrete, and even to her ears she sounded like a small animal caught in a trap.

"Yara?" The voice was far away. "Yara, it's me, Shireen. If you can hear me, make a noise. Tap the rocks." Shireen's knocks against the stones sent off vibrations in Yara's head that shot down her spine to her legs and toes. "Yara, are you there?"

Shireen, yes, yes. "I am here!" Yara struggled to pull thin, grainy air into her lungs. She coughed. It hurt to cough. The clanging in her head was getting louder.

"There is a crack. Can you see light? Look for it." Shireen's voice was controlled, low. Was Shireen lying on the rocks above her? Was she covering her, protecting her, like a blanket?

Yara inched to one side, her hands raised over her face. "I can hear you," said Yara, but there was no light.

She pushed, and then punched the stones above her face. The stones rubbed and creaked against each other and dust fell on her face, in her mouth, on her lips. She tried to prop herself up on her elbows but there wasn't enough space. And then—a thin stream of light filtered in through the crack. Air!

"Look up, Yara. I can see your hair," Shireen cried out. "You are right under me. Do not move. There are people trying to help. Ali has gone for rescuers. They have machines. They will get you out."

"My mother . . ." Yara called faintly.

"Your mama?" Shireen's voice faltered.

Yara pressed her mouth against the crack in the rocks. Her lips were coated in something. "Saad, where is he?"

"Yara, listen. Can you hear me? Saad is alive! He landed in my mother's laundry basket. He did not even cry!" Just then Yara's body convulsed in a coughing fit. "Yara, lie still," Shireen pleaded.

"I need to get out. OUT! OUT!" Yara raised her arms and pressed on the rocks above her and pushed and pushed. Sweat mixed with her tears. She was hot, so hot.

"YARA, DON'T!" Shireen was screaming.

Yara lowered her arms and crossed them over her chest. "Shireen." She coughed, and then whispered, "I will die in this place."

"Listen. Listen. You will not die. Do you hear me? The rescuers will come. More people have arrived, all our neighbors. Everyone is here. They will dig you out. Just be still, please, Yara, be still."

And then there was silence. "Shireen?" *Where did she go? Oh God no, no, no, no!* "SHIREEN, DON'T LEAVE ME." Yara hammered the rocks above her head. "Please, hurry. Please." Her cries became sobs that turned into whimpers. Her throat was on fire.

The stream of light that filtered in through the crack dimmed. "I am here. HERE! Can you see my fingers? Touch my fingers." The thin light returned. Shireen's lips were pressed against the break in the stone now. "You are my friend, my sister, my heart. Stay still. Wait. Please, Yara, wait."

"I love . . ." The words caught in Yara's dry throat. Yara could just see the tips of Shireen's fingers reaching through the crack in the stone. "No, don't. Your hand could get crushed," she cried. Suddenly Yara was outside herself. She thought of Shireen in pain. It was a separate agony, different from her own.

She loved her friend, more than anything, but where were her parents? "Shireen, where is Mama? Where's Baba?"

There were more voices from above—male voices, all yelling. "What's happening?" Yara hammered at the rocks. Was Shireen gone again?

"Who is down there?" A man's deep voice wove through the rocks and clanged like bells inside her head.

"Me," croaked Yara. "I am here."

"Who is down there?" the voice repeated.

Yara took in all the air she could and cried, "Me and Mama and Nana and Baba. Please . . ." Her voice cracked. Then she heard two words, both distinctive and thunderous.

"One below."

One? Did he say one? "No, NO! Four. FOUR!" She kicked,

she pushed. "Shireen, where are you? Four. FOUR! Mama, where is my mama?"

There was shuffling. A hammer hit the rocks. The sound drilled into her head. *Rat-a-tat.* On and on and on. Sand and dust filled the space around her. She squeezed her eyes shut and covered her face with her hands. *Hurry. Hurry. Hurry.*

And then—nothing. There was no light. There was no air. If she pushed against the stones, if she screamed or even yelled out, the little air that was left would be gone. Anyway, she was tired. A calm came over her. She lay still, very, very still, and slowly sipped air. She sipped like a baby, not too much, a little bit at a time. *Mama, can you hear me? Baba, are you near?*

A solid piece of concrete above her slid sideways. She opened her eyes wide, too wide. A beam of light bounced off a white helmet. The light stung like a thousand bees. There was more shuffling. More raised voices. Strong arms reached down and wrapped around her. Baba? No, not Baba. Her head fell against a man's chest. "You are safe," a voice whispered softly into her ear.

There were cheers and prayers. "All thanks to Allah, glory be to Him," sang a chorus. Human shadows carved out of light moved around her. She was carried away, gently lowered to the ground, and propped up against a large slab of concrete. A shawl curled around her shoulders.

"Drink this."

It was Shireen's voice. She was kneeling beside her. Yara blinked. Cold water trickled down her throat. She coughed.

"Not so fast. Can you move? Is anything broken?" Shireen wiped a cool cloth over Yara's eyes.

"I don't know." She felt stiff but there were no sharp pains.

"Mama? Baba?" Yara looked up. The panic, real panic that sent her heart racing and blocked out all other thoughts, took hold. Blinking furiously, Yara knocked the cup out of Shireen's hand and crawled on her hands and knees back towards the rubble.

"Yara, no! There are live wires everywhere." Shireen, scrambling behind, wrapped her arms around Yara's waist and pulled. "Look, Yara, look!" The balconies and even the walls of the apartment building behind their home had been cut away, sliced as if by a giant knife. Rooms were exposed; television sets and computers, even a vacuum cleaner, hung by cords. Sparking, crackling, and dancing wires dangled above her like headless snakes.

"Yara, we are taking you to our house, to your brother." Shireen reached for her.

Yara batted her back. "No, my parents . . ."

"They have found your nana. Look. She is alive. See. Look! LOOK!" Shireen held Yara tight. Yara turned her head and watched as men lifted Nana out of the rubble. Her beautiful coppery face was chalky white, her lips blue, and her eyes were slammed shut.

"Nana! NANA! Shireen, she's not moving!" Yara lurched forward.

"Yara, no. You are in shock, Yara!" Shireen tried to hold her back.

Yara shoved Shireen away with both hands and crawled towards her grandmother. "Nana? NANA?" Why was Nana not talking? What was wrong? "Wake up, Nana, wake up." Yara fell beside Nana and kissed her face. The smell of dust, spice, and honey rose up from Nana's clothes. Her thick black hair, laced with silver, was coated with white dust.

"She is breathing," whispered Shireen as she flung the shawl back over Yara's shoulders.

Yara looked past her nana, past Shireen, past Ali and the rescuers. "Where is Mama?" she whispered.

"They found her, Yara, and your father. They . . ." Shireen's words seemed to float in the air. Found them? They were not lost. They were in the bakery. Yara couldn't grasp Shireen's words, couldn't make out their meaning.

The shawl fell from her shoulders as Yara tried to stand.

"Sit. SIT! You are too weak to stand." Shireen pinned Yara back down to the ground. An ambulance pulled up, covered with mud to disguise it from the bombers flying overhead. Men were shouting. She watched as Nana was lifted up and put into the back.

"Where are they taking her?" Yara fell forward onto her knees.

"To the hospital," said the driver.

"Which hospital?" she cried. Hospitals had been bombed. Were there any left? The driver turned away. "I . . . come," she cried again. Her throat was raw and the ringing in her ears kept garbling sounds.

"No room," yelled the man.

Yara used Shireen's body to pull herself up and stand on shaky legs. She lurched forward. Did the driver shove her away or did Shireen pull her back? Shireen held tight as if to glue them together. Yara looked over Shireen's shoulder. Two white bags lay on the road. Body bags. She knew what they were, had seen them before, many times. But . . . who was in there?

An old man leaned over the body bags. She had a dim recollection of having seen him before but she couldn't place him.

"Come, Yara, we must go into the house." Shireen was sobbing but Yara took no notice.

"No, no. Get away. Get away." Yara waved arms that didn't feel attached to her body. She couldn't see the old man properly. And then there was a flicker of a memory. Was that the old man she used to give free bread to years ago? Ammo Khalid. How was he alive after all this time? And why could she remember him when everything around her was so hard to take in? What was that he was saying? "To their souls, mercy and peace." Wait, wait! That was a prayer for the dead. He was praying over the bodies.

She heard a wail. It was a long, thin shriek. Searing pain roared up her throat. Only then did she realize that the wail was coming from her. "Mama! Baba!" Yara sobbed as she fell back to the ground, her face in the dust. "Don't leave me. Don't go. Mama, I am here."

"Come." Ali lifted her up off the road in one sweeping motion. In another part of her mind, the one closed off from the pain, she felt touch. The arms around her were solid and warm. She looked up into his face as he looked down into hers. His eyes were bright with fear and something else, too, but what?

"Are you all right? Can you hear me?" he whispered in her ear.

"Ali." She mouthed his name before closing her eyes. "I have lost my family."

CHAPTER 6

S leep was deep, foggy, and filled with shadows. There was something at the edge of her dream, something dark. A monster. It held a gun.

Yara sat bolt upright. She clapped a hand over her mouth to stifle a cry. It took a moment to catch her breath, stop the screaming in her head, and slow her heart. She was coated in a sticky sweat that glued her T-shirt to her chest. She was hot and cold, both at the same time. Her hands shook as she reached out for her brother, touched his chest, and felt his heart thumping through his shirt. His soft, regular breathing made her sigh with relief. He was here, safe, and her nightmare had not woken him.

Since the explosion, since Nana was taken away in the ambulance nearly a week ago, Yara and Saad had slept side by side on mats under the only table left in Roja's house. The rooms upstairs, Ali's bedroom and Shireen's beside it, had been closed up. "My mother wants us to be together in case . . ." Shireen didn't need to add anything more. Yara knew. They lived together on one floor in case their house, too, was bombed. Live or die, they would do it together.

Everything wooden, except one shelf and the front and back doors, had been used to board up the windows, leaving the little house dark and airless. They lived like blind mice in the gloom.

Shireen lay on cushions near the shelf. Roja slept in the only bedroom, with a heavy curtain dividing her room from the main room. The kitchen was a third room at the back of the house. Ali slept in a small shed beyond the kitchen. It didn't have a proper door, more like a tall gate he slipped in and out of as if he were a house pet. He didn't seem to mind.

For the third night in a row, Yara turned on a small, battery-powered lamp that Roja had left out for her. A pool of light formed around her, bright where she lay, raggedy at the outer edges. In the dim light, the colorful blankets and pillows were shades of black and gray. The one lone shelf held family photos, mostly of Shireen's father. One photo was of him holding Shireen and Ali when they were small. He had such a kind face. Did he know how much his wife and children worried? It had been years since he was arrested. No lawyer, no trial, no judge.

Saad mewed like a kitten.

"Hush. Don't wake up," she whispered. His face was soft and milky. His sleepy eyes stared up at her. "Oh Saad, sleep,

sleep." She kissed the top of his head. He hadn't said a word since he'd flown through the air like a sparrow and landed in a laundry basket. Not a single word. How much did he understand? Likely everything.

Yara pulled him close and squeezed her eyes tight. "Uncle Sami, how do I find you? We need you," she whispered.

⌁·

"I want to come with you," said Yara the next morning. She stood in the middle of the room, fully dressed, scrunching a clump of her dress in her fist. Every day, Ali went out in search of Nana.

"It's best if I go alone," Ali said, shaking his head.

Yara was grateful to him. She was grateful to Shireen and Roja, too. How could she not be? But to not search for her own grandmother? "Her name is Maha. You must call out her name," said Yara.

"Maha," repeated Ali. "I know. You have told me." He didn't seem frustrated with Yara's constant worry. Perhaps he understood.

"What if something happens to you?" Shireen stood in front of her brother, her nose reaching to the middle of his chest. Ali rolled his eyes. This was an old argument. "Rebels, government soldiers, gangs could pick you up, put you in a truck, and we would never see you again." She spoke bitterly but her eyes glistened.

Roja nodded her head. "Listen to your sister," she pleaded.

"They won't catch me. I am fast, you know that!" Ali laughed.

"What about snipers?" Shireen was not laughing.

"Snipers shoot people who walk fast, weave, and dodge. I walk like I am already wounded." He limped around the room, grinning.

"Liar! You just said that you run." Shireen's face turned red with fury.

Ali shrugged and added (as solemnly as possible given that his mouth was turned up at the corners), "I will be back." He gave his mother a quick kiss.

"May Allah, glory be upon Him, protect you." Roja turned her head away.

Yara listened to the three bicker. Did Shireen think Nana could walk home on her own? She had to be hurt. Anyway, she was the one who should be looking for her grandmother, not Ali.

"Please, let me come with you?" asked Yara, but Ali didn't look back. "Ali!" she cried. The door closed behind him.

Shireen spent the day pacing and reading, reading and pacing. In between pacing she read. The hours dragged on.

"It does no good to worry. Lie down, Shireen," Roja pleaded.

Finally Shireen dropped onto her mat. The sweltering heat boiled the air.

"Shireen, I'm sorry," Yara whispered in her friend's ear.

"Sorry for what?" Shireen wiped her damp face with the back of her hand.

"Ali is looking for my grandmother. He is in danger because of Saad and me." She felt ashamed and grateful at the same time.

Shireen sat up, knees to her chin. "The revolution is not your fault! The death of your parents is not your fault, either, and it is not your fault that your grandmother is missing." She spoke plainly, then studied her friend's face closely. They had hardly talked about her parents, and when Roja had suggested they say prayers for Mama and Baba, Yara had turned away. Prayers? What was the point? Their bodies had been dumped into a mass grave. Dumped.

"Maybe it's not my fault, but it still feels like it is my fault. I can't stop feeling!" It wasn't that she felt she could have stopped the President from dropping a bomb on their house, it was that she was alive and they were not. Ten times, a hundred times a day she wanted to tell her mother something, and the shock that she was gone was always the same. Mama was gone and she would not be coming back.

"Listen to me, we are together. That's the important thing." Shireen cuddled close to Yara and put her arm across her shoulders. But nothing Shireen might say could stop that hollow feeling in Yara's stomach from growing and growing, like it would swallow her up. Questions went round and round in her head. Where was Uncle Sami? What if he had come to the house at night, seen the destruction, and just assumed they had all died? No, he would not do that. What if she could find him? But how? Where did he teach? Where did he live? If only she had the cellphone. Her legs and arms quivered. Sometimes it was hard to take a deep breath.

At bedtime, Yara felt Shireen kiss her cheek then move as quietly as a kitten to curl up on her own mat. Saad lay beside Yara with his eyes closed. Yara brushed his forehead, and only then realized that his ears were filled with tears. "Oh, my boy, my boy," she whispered. And he *was* her boy now.

An hour later the front gate squeaked. Yara's entire body contracted into a tight ball. The door opened. As if sensing that her brother was home safe, a sleeping Shireen twitched on her mat, heaved a great sigh, and fell back to sleep.

Yara listened as Ali removed his shoes by the door and dropped the key in a ceramic dish on the one lone shelf. She could just make out his silhouette in the dark. She sat up and opened her mouth to ask the obvious question.

"Ali, come here," Roja called from her bedroom. Yara clamped her mouth shut.

Crossing the room in long steps, Ali pulled back the curtain that hung between the bedroom and the main room. Roja's small battery light flickered on. Yara leaned on one elbow and tried her best to hear every word.

"Mother, all but one of the old hospitals in East Aleppo have been destroyed. The other places are more like clinics. Their operating facilities are so limited." Ali spoke in a whisper. "I have been to the hospital—babies and children lying on the floors, no electricity, no equipment, no lists of patients, no records . . . filthy . . . blood . . . no oxygen . . . no generators." His voice was on the verge of breaking. Yara froze in place. She could hear him gulping air. "Yara's grandmother must be dead."

A wave of nausea washed over Yara. Dead? Nana had been gone for almost a week. If she was not in the hospital, where was she? If she was dead, then she would have been buried in a mass grave, just like Mama and Baba.

She heard soft murmurings. Roja was comforting her son, making gentle, mothering sounds.

A moment later she heard Ali's feet tread softly across the room towards the shed.

A great wave of pain flooded her. Yara stuffed the edge of the blanket in her mouth to muffle her sobs. *Nana, come back. Nana, come back.*

The next morning, before anyone awoke, Yara kissed her sleeping brother, dressed in clothes and shoes that Roja had given her, pulled a headscarf low over her forehead, and left.

CHAPTER 7

The gate clicked shut behind her. Yara turned away from the ruins across the road. That was her home, or what was left of it. She couldn't bear to look.

Which way to go? She didn't know how to find the clinics Ali had talked about. She dithered. Her heart pounded. Yara looked at Roja's little house and thought about Saad, about Shireen. She felt safe in that house. No one would know if she just went back in.

No. There was one hospital still standing. Ali had been there, he'd said so. She would start there.

The hospital was to the east. The sun rose in the east. All she had to do was put one foot in front of the other.

Yara came to the end of her road and almost immediately felt turned around. Nothing was familiar. Smashed concrete, broken bricks, shattered glass, televisions, bombed-out cars, furniture—the streets were filled with rubble. She followed a narrow path cleared by a plow that had been fixed to the front of a military truck. The path ran down the middle of the street. *Tat-tat-tat.* Rapid-fire gunshots. A truck packed with soldiers barreled towards her. She had no time to think. Yara scrambled over rocks, bricks, and stacked sandbags and flung herself into a doorway. *Tat-tat-tat.* Who were they firing at? Her? Why? Crouching, she covered her head with her arms. They drove past, guns still firing. It was early morning and hardly anyone was outside. "Fools," she muttered under her breath. "Fools." Breathing deeply, she pushed on, her legs trembling.

The road ahead was blocked. She stopped to get her bearings. Wait, she knew this place. She was standing where Ammo Khalid, the old man, had sat on his overturned pail. Mounds of concrete were in the exact place where he had sat. Was it he who had prayed over her parents? *Please God, let Ammo Khalid be somewhere safe.* She used the back of her hand to clean her face. She was shaking again. She couldn't faint, not here, not now.

Yara took a left, then a right, and stopped. The shops along the street had been boarded up. And over there . . . Her legs wobbled. "No, no, no," she whispered. The apartment building Kasandra lived in had been sheared in half, sliced like a watermelon, its contents scattered like seeds. The huge, treacherous shell seemed to teeter. One good blast of wind and it would surely crumble into dust. Kasandra had not been in the building when it had been hit, though. Kasandra was safe. She had gone to Darat Izza to stay with her grandparents and had never come back.

Chuk-chuk-chuk. Instinctively, Yara cupped a hand over her eyes and looked towards the rising sun. Helicopters!

"YARA!"

She swiveled, her feet kicking up dust and stones.

"Yara, get down!" Ali was racing towards her, his arms outstretched.

Without thinking, she reached out to him. Her legs moved as if she had no control over them. The two crashed like cars on a roadway. Their arms folded around each other. He was pulling her sideways. And then they both fell onto, what was it? Cushions?

The helicopter dropped its load a block away. It was a barrel bomb. She could tell by the sound as it hit the ground: *pum, poooom.* When the bomb landed the ground rumbled as though a monster underground was turning over in its sleep. Ali fell across her, protecting her. Seconds passed.

"Let me go!" She pushed him off and shrieked to the lightening sky. "WHY ARE YOU BOMBING US? THERE IS NOTHING HERE!" she screamed, shaking her fist in the air.

"Yara, down!" Ali curled his arm around her waist and pushed her deep into the pillows. Half smothered and her voice muffled, she carried on. "YOU ARE KILLING US!"

"Yara, hush, hush," he whispered in her ear. She turned one way and then the other. *Breathe. In and out, in and out.* The dust made her cough. She covered her mouth but her lungs heaved. She needed to stand, to run.

"Will you stay still?" Ali hissed through clenched teeth.

She stopped.

"Now, take deep breaths."

"You are sitting on me!"

Ali rolled off her. Yara took a deep breath and coughed.

"What is this?" Yara twisted around. She felt beneath her. What were they sitting on? It couldn't be! They were lying on a sofa in the middle of the street. They gasped! Could anyone see?

Ali lurched to the other side of the sofa. Yara bolted up and frantically straightened the dress that hung down over her pants. Everything was very still.

They were in that silent time when the ground holds its breath, that wide, empty space between a bomb exploding and people crying for help. They sat like guests at a funeral. Ash drifted down like snowflakes.

"Why did you leave the house? What are you doing out here?" Ali, breaking the silence, barked at her from the opposite end of the sofa.

Yara brought her knees up to her chest and hugged them. Any hope for a smile at how ridiculous this was evaporated. Who did he think he was? Why did he think he could tell her what to do? Because he was older? Because he was male?

"No one has heard from your father in years," said Yara.

Ali's head snapped up. "So? We get messages. Men who have been released tell us about him. What has this got to do with your grandmother?"

"You haven't talked to him, not directly. But you believe that he is alive." She took a breath. "I believe my grandmother is alive, and I will search for her with or without you." Her fury was building.

"Yara, just listen." Ali reached across the space between them and touched her arm. "I have checked beds and ledgers in hospitals. No one is writing down names. I have walked halls and called out your nana's name over and over. She is nowhere to be found."

"I know." As Yara spoke her lips quivered. "I heard you talking to Roja last night."

He spoke quietly now, as though speaking in whispers could soften the words. "I would do anything for you . . . and your grandmother. But you don't know what it's like . . ." His voice trailed off.

"No, I don't know what it's like, and I am not going to learn what it's like by sitting in the house and waiting for you to tell me what is going on!" She was shouting, and then suddenly she felt embarrassed, and so tired she thought she might just curl up and sleep.

Ali sighed deeply, stretched out his legs, and laced his fingers behind his head. She glanced over at him. Was he trying to be funny? He looked silly!

"If this were an American movie, someone would hand me a beer right now." He laughed, or made a snorting sound that was meant to sound like a laugh. Yara didn't laugh, and anyway, Ali would never drink alcohol. They sat quietly for a moment. And then the tip of his shoe accidentally touched the heel of her shoe. Yara tensed. It was like a jolt of electricity. She didn't move. People were coming out of their homes, slowly, awkwardly, looking as delicate as paper dolls.

"I'm sorry," said Ali, suddenly serious.

"Sorry about what?" Yara asked, keeping her foot still.

People were calling out names now. There were answers, too. "I am here," and "I am alive." Some people sounded like twittering birds, others guzzled air as if they were drowning. Should they do something? Both looked around. No one was crying out for help.

Two men hugged each other in the street, kissed, and slapped each other's backs. Boys from another street came running. They cheered as a dog and her puppies emerged from a shed. A woman was on her knees thanking God.

All around there was a kind of astonished joy. Why? Because this time the bomb had landed a street away? Because this time they had not been killed? THIS TIME! She was angry, confused, relieved, everything all at once. How could anyone feel so much and not burst?

Yara turned to see Ali's profile against the rising sun. His face was bleached by ash to a papery white. She looked away, afraid that he might catch her staring at him.

"Come. The only hospital left is called Al Quds." Ali brushed his shirt and pants with the palms of his hand, succeeding only in moving the ash from one place to another. "It's been bombed many times."

Grim and determined, Yara and Ali set out towards the front lines.

Most of the streets were blocked. Looters climbed over flattened homes and stores, picking through debris and hauling away what they could carry—food, tables, beds, and chairs that were not too damaged.

They trudged on through narrow paths cleared by tractors. "Ali, the smell?" Yara held the end of her scarf up to her nose.

It was more than a smell, it was a reek, a stench. She breathed out and suddenly recognized the odor—there were bodies under the rubble, rotting bodies.

"There it is."

Yara stood still and stared at the structure Ali was pointing to. It wasn't a hospital. It wasn't anything. The shell of the building was six, maybe seven stories high, although it was impossible to tell since the top floors had been sheared off.

"The staff keep returning and reopening it." Ali pointed to a line of hospital beds on the pavement and nurses leaning over patients. "The wounded are treated in the street but there are still patients inside. Wait here." Ali bolted ahead.

What? Why? "No, I am coming, too." Head back, tears in her throat, Yara followed, her long legs easily keeping up with him.

The entrance to the hospital was oddly, horribly, unnaturally quiet, and yet there were wounded adults and children everywhere: in hallways and doorways, under beds and in offices. There were glassy-eyed nurses and doctors, all running in different directions.

"Don't ask for help. They don't know the names of the patients. Just call your grandmother's name," said Ali. A child called out, and Ali stopped to kneel beside what looked like a small bundle of rags.

"Nana, Nana," she cried. And then, "Maha, Maha." Yara, walking on, skittered around gurneys and people sleeping under them. "Nana? Please, Nana, where are you?" Her voice cracked. And the smell . . . oh, the smell! She covered her nose with the collar of her top. The farther into the building she went, the darker it became. "Nana, Maha, Nana, Maha!" She peered down a hall. The only light that filtered in came from hundreds of finger-sized bullet holes piercing the crumbling walls. For one moment, one brief second, they looked like stars in a night sky.

Yara tripped and fell to her hands and knees. She fumbled around and touched an arm. It was as cold as a stone. Yara scuttled back until she was pressed against the wall. "Ali," she moaned. "Ali, where are you?" Yara inched up onto her feet, tiptoed around the body, and tried to retrace her steps.

In the next room, light flooded in from a gaping hole in the wall. A cry caught in her throat. Ali was on his knees dripping water from a cup into the mouth of a child. She looked past him. Lined up in a long row like broken matchsticks were dozens of wounded children. They were so quiet. Most just lay there, blank-eyed, staring into space.

"Ali." She could not raise her voice above a croak. He looked so calm, while she just wanted to run away and hide. What was he saying to the children? Her foot knocked a plastic bottle. Yara wiped her face with her sleeve and filled the bottle with water from a large red jug. She sat back on her heels for just a moment. Then, crawling from child to child, she whispered, "You are loved. You are loved. You are loved."

They walked home, side by side.

"Do relatives often come for them?" she asked.

"Sometimes," he lied.

Bombs dropped in the distance. Only when the *bzzzzzzzzz* or *poooom* came too close did they take cover. And in those moments, with Ali's arms protecting her, she felt relief.

A line of flatbed trucks passed, followed by cars filled with people. Mattresses, bulging bags, bits of furniture, sometimes wheelchairs were stacked on the roofs. An ambulance sounded in the distance. Where was it going? The hospitals were gone.

"Ali." Yara pulled on Ali's sleeve. He turned. She looked straight at him. "Ali, I . . ." Her arms, face, and ears grew hot. The color in Ali's face darkened, too. The war disappeared in that moment. He needed to know . . . she wanted to say that she felt safe with him, that . . . Then something over his shoulder caught her eye. There was a child in the street. His back was to her. Why was he just standing there? Who would let a child out alone?

"Oh God, no," Yara cried. Open-backed trucks roared towards them, a whole line of them! Soldiers stood in the back with guns balanced on their hips and pointing up into the air. "Saad, get back!" Yara screamed.

Ali's feet barely touched the ground as he raced across the road. In one fluid movement he scooped up Saad. Yara, almost as fast, was right behind him. With the boy squirming in his arms, Ali ran to the side of the road and pressed his back into a wall.

"How did you get out?" Yara reached for Saad. Sobbing, the boy pitched himself out of Ali's arms and into Yara's.

"Hush, hush," she whispered. Saad clung to Yara as if she were a raft in a stormy ocean.

"He must have come looking for you," said Ali, shaking his head.

They waited until the trucks had passed and the dust had settled before Ali swung a hiccuping Saad up into his arms and again set out for Roja's house. "Hush, my boy." Yara rubbed his back. Calmer now, Saad rested his head on Ali's shoulder.

"Ali, wait." Yara tugged at Ali's sleeve. They were just feet away from Roja's front gate. "I wanted to say . . ." Now was her chance.

Hair fell over his eyes. Yara swallowed hard as Ali set Saad down. The child immediately wrapped his arms around Yara's legs. Yara and Ali stood looking at each other, Saad in between them, keeping them apart. "I wanted to . . ." she tried again.

"Do you have him?" Roja cried out from the doorway. Her eyes were wide and wild. She spotted Saad, and the look on her face went from fear, to relief, to pity. "We thought he was hiding under the table. He opened the door and the gate by himself. I have no idea how he managed. I am so sorry!" Roja wrung her hands as Yara rushed towards her.

"He is fine. We are all fine," said Yara. "Roja, the hospital, the children . . . oh, Roja . . . the children." Yara fell into Roja's arms.

"It's all right. You are safe now." Roja squeezed her tight.

"We are not safe, and it's not all right." Shireen stood in the doorway, arms crossed, fury smothering any relief she might have felt at seeing the return of her brother and best friend. "Are we supposed to wait for a bomb to drop on our heads, or to be invaded and attacked? We should fight!" Shireen's body, so small and delicate, seemed to vibrate with anger. She looked from Ali, to her mother, to Yara. "We are doing nothing but hiding in our house and trying to survive. Kurdish women fight with guns, beside men! We should be fighting with them."

Ali ducked around his sister and vanished into the back room. He was in no mood to hear an argument.

No one asked about Nana.

CHAPTER 8

T he next day they set out together, Yara averting her eyes from her own tumbled-down home across the street. She had to carry on. The alternative was to pronounce Nana dead.

They had been to the only hospital still functioning. All that was left now was to search the medical clinics. They were popping up in alleyways, empty stores, schools. Some surgical clinics were even operating below ground.

Before returning home, feeling defeated, they stopped at a street market. "My mother needs material," said Ali. Yara nodded and followed. Roja's small business of sewing *abayas* and headscarves was flourishing. They turned onto a street filled with vendors. No matter what, people still needed food and candles, batteries and tea. Life carried on in the streets of Aleppo.

That night, Yara lay on her mat and listened to the *whoosh-whoosh* as Roja's foot pressed down on the pedal of her old-fashioned sewing machine, and the *chu-chu* of the needle pushing thread into the cloth. Shireen and Yara helped with the hand sewing, but it took ages! An electric sewing machine sat in the corner.

"What good is it when we only have electricity for an hour a day? You"—Roja pointed to the machine—"are a waste of space." It was funny listening to Roja grumble at the machine. The strangest sound of all in the war was laughter.

When the electricity was miraculously turned on, Yara dragged the television across the floor so that Saad could watch Tom and Jerry cartoons under the table. When the electricity was shut off Shireen told him stories.

The next morning, Roja stacked some clothes that she'd darned and new *abayas* she'd sewn in a neat pile. "Shireen, I am going to deliver this order to Mrs. Majida." She tied her scarf under her chin.

"Ali could deliver it," said Shireen.

"Ali has gone for water. Anyway, he takes enough chances. I won't be long." Roja opened the door and great beams of morning light flooded the room. Taking a breath for courage, she plunged out onto the street. The door shut and the gloom returned.

Using the battery light, Shireen lifted the floorboards to reveal boxes of books. Almost everyone hid their books.

The government was always banning one book or another. Who could keep up? She pulled out several novels, flipped through them, and reached for more.

"What are these?" Yara reached into a box and held up four small booklets.

"They're our passports. Father got them for us," Shireen answered without looking up.

"Shireen, why didn't you tell me?" Yara was astonished. She turned them over in her hands and tapped them against her chin. "This means you can leave Syria!" she said. It seemed so simple, so miraculous!

"Mama would never leave without our father. Besides, where would we go?" Shireen picked up another book and flipped through the pages.

"But . . ." Yara took a breath.

Shireen held up her hand. "Even though we have these, we are trapped!" She snapped the book shut, gave Yara a long, hard stare, and leaned in close. "How would we get out? Hezbollah and the Free Patriotic Movement are in Lebanon. To go to Turkey, we must go north, and ISIS is in the north. Iraq requires a visa. Do you think the Iraqi authorities give visas to refugees?" Shireen's voice was full of bitterness. Yara was astonished. Hadn't Shireen just said that they had to do something?

"What about Jordan?" said Yara. It would mean going south to Damascus and then farther, to the city of Dara'a. Jordan was a good country, many found asylum there. And Uncle Sami was in Damascus. "If we all went—"

"Stop!" Shireen wrinkled her brow. "Why do you assume that I want to leave my country?"

Yara grew quiet. She hadn't meant to upset Shireen.

Shireen settled on a book as Yara fingered the passports. "Uncle Sami talked to my parents and Nana about leaving. They thought I was sleeping but I heard everything. Uncle Sami said, 'Go to Canada. Go to Australia, England, or Europe.' Nana said that she would never leave Syria. I think she meant that she would never leave Syria without Uncle Sami."

Shireen studied Yara. "Would you go, if you could?" she asked.

What could she say? Sometimes Yara imagined the world beyond Syria, and not all of it was good. She saw it on television—huge shopping centers, hamburgers as big as plates. Everyone and everything seemed big. Maybe big people needed big houses and big cars. And there were stories about drugs, drinking, and sex!

Yara traced the embossed lettering on the cover of one of the passports before swallowing hard and putting them down. "It doesn't matter what I think. Saad and I have nothing. No money, clothes, or even identity papers." There it was again, an overwhelming feeling of panic. Her legs quivered as if ants were running under her skin.

"But your uncle Sami could help you get new papers," said Shireen as she reached over and touched Yara's hand. It was such a soft, gentle touch, like a feather grazing her skin.

Yara bit her lower lip. How to find Uncle Sami? She had been over this. The cellphone was gone. And now that the house was gone, too, how could he even find them?

"My parents kept our papers in a tin box under the big table in the bakery," she said sadly.

"The bakery was separate from the house, right?" Shireen was suddenly as bright and perky as a little bird. Yara nodded again. "That's the least damaged area. Come?" Shireen stood up and pulled on one of Roja's *abayas*.

"Now?" Yara scrambled to her feet. It was midday.

"Why not now? Looters may have been there already!"

The long black dress devoured Shireen. She looked like a little girl dressed up in her mother's clothes, which was true, except that Shireen had just turned fifteen. Funny, thought Yara, Shireen would have been almost through school and looking ahead to her future if there had been no revolution.

"Come on!" Shireen knotted a scarf under her chin. She hated headscarves and did the job badly.

"Maybe we should wait for Ali and Roja to come back," said Yara. She was thinking of Saad, who was sitting quietly under the table, like a little hare hiding under a bush. She didn't want to take him outside, and she didn't want to leave him alone.

Shireen rolled her eyes. "Saad is safe. Yara, you have been out looking for your grandmother. Are you telling me you can't cross a street?"

Searching for Nana was different. Sifting through the rubble of her house—that would feel like digging up a grave.

"Come on." Shireen opened the door and bolted across

the street. Yara's legs began to tremble. "YARA, HURRY UP!" Shireen shouted.

Saad crawled out from under the table and tugged Yara's hand.

"No, Saad, let go! Stay here. I will be back, promise." She shook him loose. His face turned dark and sour. "Stay!" she repeated, and wagged her finger. His bottom lip quivered and fat tears rolled down his cheeks. "I'm sorry, but you can't follow me. You know that." Saad spun around and darted under the table as fast as a cat. "I'm just going across the street. I'll be back soon." She kneeled down and reached out to him. He scrunched up close to the wall and covered his face with his hands. "Sorry, sorry, sorry." Yara shook her head.

Yara went out and stood at Roja's gate. She scanned the sky. The street had been cleared, for the most part, anyway. The plow-truck had shoved the debris right up and over the fence. Roja's small garden was filled with broken drywall, a smashed toilet, broken chairs, shards of metal, and pieces of brick. Before anyone was awake Ali had cleared a path through it from their small house to the road.

"Yara, come on." Shireen was already across the road in front of what had once been her parents' bakery.

There was no looking away now. Crossing the street, Yara caught sight of a box Mama had planted flowers in. It was made of wood held together with just small nails, and yet there it was, surrounded by all this destruction, still intact. Purple flowers bloomed in it. Was Mama here? Was this a sign?

"What's wrong? You're green," said Shireen as she reached for Yara's arm.

"I'm dizzy." Yara clutched her stomach.

"Go home. I will look for the box. And Ali will be back soon. He can help," said Shireen softly.

"No." Yara straightened up, took a breath, and looked away from the flowers.

Two walls of the bakery still stood, although the roof was mostly caved in, so that it was hard to see anymore where anything used to be. The front door that the customers used was still intact, but right behind it was a huge heap of rubble. Picking through bricks and stones, Yara found the head of a doll Uncle Sami had given her when she was five years old. But it had been in her room, on her dresser. How had it got all the way down to the bakery? There were lots of mysteries: Nana's blanket torn into shreds, Saad's little yellow truck, the heel of a shoe, all mixed in with broken pots, mixing bowls, a cracked pipe of Baba's—tiny bits of their lives smashed into a million pieces. And then one of her sandals, the pair she kept under Baba's worktable in the bakery.

Something inside her snapped like a twig. The pain was sudden, shocking. If she opened her mouth, she was sure a howl would come out and explode in the air like a grenade.

"Yara, help me with this." Shireen, her back to Yara, stood at one end of a wooden beam.

Mourning, even grief, was a luxury. There was no time for it. Yara swallowed hard, as hard as if consuming all the pain in the world. She brushed her face with the end of her scarf and placed the sandal back where she'd found it, half buried in plaster dust.

"Yara!" Shireen groaned.

"Coming." Together they shifted the heavy fallen roof-beam. Yara moaned.

"Yara, are you all right? Is it too heavy?"

Yara shook her head. She didn't dare speak. Under the beam was Baba's tobacco tin. Yara bent down and cupped it in her hands. "Baba," she whispered.

"Yara, what is it?" Shireen picked her way over stones before dropping down beside her friend.

Yara dusted the tobacco tin with the sleeve of her *abaya* before prying it open and sniffing the apple spiced tobacco. There were a few pinches left, and beside that a little leather pouch. Baba carried the pouch with him when he went out for coffee in the evenings. Tearless, her mouth drawn into a thin line, she pinched the damp tobacco with two fingers and filled the little pouch. *Baba, Baba, Baba* . . . the picture of him holding out his arms to her . . . *must not cry, must not cry.* Yara fumbled under her *abaya* and slipped the pouch into the pocket of her jeans. She put the little truck aside, too. Maybe Ali could straighten the wheels.

Shireen started prowling around the building, scraping away rubble until her fingers were bleeding. When she got to the front door of the bakery, she dropped to her hands and knees and started knocking and tapping on it.

"Yara, come here!"

Yara made her way over to the door on her hands and knees, crawling over bricks and plaster, her hands sinking into gray ash.

"Listen." Shireen thumped the door again with her fist. They knelt down and each put an ear to the broken door. "Can you hear the echo?"

"What does that mean?" Yara crouched closer.

"It means that there is a hollow spot behind the door, underneath all the rubble," Shireen replied. "We need tools." She slapped her hands together, creating a cloud of dust.

"What are you two doing?" The voice from above was demanding and angry. Shireen and Yara, still on their knees, looked up.

"Ali, don't scare us like that!" Shireen glared at her brother and scrambled up onto her feet.

"The next street is on the front lines," he reminded them. Did he think they were stupid?

"Yara's identification papers are behind this door, or nearby, anyway, and we need tools. Are you going to help or not?" Shireen stared at Ali, daring him to challenge her.

With his hands on his hips, Ali grimaced, then shrugged. "I will find an ax and a shovel. Be careful. Be on the lookout."

By the time he returned, the girls had removed the smaller stones near the entrance and had inched the door open. Ali surveyed their work. "Look, there, the hinge is broken. It's better to smash though it," he said as he dropped the tools.

"Where did those come from?" Shireen pointed to the shovel and ax.

"Abandoned," he huffed. "Stand back." Ali picked up the ax and swung it over his head. The wooden door splintered but the movement shifted a section of the roof that was still intact. "What are we looking for?" asked Ali.

"A red metal box, under the bakery table," said Yara. She kept her voice steady and confident. She and Ali had walked half of Aleppo over the past few days. She didn't want him to see her weaken now.

Ali swung the ax again and again until he finally broke through. Now that the door was gone, they could see that the rubble had fallen around another roofbeam. If they could shift that, they might make a tunnel into the debris below.

Together, the three of them heaved at the beam until they moved it out of the way, and sure enough they saw a narrow opening.

Ali sat on his heels and chucked aside a large chunk of plaster. Yara and Shireen fell on their knees and gazed into the gap.

"It's too small to fit through," said Shireen.

"Get back." Ali took the shovel, widened the tunnel, and again examined his handiwork. He poked in his head and half his body. "I can see a table in there but I can't reach it." His voice returned as a muffled echo.

"Get out. I can fit," said Shireen.

"No, the whole wall could fall on top of you." Ali sounded like a father, not a brother.

"I will go." Yara flung off her robe and headscarf, rolled them into a ball, and threw them aside.

"No, Yara, you can't. You're still recovering. You . . ." Shireen reached out but Yara was already on her knees and crawling into the hole.

Instantly Yara's heart hammered. The tunnel was smaller, narrower than it looked. Stones as sharp as teeth poked out from the walls and scraped her sides. Breathing hard, she drew thick white powder from wall plaster deep into her lungs. The coughing started. She couldn't breathe. It was too dark to see. "SHIREEN!" she sobbed. She couldn't go forward and she couldn't go backward. She was stuck. "Help. HELP!" she cried.

"Get her out. Pull her out." Someone was yelling. Ali? Shireen? Yara felt hands grab her ankles. The coughing grew worse. She was confused. She kicked and lunged forward. Ali was telling her something. Yara reached out in the dark as if to grab a lifeline—instead, she touched, then clutched, something made of metal. When they yanked her back through to the other side, she could see her prize: the red tin box!

"Yara, drink." Shireen handed Yara a cup of water. Ali, white-faced, stood beside her, his eyes scanning the sky. Yara shook so badly that the water splashed down her chin and onto her lap. "Here, let me." Shireen held the cup up to Yara's lips.

"It seems as if you are always giving me water," mumbled Yara through gulps. She did her best to smile, and Shireen almost laughed.

A noise caught Yara's attention. Roja was walking towards them. Yara could feel herself relax a little. Roja was safe, and she was home. Then she heard the sound again. Yara spun around and looked in the opposite direction. She squinted, then shaded her eyes with a cupped hand. A thin woman, hunched, wearing a black *abaya* and leaning on a stick, limped towards them. A cry caught in Yara's throat. Hearts do stop.

"NANA."

CHAPTER 9

"But where were you?" Yara, bursting with joy, blurted out the question. Standing on the street, oblivious to snipers and the vibration of bombs landing blocks away, Yara threw her arms around her grandmother. "Oh, Nana, we looked everywhere." She buried her face in Nana's shoulder.

"Maha!" Roja, running towards them, cried out. "Praise Allah, you have returned to us."

They all heard the crack of a sniper's rifle.

"Inside," hissed Ali. He hurried them into the house and bolted the door behind them. Then he pressed his ear to a small hole he had drilled through the wood. Spotting a sniper was not about seeing so much as hearing the whisper of a bullet as it flew through the air. He heard nothing.

"Come, Maha, rest." Roja treated Nana like an honored guest. Nana paused and slowly lowered herself onto a mat.

"Come out, Saad. Nana is back!" Yara, on her hands and knees, peered under the table. Saad shook his head.

"Leave him," said Nana quietly. "He will come to me when he is ready. It is enough to see that he is alive." Nana put her hands to her eyes and rocked back and forth.

"May I?" Roja pointed to Nana's leg. Nana grudgingly agreed, and Roja spent the next few minutes inspecting the thick black stitches. "There's no infection, Maha, and the swelling is not too bad," said Roja as she rubbed precious olive oil into Nana's wounded leg.

"Thank you for your kindness," replied Nana. She grimaced at Roja's touch but did not complain.

Shireen served tea. They had very little water, and with a sniper outside what they did have might need to last a day. Still, Shireen filled Nana's cup to the brim.

"I am sorry for the loss of your daughter and her husband," Roja said quietly. Nana nodded and whispered words of thanks in return. The mention of her own daughter, now lying dead in an unmarked grave, brought a stiffness to Nana's back. Her mouth twitched and her brow became two deep furrows, but she did not cry. Yara had never seen Nana cry.

"Nana?" Yara stared at her grandmother. "How did you know?"

Nana shook her head slowly. "I saw," said Nana. "And I felt." Nana touched her heart.

"May the mercy of Allah be upon them. Your daughter helped my family when we first arrived, and now I can return the favor in a very small way by welcoming you into our home, such as it is," Roja said.

The house was in poor shape. Roja had sold almost everything of value—a beautiful copper table from Iran, books, dishes, a painting by a famous Syrian painter, a table, spare mattresses and pillows. Heaps of dreary fabric to be made into dreary *abayas*, along with a shelf of tinned food and water bottles, were all that remained.

"It looks lovely to me," said Nana.

"You are skin and bones, Maha," Roja said, ignoring the compliment.

"Nana?" Yara knew, everyone knew, that patients in the hospital relied on their family to bring food. Had she been in a hospital, or maybe a clinic, after all? Where else could she have been? How did Nana eat?

Nana looked into Roja's eyes. "I was not . . ." Nana bent in close and whispered in Roja's ear.

Yara drew back, confused. Their whispers sounded like bees hovering above a hive. Where had Nana been? What was the big secret?

Through all of this, the red tin box sat forgotten on the table like an ancient relic. It was Ali who, leaving his post by the door, presented the box to Nana like a gift to a queen.

"It is beautiful," said Roja. The red tin box was framed in wood decorated with an inlay of blue-gray mother-of-pearl.

"It belonged to my great-grandmother," Nana said as she held out both hands and accepted the box. "I took it from my home when . . ." She stumbled over her words, and paused. "I passed it on to my daughter on her wedding day." She placed it back on the table, dusted it off, then gave the latch a good yank. It held firm.

"Wait." Ali picked up a kitchen knife and, jamming it between the catch and the box, popped it open.

"Nana!" Yara gasped. Yara, Shireen, Roja, and Ali stood around the table and gaped at the contents—gold necklaces, bracelets, earrings, and gold coins were heaped in the box. Hearing the gasps above his head, Saad crawled out of his hiding place and gawked, open-mouthed, at the sparkling gems.

"It's like Aladdin's treasure!" said a grinning Ali as he picked up a long, delicate gold chain. And under the jewelry —American money! How could this be? Yara's parents were bakers.

"Nana, where did this come from?" Yara tried to catch Nana's eye, but Nana just mumbled something about it belonging to her grandmother. What grandmother? As for the American money, she mentioned that the man Yara called Mr. Baggy Pants had come to the bakery on several occasions and exchanged Syrian pounds for American dollars. But that did not explain the jewelry!

"Nana?" Yara gently touched her grandmother's sleeve, but Nana didn't seem to notice. She stood, using Roja's arm to steady herself, and dumped everything on the table. Ignoring the treasure, she delved deeper into the box. Only now did Yara notice its complexity. It seemed to have small compartments dividing it.

Under the jewelry was a handful of photographs. There was one of Mama and Baba on their wedding day. Mama, with her hair pinned up, wearing a white dress with lace, and Baba wearing a Western suit with a tie. There was another picture, creased and yellow with age, of a beautiful young woman and a very handsome man. The bride was covered in gold and wearing a silk dress, and . . . Nana plucked the photos out of Yara's hand and turned them face down on the table.

"Nana, who are these people?"

"Here they are!" Nana, ignoring her granddaughter, reached for a small stack of navy blue books imprinted with the Syrian coat of arms—passports! Five, one for Mama, Baba, Nana, Saad, and one for her, too—they all had passports! How? She opened one and saw her own picture.

"Nana, how did this happen?"

"Last year, at the *souk*. Remember, you had your photo taken in the little booth? See, you signed the bottom," said Nana as she riffled through the papers. Yara nodded. Baba had bought her candy and new shoes that day. That was a year ago. Had Baba been planning their escape all that time?

Beneath the passports were *Haweyat*, laminated green Syrian National Identity Cards, and their *Deftar Ayli*, the family register that recorded marriages, births, and deaths.

Yara reached for a pretty postcard. It seemed to be addressed to Nana but the card said, "Hello, Umm Aziz." It meant "the mother of Aziz." Aziz—she had never heard of Aziz.

"Nana, who is Aziz?" Yara held up the card.

Nana swiped it out of Yara's hand, turned her back on her granddaughter, and, after a pause, touched the top of her grandson's head. "Saad, I have missed you," she whispered. He didn't run back under the table or flinch from her touch.

Shireen had had enough of the treasure box. She walked to the door, opened it, and looked up at the stars. "Father, I am here. I miss you. I love you," Shireen whispered into the night air.

Ali leapt across the room like a cat. "Shireen, you might be seen." He pulled her from the doorway.

"I was speaking to our father. I am sad for him, and I am sad for us. How can you not miss him? All this talk about passports—you want to leave, don't you?" Shireen stared hard into her brother's green eyes.

"I would never leave our father behind. But"—he paused and closed the door, bolting it from inside—"you and Mama could leave."

"Us, leave? Mama and I?" Shireen studied her brother as if he had suddenly sprouted another head. She raced up the stairs, with Ali on her heels. Yara could hear their footsteps. They stopped on the second-floor landing outside the bedrooms they no longer slept in.

"And where do we go?" Shireen continued in a low, hard voice. "You see the television. You see Facebook and Twitter. The Germans, the French, the British, and Americans— they hate us. Once, we could get on a plane and visit any country. We were respected. But now, instead of tourists we are called terrorists. We are the same people, except now we are feared, even hated." Yara could hear tears in Shireen's voice. "Ali, I think we should fight for our country." Shireen's voice was a mix of gulps and sobs. "I think—"

"Fight? With what—sticks? There is no water, and soon there will be no electricity or food. You cannot fight for our country if you are starving!" Ali's voice cracked. What was Shireen doing? Yara wanted to run up the stairs and say something, anything, but this was between brother and sister.

She could hear him take a deep breath. "Shireen, the President cannot hold on to power forever. Do you think he will be forgiven for what he has done? Think, Shireen." He spoke more softly now. "You can return and rebuild, but first you must stay alive."

"So, you want our mother and me to leave the country while you stay and wait for our father to be released from prison? Do you know how stupid you sound? How long would it be before you were picked up by the rebels or the army?" After that there were more footsteps and a slammed door.

Yara and Roja sat silently. They had heard every word. Nana and Saad had, too. They drank tea. Yara read to Saad. The evening passed. Yara stewed in the corner not knowing what to do or what to think.

"Maha, you must be tired." Roja spoke kindly to Nana, who smiled sadly. "Your daughter . . ." Roja began, and then stopped.

Nana nodded her head. "My daughter . . ." she whispered.

Roja moved towards her, sat beside her, circled her arms around her. "Your daughter was a wonderful woman," she whispered, loudly enough for Yara to hear. Tears circled her own eyes. *Mama, Mama.* Nana bobbed her head but did not speak. And then her grandmother did something Yara had thought impossible. Even with Nana's head bowed, Yara could see her tears fall. They rolled down her thin cheeks unchecked, as if unnoticed.

"Come, Maha, you will sleep in my room tonight," said Roja as she gently helped Nana to her feet. Nana, the most stubborn woman in the world, was put to bed with tea and left to mourn her daughter.

Maybe an hour later, but who could tell, Yara inched back the curtain that divided Roja's bedroom from the main room. "Nana?" She wanted to tell her grandmother that she was hurting, too. She wanted to feel her grandmother's arms around her.

"Go to sleep, Yara," said Nana faintly.

Biting her lip, Yara pulled the curtain back across the threshold and returned to her mat beside Saad. Roja and Shireen lay side by side across the room, Ali was out back in the shed. Maybe no one heard, maybe they all did, as Yara muffled her cries in a sheet held against her mouth.

CHAPTER 10

Yara was the last to wake up. She was bone-tired, and the day had only just begun. Ali had left on his usual hunt for food and water. Shireen was reading quietly to Saad, her voice mingling with the thrum of Roja's sewing machine. Nana had switched on the diesel generator in the kitchen at the back of the house. Yara watched from her mat as Nana carefully made and poured out the tea. The water was now more precious than the tea.

Now was the time to ask, but which question first?

Yara came to the kitchen doorway. "Nana?"

Nana turned and put up a flat palm, limped past Yara carrying a tray of teacups, and slipped down onto a mat. She motioned to Saad. "Come, eat." She handed him a plate of watermelon. Saad, astonished at the treat, took the plate and returned to his refuge under the table.

"He hasn't spoken since . . ." Yara's voice trailed off. *Since Mama and Baba were killed, since we have lost our home, the bakery, the life we loved.*

Nana rested her eyes on her grandson and nodded. "It is the children who suffer the most in war," she said. "Always the children."

Perhaps Nana read her mind, or maybe the moment had simply come. Nana called to her now, and to Roja and Shireen. They all sat down on the mat and accepted her tea.

"I need to tell you something—about me, about my past. It is time you knew the truth," said Nana.

"Come, Shireen. We will leave Yara and her grandmother to talk," Roja said quietly.

Nana shook her head. "The house is too small for secrets, and we are family now." She held her head high, like a queen. "Secrets are like sparks waiting to catch fire, and when they do, they can burn down a house, or a country."

Yara and Shireen traded looks. All three sat on mats and pillows, backs straight, eyes wide.

"I lied," Nana said bluntly. She took a sip of tea. The air stilled. "The jewelry, the little money that is left—it all belongs to me."

"Nana?" Yara's voice rose in her throat.

"Hush, my girl. I need to speak, and you need to hear." Without waiting for anyone to catch their breath, Nana began her story in a low, flat voice. Everything was about to change, Yara could feel it.

"I was born in the city of Hama, an only child. I was *habibat baba,* my father's beloved daughter. Do you want to know why I am good at mathematics and speak French and English? It is because my father had visited Western countries and knew what an educated woman could accomplish. He hired private tutors, and after years of study I was allowed to go to university." If Nana noticed the shock on their faces, she ignored it. If Nana's father was not a baker, who was he?

"During my second year I met Fawzi." She spoke his name so softly, with such devotion, that both girls were startled.

"What do romance novels say, 'love at first sight'?" Nana looked up at the ceiling as if, by tilting her head, tears would not fill her eyes. "He was the eldest son of a wealthy family," she added.

Fawzi? Yara leaned forward. Who was Nana's father? Why did he travel? Nana had never, ever talked about him.

"We married, and my husband built me a beautiful home." She paused. "The city of Hama was so lovely, with its water wheels—the *norias*, wheels of pots—along the river. Such a wonderful place to raise our four sons."

Yara could only sit and stare. Four sons? *Four?* Nana had only one son, Uncle Sami, and one daughter, Mama.

"Our boys filled our home and our hearts with laughter. It took many servants to manage our big house and our family. And"—she paused—"I continued my studies. I loved French novels, Simone de Beauvoir, George Sand"—Nana's eyes suddenly brightened—"and Colette!" She paused.

Who and what was "Colette"? Yara was becoming impatient. Who cared who Colette was? "Nana, don't stop." Yara squeezed her grandmother's hand.

"Yes, yes, I'm sorry." Nana nodded. "It was 1982. Hafez al-Assad, the father of the current president, Bashar al-Assad, ruled the country. He was a monster, just like his son." She curled her fingers into a fist. "Corruption was everywhere. You could hardly cross the street without having to pay a policeman. People were angry, but we said nothing, we *did* nothing. That was our crime. I pretended that the world outside the walls of our compound was not my concern. I knew that the universities were badly run. We all knew that inept people ran the hospitals.

"Then the outside world began to worm its way into my life. Books were banned. Servants became spies for the government. I hired new servants and paid off the old servants. I was afraid they would tell the police that we had hidden foreign books under the floorboards. People were terrified of each other, of being turned in. We trusted no one except family. Men, and women, too, were picked up off the streets by the Mukhabarat, the secret police, and then they just . . ." Nana fluttered her fingers ". . . disappeared."

No one spoke. Yara was barely conscious that Roja and Shireen were even in the room. Where were her four uncles? Where was Nana's family?

"Nana, I . . ." Yara began to speak without really knowing what she would say, but Nana wasn't listening. She looked straight ahead, her eyes suddenly cold as stones.

"In June 1980 there was an attempt to assassinate President Hafez al-Assad. There was fighting between the President's regime and the Muslim Brotherhood, such terrible, terrible violence." Nana squeezed her eyes shut. Her voice ebbed and crested like sand dunes. "The President retaliated with more arrests, more murders, more disappearances. They fought on and on, and we paid for their brutality with our blood." Nana took a breath as silver tears trickled down her cheeks. "Then came the uprising in 1982. You've probably heard people speak of it as *The Events.*"

Roja's own face drained of color, and she rose to her feet. "Come, Saad." She peered under the table and motioned to the child. Saad peeked out and looked to Yara as if asking permission. Yara nodded her head mechanically, and Saad followed Roja into the bedroom. "Close your eyes, sleep," Roja whispered as she tucked Saad into her own bed, then pulled the curtain as if it would block out sound as well as sight. Roja returned and rested her hand briefly on Nana's shoulder.

"President Hafez al-Assad bombed our city." Nana looked at Roja, and the two shared a look so knowing, so painful, that Yara looked away. Roja sat, and Nana took a deep breath.

"The bombs! Explosions everywhere. Snipers were on rooftops. Tanks crushed the cobblestones of our beautiful streets. I sent the servants away. They had families of their own. Fawzi, my beautiful husband, wanted to take our sons out to buy food and petrol. He thought we should prepare to stay inside for weeks if necessary. But I would not let my boys go out. I WOULD NOT LET HIM TAKE MY SONS!" Nana clenched her fist and with each word she beat her chest.

"Nana, stop." Yara threw her arms around her grandmother. Nana cupped her hands and sobbed into them. "Nana, please." The sight of her grandmother sobbing was terrifying

102 • JAMAL SAEED AND SHARON E. McKAY

"No." Nana waved her away. "You must hear it all, and I don't want to repeat it ever again." Nana rubbed her face with the back of her hand. "My husband went out alone. What we did not know then was that President al-Assad's army was going house to house rounding up all the men and boys over thirteen years of age. *Thirteen!*

"They burst into our home. I begged the soldiers to listen to me, just listen. 'Please, we support the army. We support the President. We love the regime.' I was screaming anything I could think of. *'Just don't take my sons. Don't take my sons.'*

"I ran around the house trying to find the pin to prove that our thirteen-year-old, still in elementary school, belonged to the Baath Party Pioneers, the President's own party. My older boys were in high school and belonged to the Baath Party, too. I came running out of the house and into our courtyard with the proof, but they were gone. The soldiers, my sons—gone. Just gone! Aziz, sixteen, Kareem, fifteen, and Anas, only thirteen." She spoke each name slowly. "Sami was five years old. They left him in the courtyard. He looked so fragile, so alone." Nana glanced towards Roja's room, where Saad was sleeping.

Yara, already sitting up, wrenched her body forward. Sami? Uncle Sami? Questions ran through Yara like a speeding train. But even if she could form the questions her mouth would not utter them.

"I stood in a courtyard filled with pots of flowers, with the sun beating down and the tiles warm under my feet." Nana, almost in a dream state, continued to speak. "I stood beside my little son for a long time. He didn't cry. It was so still. Even the birds had stopped singing." Everything around Yara stilled, too. How was it possible that she had not known any of this?

"I held Sami and listened to the cries of my neighbors. There is no sound in the world like the wail that comes from the throat of a mother as her children are taken from her." Nana cupped her hands over her eyes. "It was like listening to beating hearts being ripped from breathing chests."

Roja muffled her sobs with her hands. Shireen moved closer to Yara.

"My neighbor came running. She looked half-mad. Her sons had been taken, too. 'The city square,' she screamed. 'Hundreds, men and boys—in the city square!' And then the woman ran off! I thought that, maybe, maybe, the soldiers were going to make them all join the army." Nana stopped. The heat in the room closed in. Shireen held on to Yara as if trying to pin her to earth. She wrapped her arms around her and began to rock Yara gently back and forth, back and forth.

"My husband came running home," said Nana. "I was shaking. I couldn't stop myself. Words tumbled out of my mouth. When I told him that our sons had been taken, he went mad. He ran to the square. I couldn't stop him. I wanted to go, too. 'Stay with Sami,' he cried. 'Protect him. No matter what, protect him.'

"Two days I waited in our house, our beautiful home that was now my prison. Finally, I locked Sami in a closet and went looking for my children and my husband. And I found them." Nana held her hands up, palms to the ceiling. "I found them all. They had been executed. Their bodies were still there—

in the square, baking in the sun. My husband was spread over our boys as if even in death he could protect them." Nana, defeated and exhausted, looked as small as a bird. "Every male over the age of thirteen in the entire city of Hama had been murdered," she said in a small, tired voice.

Roja knelt down beside Nana and folded her arms around her. Yara and Shireen sat in stunned, pained silence. Taking another breath, Nana continued.

"There were rumors that my in-laws had supported the uprising. How was I to know truth from lies? What truth is there in war?" Nana's voice was now low and flat. "My own dear father, the man who raised me, educated me, had suffered a fall the year before. He could barely walk. I knew my mother would not leave him. I wanted to run across the city to my parents' home but the streets were dangerous and Sami was so little. Even with the shelling and the tanks rolling through the streets, one of my parents' servants made his way to my house. I had known him since I was a child. He said the government had called for the city's surrender. Was I to surrender? To whom? I didn't understand. The government said that those remaining in the city would be considered rebels and shot. I had to leave. But leave and go where? I thought perhaps all of Syria was under attack. I wanted to die with my husband and sons, but there was Sami, and my promise.

"This servant, he gave me a scribbled note from my father. It said that I was to run, hide, and to never come out of hiding. Was my father a rebel? It was dangerous to ask questions. It still is.

"Later, I heard that my parents had been killed. I have never learned exactly how they died. Sami and I ran to my in-laws' house. The army was everywhere, in every doorway, on every rooftop, even in the mosques and shooting from the minarets.

"The home of my husband's parents had been destroyed." Nana stopped, took a breath, and again, as if trying to get the story told, never to be spoken of again, she charged on. "They were there, in the courtyard. My in-laws had been executed. I had loved them, and they had loved me. Sami and I were in danger, it was obvious. I could be accused of supporting the uprising, and what would happen to my boy, my last son, if I was killed or arrested? Who would protect him? I ran home.

"After a few days I ventured out again. Our money in the bank was frozen. Majed, a baker—your grandfather, Yara—came to the gate one day with bread. I did not dare let him in. We talked through the gate. Through all the chaos, through all the horrific sounds, I heard this gentle voice. He had lost his wife and daughter, his home and business, in Hafez al-Assad's ruthless shelling of our beautiful city. I told him about my husband and sons. We cried.

"Majed came back the next day, and the next, and the next to give us bread. My trust grew and I let him in. He was a kind, intelligent man. On the fourth day, although I can't be sure, he offered to marry me and take us away. I was desperate, alone, and I had to keep Sami safe. I was grateful. Do you remember him, Yara? You were only four when your grandfather died."

There was a shadow of a memory, of a man with soft brown eyes lifting her up onto his shoulders. Yara nodded, and Nana carried on.

"I gathered Sami, and all the jewelry and money I could find in the house, and the three of us left Hama forever. We waited four months after the death of my husband to marry, as required by Islamic law. Later your grandfather and I sold enough jewelry to buy the bakery here in Aleppo. I learned how to bake. Later your mother was born. I began a new life. Sami was my only connection to the old life." Nana simply stopped speaking. She was clearly exhausted.

"I'm sorry. I'm sorry," Yara whispered. Nana had lost a family, a husband, sons, her home, and then to become a baker after having many servants! Yara was the granddaughter of bakers, but now she was something else besides. Uncle Sami and Mama had different fathers. That meant that she had great-grandparents she had never heard about. It was confusing. One day she would think about it but not now. She wiped the tears from her face with open palms.

"Nana, about Saad . . ." Yara stopped. She remembered the day Saad was born, and how Nana had looked at him and left the room, shoulders slumped.

Nana looked towards the bedroom. "I saw it the moment he was born. He looks like Anas, my most beautiful son, the sensitive one, my poet. Every day I look at my grandson and the face of my third son flashes in my mind. It is uncanny."

Nana had never held Saad unless it was to keep him from falling, and now Yara understood why. She felt Shireen's hand cover her own, felt her friend's strength spread from one body to another.

"I thought you were always angry at me, at us," Yara murmured through tears.

Nana put up her hand. "No, never!" Her voice rose to a cry, her eyes wild with alarm. "You are my heart. Without you, your brother, and Sami, there is nothing. Nothing!"

Yara lurched towards her tiny grandmother, who seemed so small in her arms.

"Wait, wait. There is something else." Nana pulled away from Yara. She looked from Roja to Shireen, and finally her shining eyes rested on Yara. *No, no, no more.* Yara held her breath.

"I met a man," said Nana. Yara slapped a hand over her mouth. Nana sat tall, suddenly composed, eyes expressionless, revealing nothing. "The hospital I was taken to was bombed. I was confused . . . For a woman to go and live in a man's house—a man who is not her husband . . ." Nana shook her head. "His name is Rifa'at. He helps people escape Syria."

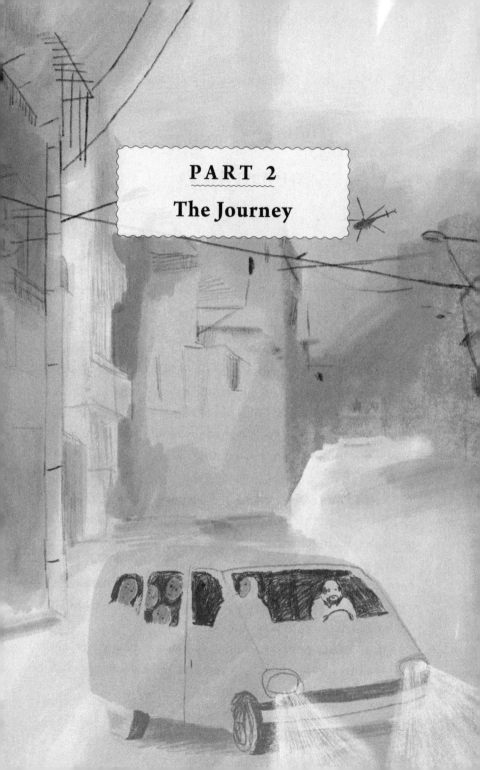

PART 2
The Journey

CHAPTER 11

ALEPPO, SYRIA

2015

Yara stood at the peephole. She had been waiting all day for this mystery man of Nana's. It was late, just before sunset, when she saw an old, bent man creeping along the road, tapping his white stick against the stones and rocks that littered the ground. He was coming directly towards their door!

"Nana?" Yara stood back as he knocked.

Nana peeked through the peephole. "That's him," she said.

What? Their guide was blind!

The old man crept inside and, with a flourish, flung off his shawl, tossed aside his cane, and straightened up. There were many ways to try to fool snipers, and disguising oneself as an old, broken, blind man was one.

Rifa'at had a nose as straight as a blade planted firmly between two narrow, hooded eyes, and the hair on his chin stood up like bristles on a wire brush.

"*As-salaamu 'alaykum.* Peace be upon you." His voice was so low and gravelly he might have had pebbles trapped in the back of his throat. He nodded first to Roja and then to Nana. His eyes softened when he looked at Nana. Yara's eyebrows shot up.

"*Wa 'alaykum as-salaam.* And peace be upon you," Nana responded, her voice also low and respectful. She introduced Ali, Roja, Yara, and Shireen. Saad ducked behind Yara. Shireen did not greet him; instead she gazed at him with a mixture of curiosity and suspicion.

"Sit, Rifa'at." Nana motioned to a pillow. As he lowered himself to the floor, his knees cracked like gunshots. Saad flinched.

"He is easily frightened," explained Nana.

"Come, come." Roja took Saad by the hand and settled him in the bedroom, returning to the kitchen to make tea.

"And how is your grandson, Rifa'at?" Nana asked politely.

"My grandson is not the carefree boy he once was. What will happen to the children in Syria once this war is over?" Rifa'at shook his head. His eyes were black and watery.

"Can it be worse than what is happening to them now?" asked Nana.

Rifa'at gave what might have been a sad smile, had it been possible to see any real expression under his overgrown mustache. He turned to the small group that surrounded him and said, "Are you aware that your grandmother saved the life of my grandson?"

Yara and Shireen exchanged glances.

Rifa'at did not wait for a response. "The hospital was bombed. When everyone else ran for their lives, your grandmother, with a leg that could barely hold her up and a bump on her head the size of a melon, carried my grandson down hallways, three flights of stairs, and out onto the street. I found them there, holding on to each other." Here Rifa'at turned to Nana and added, "I owe you everything. I have only his mother and the boy left. The rest of my family"—he paused to clear his throat—"were killed in a car bombing a year ago. They were together, on their way to a family picnic."

No one spoke for a moment. It seemed everyone had a story like this.

"It is I who owe you, Rifa'at," said Nana. "When Rifa'at found us, I did not even know who I was." Nana turned to Yara. "After the bombing, Rifa'at took me to his home, where his daughter-in-law cared for me." Yara and Ali stared at each other, eyes wide. It all made sense now.

Nana clapped her hands together as if to say, *Enough of this, let us get on with it.*

Rifa'at unfolded a map that had gone soft from folding and unfolding. As he spread it out, flattening it with the heel of his hand, all of Syria and the surrounding countries were laid out in front of them.

"A map, Rifa'at? Why do we need a map?" asked Nana. Syrians did not use maps. The shape of their country was imprinted in their minds, maybe even stamped on their souls.

"It is from a hotel. There are not many tourists in Syria now." He shrugged. "You should see, not only hear, about the dangers ahead." Rifa'at tapped the map with a long fingernail. "Here are Turkey, Iraq, Jordan, and Lebanon, the four countries that surround Syria."

Ali rolled his eyes. Yara caught it and almost giggled. Did this man think they were all stupid? Yara then looked over at Shireen. They had talked before about all the countries, about the dangers of each. But Shireen's eyes were blank, as if she were looking inward. Was she still being stubborn about staying in Aleppo? They would all leave together, they must. Yara had already lost Mama and Baba, how could she lose Shireen, too?

Roja set down a tray of tea and cups, poured herself the first cup, tasted it, and then poured a cup for Rifa'at. "You must be thirsty," she said quietly. Rifa'at nodded.

As Roja continued to pour, Yara tugged on Nana's sleeve. "Nana, we must go to Damascus to see Uncle Sami. From there we can go to Dara'a, then cross the border into Jordan." Yara took a deep breath. "Please, Nana, think of Uncle Sami."

Nana looked into her granddaughter's eyes. Yara looked away. Of course Nana was thinking about Uncle Sami.

Nana turned back to Rifa'at. "My granddaughter is correct. First we go to Damascus. Then we go into Jordan."

"Do you think it is that easy? Do you think you will just show up at the border and wave your passport and they will let you in? 'Come, welcome,' they will say. 'Have tea.'" He flapped his hands in the air. "Listen to me, the Jordanians will stop you at the Nasib Border Crossing. Why should they let you in? You could be with ISIS for all they know!"

Nana waved a hand. "Never mind that. First we go to Damascus."

Rifa'at shook his head. "The M5 highway that connects Damascus to Aleppo is under government control. The soldiers on patrol are like pirates on the high seas! They watch. The government knows if a bird flies over the road," Rifa'at growled.

"But my uncle is in Damascus." Yara was persistent.

"Do you know where he lives? Are you going to walk the streets yelling your uncle's name?" Rifa'at waved his hand in the air as though he were shooing away flies. "When did you call him last?"

"Numbers change. Phones get lost." Two distinct ridges, as deep and straight as if carved with a knife, formed above Nana's nose. "Leave my son to me," said Nana sharply. Everyone was getting tense.

"How long would it take to drive from Aleppo to Damascus?" Ali interjected. Yara shot him a sideways glance. He was interested. That was a good thing.

Rifa'at shrugged. "How long? Is this Switzerland? It takes as long as it takes to drink a river or a glass of water."

Yara and Shireen exchanged looks. What did that mean?

He continued. "In normal times, four hours by bus. But now, who knows? It can take weeks." Frustrated, Rifa'at slurped his tea. Then he set down his cup and held up a finger.

"There are explosions, long checkpoints, breakdowns, accidents. We might have to leave the highway and take back roads. And who might we meet? The Queen of Sheba? No, more likely the al-Nusra Front—do you know them? Of course you do, al-Qaeda's military wing. And what about the Free Syrian Army, the rebels? They need money to survive. Where will they get it, hmm? Well, where do you think? Hezbollah—they descend like dust storms—they want to rid both Lebanon and Syria of all 'non-believers,' but who are they to decide who is or isn't a good Muslim? Only Allah knows, Glory be to Him." Rifa'at was getting more agitated with each breath. "The Kurds are fighting for a homeland. The Shabbiha are just thugs paid by the government to harass us. And there are gangs everywhere. How are we to survive?"

"But the Free Syrian Army want to liberate us, give Syria democracy, like Europe and America," Ali interrupted.

Rifa'at lifted his hands, palms raised to roof. "Many in the FSA are good, but many have broken away to form gangs. As for the others . . ." Rifa'at shrugged.

"But there is still hope," Ali piped up.

"Hope, yes, but do you care who robs you?" asked Rifa'at. "You have still lost your possessions. And do you care who shoots you? You are still dead."

"But . . ." Ali, red-faced and confused, raised his voice.

Rifa'at shook his head. "Are you looking for heroes in a war? There is no such thing. But if you are searching in your mind for goodness, then think of the Syrian people themselves. There are many, many peaceful activists who are caught be-tween the hammer of government and evil fanatics and armed militias. Your husband"—Rifa'at nodded towards Roja— "I have heard of him. Word gets out even from the prisons. He is a good man, a peaceful man, and he is not forgotten."

The kind words were unexpected. Roja, who was not given to showing her emotions, teared up. Shireen reached over and took her mother's hand.

Yara looked from Ali to Rifa'at. Why were they talking politics? They should be planning their journey, their escape!

"Once we pass Damascus, it is one hundred kilometers and seven checkpoints to Dara'a, and then on to the Jordanian border," said Yara. "I saw it on Facebook," she added.

"This you got from *Facebook*? Would you find the date of the post?" Rifa'at asked, and shook his head.

Yara nodded, picked up her tea, and held the cup high to hide behind.

Rifa'at took a long, cooling breath. "I am telling you, it costs money to get into Jordan, big money. If you do get in, you will live in a refugee camp, possibly for years. There you could apply for a visa to some country. But what skills do you have? What money? Why would they want you?"

"Leave our immigration problems to us, Rifa'at. We need you to take us to Damascus. That is all." Nana's words were as blunt as a hammer on a nail.

"That is all? And what do you do there, have coffee in Damascus with the President and his British wife?"

For a moment no one talked. Rifa'at turned to Roja, who was sitting quietly, her hands folded, her thoughts seemingly far, far away. "What about you?" he asked, not unkindly.

Roja looked around the room, first at her children, then at Nana, before turning to Rifa'at. "I will not leave the country without my husband. In time my brother will come for me. I will return with him to Hasakeh, up north, near the Turkish border." Roja spoke slowly but with a certainty Yara had never heard before.

Startled, mouth agape, Nana stared at Roja. Shireen and Ali, too, looked stunned. Ali's mouth was drawn into a hard, pale line and his nostrils flared. Yara knew what he was thinking. Ali's mother had made plans without consulting him. With his father in jail, he was the head of the family.

Shireen found her voice. "No, Mama," she said. "We can't go there. Hasakeh is near the city of Raqqa, the capital of ISIS! We can't . . ." Shireen looked to her brother, to Nana.

"Roja, my friend, please think more carefully about this," Nana said.

Roja gave Nana a small smile. "Dangers are in every corner of this country. Allah wills if I am to die, and if it is so then I will die with my brother and his family." Her words hung in the air. "And, if Allah wills, my children will not be with me."

"I don't understand," cried Shireen. "We are your family! *We are your children!*"

Roja ignored her daughter and turned to Nana. "Maha, will you take Ali and Shireen with you?"

Ali cried out in disbelief, "Do you think I would leave my father in prison and you, my own mother, alone?" The look on Ali's face sent a chill down Yara's spine. The muscles in his jaw were clenched.

Roja turned on her two children with the terrifying focus of a cannon. "Your father wants you out of Syria. Do you not understand what hell he is in, thinking that you two are in danger? Do you not know what it is for a parent to not be able to protect his children? We raised thinkers and scholars, not soldiers. You will not defy him! YOU WILL NOT!" Roja's voice was as powerful as any weapon.

Shireen's mouth gaped open.

"How do you know this?" Ali leaned towards his mother.

"I have received word. It cost him a great deal to get a message out of the prison. You will NOT defy him!"

"But Mama . . ." His voice was softer now.

"YOU WILL NOT!" Roja repeated, and she turned back to Nana, clear-eyed and determined. "Maha, I have money put aside. Will you take my children?"

"Yes, yes, of course, my friend," said Nana.

Strong, beautiful Roja, with liquid brown eyes, turned back to stare boldly at her two children. Shireen looked down. Yara could see tears caught in her eyelashes. Ali stared at his mother, as defiant as ever. Neither said another word.

"There will be five of us traveling," said Nana to Rifa'at.

Bubbles looped and twisted in Yara's stomach. She was sorry, really sorry, that Shireen and Ali were upset, but now they would stay together! *Thank you, thank you, thank you!* She murmured the words in her heart but she, too, said nothing.

Rifa'at peered at the twins, at Yara, at Nana, and then looked to the bedroom where Saad slept. He shook his head. "You don't know how dangerous this journey is," he said. "Boys, even little ones, get abducted, and girls . . ." He did not finish his sentence. They all knew what could happen to girls.

"You yourself said that all routes out of Syria are dangerous," Nana added, although she was still looking at Roja. "And my granddaughter is right. We must go first to Damascus." Nana, in a gesture that would never have happened even a month before, brushed Rifa'at's hand, and added, "Put away your map, my friend, and tell me how we can get there and how much it will cost."

CHAPTER 12

The sound of Shireen rising from her mat was muted and soft, like a moth's wings flapping against glass. Without turning her head, Yara knew Shireen was making her way to the spiral stone steps that led to the roof. No one noticed, or possibly cared, as Yara followed Shireen up to the second floor, past the two shut-up bedrooms, then up more stairs to the roof. Shireen and Ali would come with them, she was thinking. They would go to school. Saad would talk again. Yara was so happy she thought she might fly up the steps.

Yara stood at the doorway to the roof. It was already cooler up there. The oppressive heat of the day would soon lift. Instinctively, she searched the sky for helicopters or planes.

Shireen stood close to the lip of the roof. She had no fear of heights and was always too near the edge. The dying light outlined her profile with the exactness of an artist using the thinnest of pen nibs. *She is so beautiful,* thought Yara. In the West, they would put Shireen's face on glossy magazine covers. Maybe that could still happen. In the West, people could do what they liked, become whatever they wanted to become, there were no limits. That's what she'd heard.

"Shireen?" Yara called out.

Shireen didn't turn around. "I miss my beautiful city," she said.

Yara stood beside her and looked out. "I will miss it, too." A golden sun was setting as fingers of light curled back into a fiery orange fist. The sky above was darkening.

"No, you don't understand," said Shireen, her voice suddenly hard and laced with resentment. "I miss it now. I miss the Umayyad Mosque, the Citadel, the beautiful al-Jadidah neighborhood, the scents of the perfumers' market, and the people who have disappeared, who have left, and who have died." Shireen wrapped her arms around her waist as if trying to hug herself. "Most of all," whispered Shireen, "I miss my father. He . . ."

Then neither spoke. Black dots were flying out of the sunset. Yara pointed to the helicopters, a half dozen or more, coming towards them. They stood, transfixed. Yara reached for Shireen's hand. They waited, counting the seconds. Which way would they go? *Which way?*

And then . . . *and then* . . . the helicopters veered towards the southern part of the city.

Boom! Boom! Boom! Puffs of gray smoke rose up in a thin stream.

As they watched, the wind blew and the smoke stretched out and lay like a rumpled, dirty blanket across the sky.

Shireen's face contorted in fury. "You see? We are being bombed out of existence—forever! It is not enough to take our lives. They want the lives of our ancestors. Buildings and streets that have been walked on since the beginning of time are gone in an instant. In a thousand years, in five thousand years, no one will find our treasures in the sand. We are being removed from history. And now my parents want us to be removed, too." Shaking with emotion, Shireen sank down to her knees and dropped her head into her hands.

"Yara, leave us, please." Roja, her mouth set hard as stone, stood on the roof by the door.

"Shireen?" Yara whispered.

"Leave us, Yara," repeated Roja.

Yara walked past Roja and paused on the stairs, her back against the cool stone wall of the stairwell. Peeking around the corner, she saw Roja bend down in front of Shireen and fold her hands around her daughter's hands. Yara knew she should not eavesdrop, but it was as if her feet were rooted to the spot.

"Do you know how much you are loved? Do you? Why do you think he got us passports? Your father loves you more than the earth." Roja's voice softened. "This is your chance for life, your best chance. All parents want their children to be safe and happy, and that's not possible in this country."

Quietly, Yara tiptoed down the stone steps.

She found Ali sitting across from Rifa'at, listening so intently that he did not notice when she entered the room. Nana sat close to her friend.

"I cannot guarantee your safety, Maha," said Rifa'at with a shake of his head. "You will need at least one million Syrian pounds, that's two thousand American dollars, just for bribes. And it costs money to leave Syria and enter Jordan." Rifa'at peered at Nana under eyebrows so thick they could have been two mustaches joined in the middle.

"We will find my son. He will help us." Nana gave Rifa'at a knowing smile that seemed to irritate him even more. "There is hope, *inshallah,* if God wills it we will all survive."

"And will God do something about this heat?" Rifa'at grumbled as he scratched his neck.

"Yes, yes, water could boil in a jug." Nana's mouth twitched. She gave Yara a small smile.

Rifa'at shrugged. "You saved the life of my grandson. I am in your debt. But know this." He waggled a finger. "It is rumored that Aleppo will soon be lost to al-Assad and his government, by June perhaps, August at the latest. The rebels are beaten, at least here in this city." As Rifa'at stood, his knees snapped and popped. "Tomorrow I will come for you. Watch for my van. Day or night, I will blink the lights if it is safe. Now I must go. My grandson and daughter-in-law will worry." He placed a hand on his back and groaned.

"Yara, look out to the road," said Nana.

Yara could have skipped across the room. They would see Uncle Sami very soon and they would all be together! She peered through the peephole. A half-moon cast ghostly shadows on the empty street. Roja cautiously turned off the battery light as Yara opened the door.

With his stick in hand and his head covered with a shawl, Rifa'at turned to Yara. "You are very like your grandmother," he said softly, before walking out into the night. He mumbled something else, too, something like, "You are both stubborn as rocks."

CHAPTER 13

The night passed and the next day dragged on. But who could tell? With the windows boarded up it was always dark inside. Ali was at his post by the door, on the lookout for Rifa'at.

"I hear something—it's distant—a truck, maybe a van. Quiet." Ali pressed his ear to the door.

"Is it him?" whispered Yara. "Is it Rifa'at?" And then they all felt a slow, continuous rumble. The vehicle wasn't stopping. It was not Rifa'at.

Shots were fired up into the air. They didn't need to see in order to know. Army? Rebels? *Tata-tat-tat*. And then came the grinding sound of truck tires spewing stones. Shrapnel pinged off the roof.

"Down," Ali ordered. Yara grabbed her little brother, pushed him down, and lay on top of him.

A sound system squealed. "You, in your homes, listen to me," thundered a voice through a speaker. "If there are men or boys of fighting age hiding in your house, tell them to come out now."

Who were they? Government soldiers? Rebels? Gangs? Ali put his eye to the peephole.

"HEAR ME! Tell them that only by fighting will their lives have meaning. Tell them that they will go to paradise if they are killed fighting for our faith." More bullets were fired into the air. *Tat-tat-tat.*

Blood rushed up to Yara's face. It was hard to breathe. "Who are they?" she whispered. Ali shook his head.

"If we come into your house and find you hiding behind women it will be bad for you, and your family," the voice continued.

They were rebel soldiers, Yara was sure of it. Ali had said he wanted to fight with the rebels. He would do anything to get his father out of jail.

Breathless, Yara stared at Ali. *Don't listen, Ali, don't listen.* She wanted to sit beside him, to put her arm around him, to tell him . . . something. He was glued to the door. She couldn't tell what he was thinking. *Don't listen.*

There was a pause and another high-pitched squeal of the sound system, and then the disembodied voice carried on. "A great battle will take place here, on this street, during the coming week. Wives, mothers, send out the fighting men and leave your homes! We are fighting to satisfy Allah." The guns went off. *Tat-tat-tat.*

Ali gazed first at Yara, but then focused on Shireen. Even in the dim light, Shireen's naturally light olive skin looked pale, almost blue, as if she were cold. Yara buried her face in Saad's hair.

Thoughts of Mama and Baba rushed in. She gulped hard and held her breath. And then there was a rumble and a squeal of tires on the road as the truck, and the voice, pulled away.

"Rifa'at will come for us. You will see," Nana whispered.

All day Nana and Roja, and Shireen and Yara, too, had worked frantically sewing bits of jewelry into their clothes. Shireen had objected. "This does not belong to me," she'd said, holding up a ruby ring.

Nana had wagged a finger at her. "What if something happens and we are split up? Do you think I would want you to be without resources?" Nana clucked her tongue like a chicken. Roja continued sewing, her face soft with gratitude.

An emerald ring and a gold chain were sewn into Ali's secret pocket. Yara didn't even know what baubles went into her clothes. Nana held on to the cash. Gold bangles and a few bits were left in the tin box. A thief needed something to steal.

Yara handed around bread. Ali whispered to his sister. Shireen took his place by the door as Ali quietly walked across the room to the back shed. Soon they would have tea. That would be her chance to talk to him. After the journey began, who knew when she would find a moment to say . . . say what? She would think of something, anything!

Yara smoothed her long, dark hair and straightened the dress Roja had made her. It fell over her jeans to her knees.

Her heart thumped madly with excitement. Nana and Roja were huddled around the lamp, stitching the last of the jewelry into cuffs and hems.

"Ali." Yara held back the curtain that divided the living area from the shed. She blinked. He had taken down a board that covered a smashed window. Streams of light poured into the room. In the dimness of the house his hair was dark but now, in the light, she could see strands of gold, cinnamon, and even ruby red all mixed in. He had grown taller despite his poor diet.

"Ali?" she tried again. Her tongue stuck to the roof of her mouth. He moved towards her without speaking. Beads of sweat gathered on her neck behind her hair. She walked towards him as if being pulled by a magic thread. Her heart hammered. She should turn around right now. Go back into the main room. What if Nana saw her here? But she wasn't doing anything wrong. Not yet.

"I wanted . . ." She had no idea what she wanted. He stepped towards her. They were inches apart.

She lifted her hand and gingerly touched his chest, then pulled it back as if she had touched hot coals. A shiver shot down her spine. He put a cool hand on the back of her neck.

"Yara, I . . ."

"Yara, come and choose a bag," Roja called from the other room. Yara and Ali stood still, as if caught in a beam of light. "Yara, where are you?" Roja called again.

"Coming." Yara spun on her heels and walked into the main room. Could they see her red face? Could they hear her heart banging?

Roja stood next to a pile of bags. "Take this." She handed Yara a backpack. Shireen, who was stretching, was given a string bag. "This is for you, Maha," said Roja. Nana graciously accepted a small roller bag.

Yara's hand trembled as she clutched the backpack to her chest.

"What's wrong with you?" whispered Shireen.

Yara shook her head and turned away.

"This one is for you, Saad." Roja held out a Woody Woodpecker backpack. Saad rolled off his mat and wandered over, two curled fists rubbing his eyes. He studied Woody's red hair and smiley beak. *Say something, Saad,* thought Yara. *Say anything.* He gave Roja his approval with a grin.

"Here, you can have this. It was mine!" Shireen took a little stuffed bear off the only shelf left in the room and handed it to Saad. His small face brightened. He held it against his chest, then slipped it into his Woody Woodpecker backpack. He added the yellow truck with the loopy wheels. Ali had tried to fix it. The wheels turned now but in a lopsided way—as though the truck needed crutches.

Ali had come in from the shed. Goose bumps traveled Yara's body. Where was Rifa'at? Water bottles, a first aid kit, food, thin blankets went into their bags. There was underwear, too, and a pair of leggings. She wished she had another pair of jeans, but at least the ones she had on were clean.

Yara drew her father's tobacco pouch out of her pocket. She opened it and inhaled. Baba was suddenly as real to her as if he stood beside her.

Shireen tucked her father's Quran, covered in a red velvet sleeve, into her string bag, along with a change of clothes. She looked angry. Every time Roja approached her, Shireen turned away.

Roja moved around the room at lightning speed, her movements sharp and jerky. She was sending her children away, thought Yara. But it was the right thing to do. If only Shireen understood.

The red tin box went into Nana's roller bag. And then Nana grasped her friend's hand. "Roja, come with us." Nana was pleading.

Again, just like the last time and the time before that, Roja shook her head. "We have been over this. I cannot leave my husband. Who would feed him?" She looked into her friend's eyes.

"You cannot help him."

"But he could be moved to another prison. Things change, Maha. I have to hope. And what if he is released and I am not even in the country? No, I will stay. My brother is coming for me at daybreak tomorrow." But her wobbly voice betrayed her. Even Roja's confidence was slipping.

"What if your husband is never released, Roja?" Nana asked bluntly. The two stubborn women stared at each other.

"What if he is?" replied a defiant Roja. And then her head dropped. The fight in her was draining away. "Maha, it is enough that my children are with you," she whispered. "I will find a way to get word to him, to tell him that his son and daughter are on their way to safety. Prison guards can be bribed." Roja looked at Nana with soft, pleading eyes, as if silently imploring her to stop.

Nana nodded and said nothing more. Shireen listened, and then turned her back on them all.

～•

Minutes turned to hours. Rifa'at could come anytime, but likely it would be after sunset when the chances of being hit by a sniper were small. They had waited, ready to run out the door, the entire day.

"Listen," hissed Ali. They heard a motor running. Ali looked through the peephole. "I see the van. It's him. He is blinking his headlights." Ali inched the door open as Nana and the girls pulled on their *abayas* and *hijabs*. "Hurry."

Roja dimmed the battery light, flung open the door, and stood under the threshold holding a copy of the Quran high in the air. Ali kissed his mother as if he would see her later, tomorrow maybe, ducked under the Quran as she whispered a prayer, and raced towards the headlights.

Yara and Saad, too, passed under the Holy Book as Roja repeated the prayers for safe travel.

Nana stopped and faced Roja. She handed her a small bag. "For bribes," she said, and then added, "I will give my life to save your children." The words were said in a whisper but the night air carried them to Yara. Roja's legs shook under her. Trembling, still holding the Quran in one hand, she stepped back and leaned against the door.

"You are my eyes," Nana said softly to Roja, leaning on her cane.

"You are my heart," replied Roja. Streaks of tears ran down her face. "Thank you, my friend. *Salamtik*. My prayers will all be for your safety."

Again, the headlights of a van flickered and then went dark.

"Go with Nana." Yara gave Saad a gentle push. Nana and Saad followed Ali down the road, her cane *tap-tapping* on the uneven ground, creating a sound path for Yara to follow. But Yara didn't follow. She stood on the path outside Roja's door.

"Come, come, Shireen," she called out softly, her eyes darting from the faint light in the doorway to the van parked down the road. Nana was now sitting in the front beside Rifa'at. The lights of the van flickered, the signal to hurry. "Come on, come on," Yara urged her. And there she was. Shireen stood in the doorway. Yara hadn't realized that she had been holding her breath. Shireen's jaw was clenched and her mouth was pursed into a tight bud. In this light, in any light, angry or happy, Yara thought Shireen was beautiful.

"My dearest daughter," said Roja. "Remember, 'Male or female, a lion remains a lion.' Those are Kurdish words," she whispered as she wrapped her arms around Shireen. "I love you, my daughter, I love you. Live a good life. But no matter what happens, your father and I will be proud of you forever."

"Mama!" Shireen let out a strangled cry.

Yara shrank back into the shadows. Roja was casting her children out to fate. Shireen would likely never see her mother again. Yara felt sick.

In the distance a bomb fell and the ground vibrated under their feet.

"Go, go now." Roja gave her daughter a nudge, then stepped back into the house and closed the door.

"*Inshallah*, I will see you again, Mama, I will." Shireen, sobbing, the tears running in rivers down her face, placed her hands on the door.

"Come, Shireen." Yara stepped out of the shadows, took Shireen by the hand, and pulled her along. Shireen stumbled behind.

It was a small van, like a baker's truck. Baba and Mama had talked about buying one once, years ago, in another life. There were windows at the back.

The back of the van gaped open like a toothless mouth. The two girls tumbled onto the metal floor. A few mats and thick, coarse blankets were all that protected them from the ribs of the van's corrugated steel floor.

Yara crawled to her brother and tried to hug him. "It will be fine, Saad, you'll see." Saad pulled away. He had never been in any vehicle before. It was too dark to see his face but she could feel his body quiver. He laid his head on a mat and pulled his knees up to his chin. Shireen sat as still as a stone.

Ali slammed the back door shut and climbed into the front seat beside Nana and Rifa'at. Yara pressed her nose against the back window and looked at the rubble that was once her home, her place in the world. It was likely that she was leaving forever. "Baba, Mama, I love you," she whispered, her breath making a foggy cloud on the window. She sank down and doubled over in pain.

The van jolted backward and then rocketed ahead. Shireen, Yara, and Saad bounced around the back like marbles in a soup tin. Breathing hard, Yara pressed against the wall of the van. For the first time the *abaya* was not a long black gown but her protection. It surrounded her, hid her, and formed a barrier between her and the world.

They were slowing down. Yara sat up on her knees so she could see through the front windshield. Wait, they were heading towards the blockade of three buses standing on end! Weren't there other roads that would take them from East to West Aleppo?

"Shireen, look," Yara whispered. Shireen, too, sat up, and both girls peered ahead into the dark.

The headlights of the van flashed over the underbellies of the huge buses. They looked sinister, like the skeletons of monsters. To the right of the buses was a walkway only big enough for pedestrians, or maybe a donkey cart. How would the little baker's van fit?

"Nana, why . . . ?" Yara reached forward and touched her grandmother's shoulder.

"Hush." Nana patted Yara's hand. "Rifa'at has made a bargain . . ."

"Get down," Rifa'at barked.

Yara, Shireen, and Saad huddled together and waited.

The van came to a stop. Yara heard muttering, two men speaking, and then Nana whispered something, too. Were they bribing the man? If only she could see!

The van inched forward. No sound of nails scratching on a blackboard could match the high-pitched vibration as the thin walls of the little baker's van scraped and crunched through a passage meant for a pushcart. The girls moved closer and clapped their hands over their mouths. Saad whimpered and buried his head in Yara's shoulder.

And then it was over! "Are we in West Aleppo?" Yara called out.

"Yes, but remember, there are checkpoints every few blocks. Be quiet. Do as you are told," said Rifa'at, his voice raised only enough to be heard over the sound of the engine.

Yara touched Nana's shoulder. It was reassuring. The warm night air poured in through the front windows. Yara sat back then and closed her eyes against dizziness, a queasy stomach, and the sight of the President's soldiers who waited for them around the corner.

CHAPTER 14

"STOP!" A beam of light shot across the windshield like a bolt of lightning. Rifa'at slammed on the brakes. They had been driving for only a few minutes.

"Who are they?" Shireen's voice, usually bird-like and sweet, was as cold as ice.

"Government soldiers," Rifa'at hissed through his teeth.

Yara covered her mouth and nose with the end of her headscarf. Her body shook as if she had been picked up by a giant and rattled like a toy.

"Papers." A soldier, a commander by the stripes on his sleeve, came to the driver's side window. Standing tall and square in the headlights of a military vehicle, he looked like a cardboard cutout. He was not old, maybe Baba's age. His nose was beak-like and his black eyes were small and piercing. There were three more soldiers behind him, feet apart, hands gripping AK-47s.

Nana passed Rifa'at the little blue passports and green identification cards. He added his own identification to the small stack and gave them to the commander. No one in the van spoke; they were scarcely breathing.

The crossing from East to West Aleppo was just behind them. Could it all end here, just blocks from the house? What if the commander did not give the papers back, arrested them, sent them to prison, or just shot them on the spot?

"Saad, come." Yara mouthed the words while holding up the end of the heavy, rough blanket. Like a rabbit he burrowed down. Yara fumbled through her *abaya* and blanket, found his small hand, and squeezed it tight. She felt another hand. It was Shireen reaching over to stroke her shoulder. Her touch was soothing.

"Why are you leaving Syria?" The commander's voice vibrated in the thin night air.

"We are not leaving Syria. I am taking this woman to visit her son," said Rifa'at, adding, "*bi-idhn Allah,*" with God's permission. Was there dread in Rifa'at's voice? Anger? Fear? Of course, fear.

The commander whipped the flashlight around the inside of the van. The beam stopped on Nana. "Where does your son live?"

"Damascus. He is sick and he needs me. I could not leave my grandchildren behind. Their parents are dead." She spoke clearly and calmly. Yara shrunk even deeper into her *abaya*.

Snorting, the commander shouted over his shoulder, "Do you hear that? They are going to Damascus!" The other soldiers, impossible to see clearly from the back of the van, belched hollow laughs. They didn't care that their parents were dead. Orphans were as common as grains of sand.

"Search them." The commander pulled out a crumpled package of Marlboro cigarettes, lit one, and then dissolved into the shadows.

Two young soldiers, teenagers really, flung open the back door. "Out! Out!" they yelled.

Shireen leapt out first and reached back for Saad. Yara jumped to the ground. They stood together with Nana, Rifa'at, and Ali, facing the barrel of an AK-47.

Their backpacks and bags were tossed on the ground and searched. Saad's yellow truck was broken into pieces. "Never mind the truck," Ali whispered. "I will get you another one." The teddy bear Shireen had given him landed at Saad's feet. Yara snatched it up for him. "Don't cry," she whispered. Saad hugged the toy, then buried his head in Yara's gown.

In those same moments Shireen scooped up the velvet-covered Quran. She held it for only a second before a soldier yanked it out of her hands.

"What's that?" He held the book over his head.

"That Quran belonged to my father, and my grandfather before him." She made a grab for the book. He was tall, she was tiny, it was a futile attempt.

"Shireen, stand back," Yara whispered.

The soldier shoved Shireen backward. Ali lurched towards his sister, but Nana's arm came down in front of Ali like a cold blade. She said nothing. He stopped, but his eyes tracked every movement the soldier made. They wouldn't attack Shireen here, not out in the open. Would they?

"Are you part of the Muslim Brotherhood?" the young soldier snarled at Shireen.

"Of course not!" Contempt turned into fury. Bashar al-Assad's father had banned the Muslim Brotherhood more than forty years ago. To be a member meant life in prison, or even execution!

Yara felt her own stomach contract. *Please, please, Shireen, don't provoke him.* She could hardly hear her own thoughts over the thundering of her heart.

The commander held the passports. *Give them back, give them back*, Yara thought. He paused for a long moment, then turned his cold, reptilian eyes on Ali. "You should be fighting." He spat out the words. Just then, Yara saw Nana step back and slide something into the palm of Rifa'at's hand.

Ali opened his mouth to protest, but Rifa'at stepped forward. "Brother, I am but a poor driver. He is a boy, an only son. He is also the head of this family. This boy has three women and a small child to care for. What are they to do without his protection? Please, brother, take this small contribution for your men. We, the people of Syria, support you and our President." Rifa'at slipped money into the commander's palm.

There was a moment, a pause. They all held their breath. The money vanished into the commander's pocket. "Go," he snarled. Shireen, her lower lip quivering, snatched up the Quran and held it with all reverence. They climbed back into the van without a word.

"Wait!" The commander leaned the barrel of his gun on the van's window frame and peered inside. "You are all fools.

Go to your deaths!" He tossed their passports in through the window and thumped the roof of the van with a closed fist. Rifa'at gripped the wheel and put his foot down hard on the gas.

Through all this, Nana's own suitcase containing the red tin box was ignored. Perhaps they had thought an old woman would have nothing of interest.

~ •

They waited in lineups at three more checkpoints just to leave the city. The soldiers took their time, occasionally stripping cars or trucks down to the frame, sometimes waving vehicles through without even looking at them. Before dawn, Rifa'at turned the van onto the M5 highway, a road that ran like a river through Syria.

It was too hot to think, let alone speak. The sun had no sooner risen than it beat down on the roof of the van with a closed fist. The traffic was bumper to bumper. Drivers leaned on their horns. Why? Where was anyone to go? They followed a truck filled with crates of squawking chickens. The stench wafted back into the van. Yara covered her nose and tried to breathe through her mouth.

Seemingly endless flat plains surrounded them. Women covered in dark *abayas* stood on the roadside selling food. Twice, Rifa'at pulled over and Nana reached through the window and selected red, juicy tomatoes from their baskets.

Yara peered out the back window to see miles and miles of trucks following at a snail's pace. "Where are they going?"

"To the vegetable markets in Damascus," said Rifa'at, in a slow, dreary voice. It was too hot to talk, too hot to even think.

"Here is the first highway checkpoint. Get ready," Rifa'at said sharply. Yara scrambled to the front of the van and looked over his shoulder. Snipers, standing in the distance, had their automatic weapons trained on the vehicles in the line-up. The words "Either al-Assad or Nobody" were painted in a childlike scribble on the side of a small hut beside the road.

"Listen now." Rifa'at spoke quickly. "The government soldiers are looking for suicide bombers. The old soldiers send the young soldiers to check the cars. The young ones are untrained and scared, and that makes them unpredictable. They will make us get out of the van. Pull back your sleeves and show them your hands and arms. They want to make sure you are not holding a detonator. Do not make eye contact. Do not move quickly. Do not move at all! And do not speak." Rifa'at's voice was fast and urgent.

The truck ahead filled with chickens was waved on. It was their turn. Two young, grim government soldiers approached the van holding AK-47s. Yara dropped her head. A third soldier motioned for them to get out of the van. "Palms up," he yelled.

Standing on the roadside, a soldier used the barrel of his gun to separate Yara and Saad. "Stand apart," he bellowed, as if they were far away, as if they were deaf. How old was he? Maybe eighteen?

Saad leaned against her leg. "Stand still, Saad," she whispered as she pushed him inches away. He hung his head and stood still. Yara tried to take deep breaths but could barely get air past her teeth.

Somewhere, Syrian music blared out of a radio or cellphone. Another young soldier came out of the hut with a German shepherd straining against its leash. "Don't look," Yara whispered to her brother. Saad again buried his face in Yara's *abaya*. The dog's head was as big as a bear's. It bared its sharp, pointy teeth, jumped up on its hind legs, and pedaled its paws in the air. Shireen inched closer to Yara and reached for her hand.

"Don't move!" yelled a soldier. Shireen drew back her hand. He looked to be the youngest of all. He held a wand as long and thin as a shovel and he ran it under the van.

"What is he doing?" whispered Yara.

"Checking for explosives, I think," Shireen whispered back. "Look." She nudged Yara. Just ahead, a car was wedged between large concrete blocks. A boy of maybe fourteen or fifteen crouched behind it. His face was a bloody mess and one eye was swollen shut. Another man, perhaps the boy's father, was pleading with a group of young soldiers.

"Brothers, please, he is a boy, just a boy. He means no harm. See, he has his schoolbooks with him." The father fell to his knees and begged. He was ignored. Yara took in a breath. Had he no bribes? But then they looked poor.

A sneering young soldier snapped handcuffs on the boy. "Congratulations! You wear the bracelet of freedom. No more school for you." The young soldier laughed.

"Baba," the boy cried out to his father. "Baba, help me!" Blood, mixed with sweat and snot, dripped from the boy's nose.

"Please, have pity. God will bless you. Please . . ." The father twisted and turned as if in a strong wind. Another soldier who stood behind the father rammed the butt of his gun into the man's back. The father fell flat on his face.

They are your countrymen. The boy could be a schoolmate. Why are you treating them like this? Yara screamed in her head. She opened her mouth. She couldn't just stand by! But Nana, as if reading her mind, shot her a look as sharp as daggers. Yara lowered her head. She knew. She knew. Do not speak. Do not move.

Rifa'at handed over their passports. The books were passed back to a soldier behind the barricade. Rifa'at gave Ali a hard, meaningful glance. Ali stepped back, as if trying to make himself invisible.

"What are they doing with the passports?" whispered Yara, her voice unsteady.

Rifa'at waited a moment and then muttered, "They are checking our names against a list. If someone is on the list, they are arrested immediately."

Yara looked over at the boy. Was his name on a list? What if two people had the same name? *Oh God, please help him,* she prayed. The boy was being hustled towards a van. He stumbled and fell. The sneering soldier kicked him, shouting, "Get up. Get up." He pointed his gun inches from the boy's ear. Yara saw hatred on that young soldier's face. And something else, too—enjoyment.

It was then that Yara understood. It was so simple. That boy's death, their deaths, her death meant nothing. They could all vanish with the touch of a trigger. Yara's feet went numb. Her legs started to shake. What gave them the right?

Shireen grabbed Yara's arm so tightly that her nails dug into her flesh. "Look," she whispered.

Head high, walking with her cane, Nana was calmly approaching the hate-filled soldier. She began speaking calmly to him, like a grandmother chatting to a favored grandchild.

Dogs barking, radios blaring, bleating goats, engines revving—it was almost impossible to hear what she was saying. Rifa'at was watching, too, and he was furious. His eyes were drilling holes in Nana's back.

The soldier returned with their passports. He looked around, his eyes skimming from one scene to another. Was he looking for Nana? Suddenly, Rifa'at ran up to the soldier and began to ask questions. "What is the traffic ahead like?" "What is your name? You look familiar." What was Rifa'at doing?

Yara's head swiveled from Rifa'at to Nana. Yara caught bits and pieces of the conversation: "my neighbors"—Nana pointed to the man and his bloodied boy—"support the President." She was reaching into her pocket.

Shireen tipped her head towards Rifa'at. Clearly sick of Rifa'at's gibberish, the soldier slapped the passports against the old man's chest. Clown-like, as if he were a blundering fool, Rifa'at let them fall on the ground. "Sorry, sorry, sorry," he prattled.

Yara looked back at Nana. She watched as Nana took a roll of American bills out of her pocket. What if she got caught? The soldier snatched the money out of Nana's hand like a snake swallows prey.

Rifa'at had fallen on his knees and was making a poor attempt at gathering the passports. The soldier shouted that he was a useless old man.

"My apologies, brother. I am deeply sorry for my clumsiness."

As Nana watched, the sneering soldier who had pocketed the money unlocked the boy's handcuffs. The father stared open-mouthed at Nana.

"Good journey, old friend." Nana, not catching his eye, waved him off as if he were going on a picnic. His eyes shone like the sun. As cool as a queen at her coronation, Nana strolled back to her family.

Rifa'at, on his feet and clutching the passports, gave Nana a murderous look. Nana ignored him.

There was an uproar down the line. "What's happening?" Yara whispered in Shireen's ear. Was it an attack? Soldiers were taking aim at some distant target.

"Get in the van, NOW!" Rifa'at waved them on. "Go! Go!" His face was purple as he, too, jumped into the van and turned over the engine. It gave a frightening roar. Nana, leaping like a girl, climbed in beside him. Shireen, Saad, Yara, and Ali piled into the back, flopping on each other like fish in a bucket. The van took off even before the doors were closed.

A maze of concrete blocks, meant to slow traffic, lay ahead. Rifa'at charged through as if he were in a racing car. The engine jerked back and forth like a donkey trying to break free of its harness. Finally, the old van rolled out onto the highway.

Rifa'at's face was red with fury. "Maha, what you did could have got us all arrested! Only by the grace of God did we survive." If Rifa'at had clutched the wheel any harder it would have snapped in two.

"That is what I was counting on," said Nana, wisely.

Shireen and Yara exchanged shocked looks. Ali hid a smile behind his hand.

Minutes ticked by before a calmer Rifa'at said, "The worst is over. They will radio ahead that we have been cleared."

"Nana . . ." Yara, in the back of the van, reached over and touched her grandmother's shoulder. Nana grabbed her hand, squeezed it for a moment, and, sighing deeply, let go. "Oh, Nana," Yara whispered. "Thank you." She started to cry. "Thank you."

CHAPTER 15

A truck coming in the opposite direction slowed down. Rifa'at watched it carefully, then put his foot on the brake. The driver and Rifa'at spoke.

"There has been a suicide bombing at your next checkpoint," the truck driver warned him. "The road is shut down." Thanking the man, Rifa'at veered off the paved highway and the old van bounced onto a side road. No one said a word.

They passed through town after town. They passed thin, dusty boys trailing behind ragged herds of sheep and goats. And occasionally they saw women and children walking slowly along the side of the road. What would happen to them, without the protection of a man? Yara couldn't look at them, but she couldn't look away, either.

Up in the hills, Bedouin tents dotted the dry and sandy landscape. The tents were made of black cloth, old rugs, sheets of cardboard, and strips of plastic pinned to the ground with a

146

tangle of ropes. And yet Yara could see the beauty in the land around her, and it made the loss of Mama and Baba feel even worse. The empty place in her middle was expanding.

Defying the heat, she wrapped her *abaya* around her and listened to the rhythm of the tires as they went round and round on an asphalt-paved road. She could hear the rhythm in her spine, in her bones, from inside out. *Your mother is dead. Your father is dead. Your mother is dead. Your father is dead.*

"Yara?" Shireen scooted over and pushed back Yara's headscarf. "Oh, Yara," she said softly, then she took off her own headscarf and mopped up Yara's wet face. They lay side by side as the tires continued to sing. *Your mother is dead. Your father is dead. Your mother is dead. Your father is dead.* Exhausted, and tired of crying, Yara let Shireen hold her tight.

"Your mother must be with her brother now," said Yara, above the sound of the singing tires and the wind streaming through the open windows. She patted Saad's hair. He had fallen asleep on a blanket.

"My mother's brother is ten years old," said Shireen.

"I don't understand . . ." Yara stared at Shireen's profile. "But . . . but your mother is from a big family!" she sputtered.

"Some have been killed, and others have left Syria. Her older brothers were forced to join ISIS. If they didn't join, what was left of my mother's family would have been murdered. The only ones left now are my old grandfather and the son of his fourth wife."

"But that means . . ." Yara knew exactly what that meant. Roja had lied. She was alone. To come with them would have meant abandoning her husband in prison. But to stay . . .

What happens to a woman without the protection of a man? She thought of beautiful, proud Roja, who glided across a room. Who read poetry and novels. Who loved her husband and children more than her own life.

"That's why you wanted to stay in Aleppo," said Yara.

Shireen nodded. "But if I'd stayed, Ali would have stayed, and how long would it have been before he was picked up and forced into one army or another?"

"Does Ali know about your uncles?" Yara knew the answer to that, too.

Shireen shook her head. "She never told him that they are with ISIS. She never had the heart."

Yara rested her head on Shireen's shoulder. There was great loyalty to be found in war, and great sacrifice, and among all the killing, great love. *Your mother is dead. Your father is dead. Your mother is dead. Your father is dead.*

After a while the van jolted, bucked, and came to a sputtering stop. Startled, both girls sat up. Rifa'at slammed his hands on the wheel and climbed out. Ali joined him, and the two gazed under the hood with perplexed expressions.

"Why do all men think they can fix engines?" whispered Shireen. She smiled as she wiped sweat from her face. Nodding, Yara smiled, too. And as they listened to Rifa'at thunder to the sky, their smiles turned into nervous giggles, and the giggles turned into laughter. Nothing was especially funny, but why not laugh?

Rifa'at took out his phone and wandered away to make a call. Finally, and with the look of a defeated man, he came around to Nana's side of the van, crossed his arms over the lip of the window, and spoke. "We are close to Ar Rastan. I have a friend nearby. We served together in the army." With a few exceptions, all Syrians served in the army. It was the law. "He will come for us when it is safe. There are patrols in the area." Rifa'at flipped opened his phone again. "Meanwhile, hide over there." He pointed to an olive grove. Once again, he jabbered into his phone.

Hide? Yara looked over at the scrubby, bent trees. It would be like trying to hide behind a telephone pole.

Darkness came with the swiftness of a door slammed shut. The ground was still warm, but that wouldn't last. The sky grew bigger and bigger, expanding with the light of each new star. They bundled up in the blankets from the back of the van and waited.

Rifa'at slept in the van when it got truly dark. Ali was on lookout a few yards away, and Nana, with half-closed eyes, leaned against the trunk of an olive tree.

Sleepy, silent Saad rested his head on Yara's lap. His hair curled around his ears and lay against his neck. Haircuts were hard to come by in a war, but Roja had done her best with her large sewing shears. Saad reminded Yara of a video she had seen when she was small. What was it called? Ah, *The Shaggy Dog*. She loved that movie.

"Oh, Saad," she whispered, "I'm so sorry." He was so little. He needed friends and toys and stories, lots of stories. He looked up at her curiously. "You know nothing but this war, don't you?" Yara bent over him. "Do you remember Mama telling silly stories and making up funny voices?" She could feel his whole body stiffen at the mention of Mama's name. And so she told him a story of three mice and some candy and none of it really made sense. In the end, she fluttered her fingers skyward and Saad laughed. It was a sweet laugh.

"Can you say 'three little mice'? Can you just try?" Yara begged. The smile on Saad's face vanished. His eyes, so full of light, quickly dimmed.

Sighing deeply, Yara hugged him. "It's all right. Everything will be all right." She kissed the top of his head.

Ali sat in the distance, scanning the horizon. He sat like their protector, straight, tense, ready to leap up and defend them. If only she could sit beside him, talk to him. Yara looked over at Nana. She didn't dare.

Yara noticed that Shireen was lying too rigidly, too tensely, to be asleep. She lifted Saad's head off her lap and laid it gently on his Woody Woodpecker backpack, then crept over to her friend.

"What is it?" Shireen sat up, pulled her knees to her chest, and wrapped her arms around her legs.

"Shireen, your mother will be proud of you, you'll see. She's strong, stronger than you know. And you *will* see her again." Yara tried not to sound like a child. Shireen's profile, lit only by starlight, was as perfect as an artist's paper silhouette. Her bottom lip quivered. They both looked over at Ali.

"*He* must be the one to get out," whispered Shireen.

They waited all the next day in the olive grove. The air was dusty, and when the sun set again it had the sickly yellow look of the color that surrounds a bruise.

It was on the second night that they heard a voice coming from the road. "Rifa'at, are you here?"

The two girls jumped. "Saad, come to me," Yara whispered. Ali was up on his feet.

"Omar, is that you?" Rifa'at called out.

"Yes, yes. I am sorry it took so long, my friend." The stranger's voice seemed to vibrate warmly in the night air.

Rifa'at opened the van door and, standing in the glare of the car's headlights, he kissed the man on the cheek three times, right, left, right. "It does not matter. You are here now." Both men smiled, their teeth blazing white against their dark beards. "Come, come," Rifa'at called cheerily to the others.

Stiff and thirsty, they gathered their blankets and belongings and piled into the stranger's car.

"Ar Rastan is near. You will see. Nice house. Good people," said Rifa'at. The car kicked into gear and lurched off into the night.

They drove for a mere twenty minutes. Nana grumbled. They could have walked that far had they known! Omar, the driver, stopped in front of a large steel door.

"Look!" Yara nudged Shireen. There were men with guns perched on a wall that had to be two stories high. "Saad, come close." Yara reached for him.

Almost instantly the metal door rumbled over iron tracks to reveal a courtyard. She could make out a dimly lit fountain, large lemon and olive trees in pots, elaborate tilework on the floor and walls, seating in small alcoves filled with chairs and pillows and Persian rugs. A beautiful tree surrounded by a circular bench was off to the side. And beyond, she could see by the light of swinging lanterns, were outbuildings— some elegant, others rather plain, perhaps for the guards or servants. All together it was, Yara thought, beautiful.

"Yara." Shireen gave her a push. "Look over there!"

Two men stood in the path of the headlights, both pointing AK-47s directly at them.

"*As-salaamu 'alaykum*. Blessings on you, my friends," one of the men called out, recognizing Omar immediately.

"*Wa 'alaykum as-salaam*. This is Rifa'at, a brother," Omar called back. The men relaxed and slung their guns over their shoulders.

The door slid closed behind them with a thunderous thud. "Come, come!" Omar motioned for them to get out of the car.

"You are safe," Rifa'at announced, grinning from ear to ear. Then he turned and introduced Ali. One by one the men patted Ali on the back like an old friend. The woman were ignored.

"*Ahlan wa Sahlan*. Welcome, as family, to our home." A woman dressed in black and framed by light emerged from a far house. She held up a small lamp. As she came closer, Yara could see her twinkling eyes, almost hidden in a nest of wrinkles. "My name is Haya. Do not be frightened. Nothing will happen to you here. My husband and sons will protect us."

Yara grabbed Saad's hand. "Come, don't be scared," she whispered to him.

"Ali, come back," Shireen called. Ali shrugged and grinned before being swept away by the men towards a far building. The door of the building opened and blue smoke from *shisha* pipes streamed out and into the cool night air. "Ali, don't," Shireen cried. If he heard her, he did not let on.

"Come, Shireen," Nana said. Shireen looked at Nana, her forehead creased with worry.

"Yara," Shireen whispered, "we do not know these people. Ali could be made to fight with them. What if they recruit him? What are their politics? Who are they?" She gripped Yara's hand.

"They are friends of Rifa'at," said Yara, quietly.

"Yes, but how well do we know Rifa'at?" asked Shireen.

Yara shuddered and put an arm across Shireen's shoulders. All they could do now was trust.

Haya reached out to Nana and almost immediately the two women were bobbing their heads like birds in a newly seeded garden. Nana, who so often said that all strangers were spies, who told Yara every day of her life to *trust no one*, rested one hand on her cane and the other on Haya's extended arm—more proof that the world was upside down.

"I am Maha, and this is Yara, Shireen, and my young grandson, Saad." Nana pointed to each in turn. "And that young man was Shireen's brother, Ali."

"Welcome," said the older woman.

Yellow lamplight from the house guided them across the courtyard and past the well. Cozy benches were tucked underneath olive trees, and pillows and children's toys were scattered everywhere. The two-story house ahead was made of cinder blocks surrounded by sandbags.

They removed their shoes on the threshold of Haya's house. A young woman wearing black and a headscarf stood smiling in the doorway.

"My name is Rahaf. I am Haya's oldest daughter. Come." The young woman beckoned to Yara and Shireen. A little girl with dark hair peeked out from behind Rahaf. Yara smiled at her as they stepped into a large, beautiful, but poorly lit, room. Yara could only guess but she imagined the walls were covered with bright material, and the sofa and floors with colorful pillows.

"As-salaamu 'alaykum," Nana said to the children, who bounced up and down, cheering, clapping, and giggling.

"Look! I lost two teeth!" A little boy opened his mouth and proudly displayed his toothless upper gum.

Saad ducked behind Yara. "He is shy," Yara explained. She smiled at the toothless boy and bent down to peer into his mouth. "I can see new teeth already coming in!" she exclaimed. He bobbed his head so hard Yara was afraid he might lose a few more teeth.

When everyone had been introduced, the mothers gathered up the children like chickens in a yard and hustled them off into a far room to wash their hands and feet.

A smiling Rahaf led Shireen and Yara towards the washroom. A fat bar of pale-green laurel soap sat on a towel beside a washbasin.

"Thank you." Yara could have cheered. Soap! Both girls washed their hands, arms, faces, and, in a separate bowl, their feet. How good it felt. But Shireen still looked sour, as if she had swallowed a lemon, maybe even the whole tree!

"Ali is fine," whispered Yara. Shireen made a face.

"Come, Saad." Yara gave her little brother a scrub that left his hair standing on end. It had been a long time since they had had so much water.

Smiles and platters of food awaited them when they returned to the big room. Children hovered about, squeezing in around a large cloth spread on the floor. The children in East Aleppo were hungry, some starving and thirsty, but here the children were all happy and healthy.

Yara folded her legs beneath her and pulled Saad down to sit beside her while Shireen sat on her other side. Yara looked across the cloth at Nana and smiled. Nana, too, had washed and seemed brighter, and, if not exactly relaxed, at least calmer. This was nothing short of a miracle!

There were other young women around the food, Haya's daughters and daughters-in-law. Their long, dark hair curled around their shoulders and flowed down their backs. This was the Syria Yara knew—kind people treating strangers like family.

Minced beef and salty cheese pies called *manaqish* were laid out on the cloth, along with dishes of sweet olives and bread. "Look, Saad, a *zaatar* swirl, just like Mama made." Yara picked up the pastry, breathed in the scents of oregano, sweet basil, and thyme, and took a small bite. The face of her mother was before her. Suddenly overwhelmed, she closed her eyes and once again heard the *chu-chu-chu* of helicopter blades. The sound of the explosion, the sensation of flying through the air, of her limbs trying to detach themselves from her body, of a scream caught in her throat, of being buried alive. *No, no, no!*

"Yara?" Shireen touched her hand. Yara's head fell to her chest. "YARA!" Shireen gripped her arm. "Yara, stop!"

Shaken, Yara looked down at the smashed pastry balled up in her hand. The room was silent. Shireen's arms were wrapped around Saad, who was whimpering softly.

"I am . . . I am so sorry," Yara mumbled. Her face grew so hot her ears tingled.

Rahaf reached over and squeezed Yara's hand. "Do not worry. We understand." The beautiful woman smiled. Yara wanted to cry. The food, the water, the kindness—it was overpowering. She looked over at Shireen, who nodded. The lemon-face look was gone.

"*Bismillahi wa'alaa barakatillah.* In the name of Allah and with the blessing of Allah," said Haya. They ate.

They enjoyed the meal in a relaxed, leisurely way, and when it was over Yara sat and rubbed her belly. She had not eaten so much in a long time. Two young women removed the dishes to wash in an outdoor kitchen. Shireen found a book to read. The young mothers put their children to bed in another room, and even Saad was comfortable enough to lie quietly on a mat, although against the wall and close enough to see Yara.

Haya and Nana retreated to a corner of the room and sat comfortably on a wooden sofa surrounded by pillows.

As they talked together their faces glowed like small moons around a battery light. Bits of their conversation drifted across the room. "We joined with other families in the village . . . We are armed and ready to fight for each other and our lands. We are against al-Assad's regime, but we have no desire to trade one tyranny for another. We will not be controlled by ISIS or al-Nusra or these gangs that are everywhere," said Haya defiantly. This was her house and she spoke freely, but Yara shuddered: *Walls have ears.* "As for the Free Syrian Army, we support them, but many have broken off into gangs and now take bribes," Haya explained. "They call them *war gifts.* This, they say, is 'God's will'!" Haya scoffed, but Nana stayed silent.

As the two older women talked, Rahaf served Nana and her mother coffee in small china cups. "Before the revolution, Rahaf was in university. She was exposed to modern ideas." Haya sniffed. "It was a worry. Real beauty is the beauty of morals!" she added.

Rahaf set the tray down and looked at her mother sternly. "Beauty is everywhere, Mama," she said with a small smile. Yara thought she was the most beautiful woman she had ever laid eyes on.

"And ugliness is everywhere, too," Haya answered briskly. She turned back to Nana. "But now all our daughters are home. It is hard finding suitable husbands, so many men are dead." She sighed deeply.

Rahaf caught Yara's eyes and rolled her own. Yara giggled.

CHAPTER 16

The next day, Rifa'at went back for the van and returned with the news that it needed new parts.

"I will have it fixed," he said quietly to Nana. They were standing in the courtyard near the well. "Meanwhile, you are safe and welcome here," he added.

Yara heard her grandmother say something about Uncle Sami. "I will keep trying," Rifa'at whispered to Nana.

"Say nothing to Haya about Sami," said Nana. Nana did not trust Haya with the name of her only son. No one in Syria gave total trust to a stranger. Rifa'at nodded and walked back towards the men's house.

"Yara, are you listening in on a private conversation?" Nana sniffed.

Yara opened her mouth to defend herself, to say that she had a right to know what was going on, but Nana just sailed past her with a dismissive wave of her hand.

⌒•

They went on living in Haya's house for three days. The children were homeschooled in the morning before the heat of the day became oppressive. Even Saad attended the lessons. There were brief moments when Yara thought he might even say a word or two. The moments passed.

Shireen sat under the olive tree in the middle of the compound. Green, nubby, thick-skinned olives were beginning to grow on the crooked, stubby trees. The young wives and sisters sat under trees or walked around the courtyard, often arm in arm. All the women dressed in jeans and loose shirts. There were chickens, and an annoying rooster who strutted around like . . . well, a rooster. In the distance Yara could hear clanging goat bells. An old dog lay out as flat and thin as a rug. The children used him as a pillow, read to him, poked him. He was a gentle old pet.

Occasionally, Yara caught a glimpse of Ali, but except for nodding to his sister he seemed to ignore the girls entirely.

"Are you really going to go to a Western country?"

Startled, Yara looked up into the eager face of a young girl, and nodded. "Maybe," she said, but Rifa'at's words were always in her mind: *You will live in a refugee camp, possibly for years.*

"I don't know how it works," Yara said simply. It was not as if she hadn't thought about it, and she'd even seen pictures of the camps on Facebook. There were rows upon rows of tents, and some kind of metal shelters shaped like trains. The camps looked clean and tidy but temporary. How could anyone stay there for years? When they entered the camp, would they just ask to go to a foreign country? Australia, maybe? Or Germany?

"Are you afraid of the West?" A girl with long eyelashes, sparkly eyes, and hair tied back in a blue bow sat down beside Yara.

Before Yara could answer, a young wife asked a question. "Is it true that boys in the West are corrupted with drugs and play computer games all day?" With one hand on her big baby-belly she slowly lowered herself to the ground. Yara giggled. How was she to know the answer? "And girls have sex before marriage, and not even their fathers or uncles care?" She patted her pregnant belly protectively.

The questions, the statements, the observations came fast and furious now as more girls and women chimed in. Soon Yara was surrounded with warm babble. "In the West, people can do as they like." "But is that good?" "What if a boy wants to marry a woman who is unsuitable?" The babble was now a chorus. "In the West, children are not taught respect." Heads bobbed. "They are rude and do not care about their elders." One of the youngest women piped up with, "Old people are shut up in buildings and left to die without family." Could all this be true? She had seen many Western television shows, *Days of Our Lives* and *The Young and the Restless*. In these shows, women had money and wore very tight clothes.

"In the West, women have respect under the law." And, "In Canada, there is snow up to your eyes!" Everyone considered that for a moment.

"In Australia, I hear that everything that crawls can kill

you," one young woman announced. Everyone seemed to agree. "There are frogs the size of dogs! I saw it on television," she added. Yara bit her lip. Could someone drown in snow? Did giant frogs bite?

"The sun goes to the West to die," announced a small voice from beyond their circle. The babble stopped. Every head turned towards the small boy with the missing front teeth.

The mother of the boy leapt up and wrapped her arms around him. "The sun does not die, it rises again in the East!" She tried to sound triumphant but she looked at Yara, her eyes wide. Slowly, one by one, heads turned and peered at Yara. This was just silly. Why were they looking at her? Shireen was staring, too. But what did she know about living in the West? The truth was she hadn't given it much thought. She thought of today, tomorrow. She thought of finding Uncle Sami. The West was like thinking about dying and what might happen after! It was—she tried to think of the word—unfathomable! And scary.

In the distance, from somewhere in the village, they heard the call to prayer. "Thanks to God," murmured Yara with a sigh.

Yara had spotted the computer the first time they'd entered Haya's house, but it took four days before she found the courage to ask if she could use it.

Rahaf sat in front of it, tapping away with graceful fingers. Yara came up and stood beside her. "Excuse me?" She didn't want to be a nuisance.

Rahaf looked up and beamed. Just being the focus of Rahaf's attention made Yara blush. And how did she get her eyeliner on so straight?

"Can I help?" Rahaf asked.

Yara stumbled over her words. "I was hoping to learn about . . ." She bit her lip. "Australia!" She might as well start somewhere, and "A" for Australia was right at the beginning of the Western alphabet.

"Can you read English?" asked Rahaf.

Yara nodded. "A little bit. My grandmother is teaching me."

Rahaf's eyebrows peaked. "Your grandmother speaks English?"

"Yes . . ." Yara began.

"Helicopter!" a male voice shouted from the wall.

"The children!" cried Rahaf. She was gone in a blur.

Yara was on Rahaf's heels. "Saad!" she screamed. He came running, his eyes round with terror. "Come, Saad, come." She held out her arms.

Men and boys scrambled up ladders and loaded up rocket launchers. Giant guns were pointed to the sky.

Ali, don't die. Don't leave us!

The first bomb fell not far from the compound. The peaceful yard erupted into chaos. Skipping ropes, bikes, and toys were abandoned as screaming women and crying children scurried deep into the house. "Get the dog," someone called out. Nana and Shireen, herding children like goats, came in last. Haya bolted the door, as if that could keep a bomb from falling on their heads. They huddled together in far bedrooms that were as dark as the bottom of a well.

"Stay with me. We are safe," Yara whispered in Saad's ear. *Liar,* she thought, *liar, liar, liar. Remember when you told Baba you would never tell a lie? Remember?* But Baba had said he would keep her safe. No one was safe.

Shireen sat beside her, stiff with anger and fear. "Ali is with the men," she muttered, as if reading Yara's mind. Yara looked at Shireen, wide-eyed. Of course he was with them, but doing what? Did he carry a gun? Was he up on the wall? Was he a target?

Prayers were whispered around them. "God, I seek refuge in You from the evil in myself and every creature that You have given power over us." Yara closed her eyes. As the bombs dropped closer the prayer was said faster. "Whatever God wills happens, and whatever He does not will does not happen."

"Please stop the bombs, please stop them," whispered Yara.

The bombs did stop. Haya's house was spared. It was just as she had said: *Nothing will happen to you here.* But then came the eerie quiet, the rustle of small fires, the crackle of wood burning, and the occasional *pop, pop, pop* as gasoline tanks exploded.

Shireen flung back the door and held up an arm as a shield against the ash that fluttered down from the sky. "Ali!" She ran out into the middle of the compound. "ALI!" she cried, as though her heart was breaking.

On the other side of the great steel door that led to the road, fires shot up like hundreds of spears. The flames licked the walls and torched the surrounding olive groves.

There were shouts and cries for water, and the frenzied clang of goat bells. Boys were sent out to gather the animals.

Haya's daughter and the wives of her sons kissed their children and set to work. There would be wounded.

"Saad, stay with the children. Do you understand? Stay here," Yara barked at him. She took a few steps away, then turned back and kissed him before following Shireen out into the compound, searching, searching, her eyes stinging from the smoke.

"Where is he, Yara?" Shireen cried as she spun in circles.

"There!" Yara pointed. Ali emerged from the haze like a ghost. A gun was slung over his shoulder. He gave his sister a nod, Yara a penetrating look, then he ran out onto the road towards the flames and the injured.

There was yelling. Someone cried out that a doctor and nurse had been called from another town. Instructions were given. The dead were taken to a makeshift morgue, and the badly wounded were carried to a distant house to wait for medical support.

A man Yara had never met barked out a command. She was told to carry buckets of water from the well out onto the road to the wounded. Within an hour the thin wire handles on the buckets cut into her hands. She found a cloth on the ground. Maybe it had been a headscarf or a piece of curtain. She ripped it into strips and wound it around her palms. The stink of cinders and ash went up her nose. Somewhere in the distance goats bleated, donkeys brayed, dogs barked, and boys' voices called out. She didn't stop. She kept herself steady by looking at the ground.

"Nana?" Yara called out. Nana, kneeling by a house that was still belching smoke, did not turn around. "Nana?" Yara set the buckets down and called again. What was she holding? Yara walked towards her grandmother.

"Go." Nana waved her away. "Go, Yara, now."

Staggering backwards, Yara turned away. Nana was trying to stop her from seeing a child die. It was too late.

As the sun dropped below the horizon, camp beds were set up in the courtyard for the wounded who could walk or be moved. For the moment, anyway, there was quiet. Every bone in Yara's body seemed to vibrate with exhaustion. She sat on her mat beside Saad, not far from a sleeping Shireen, and tried to breathe. Sweat glued her shirt to her skin. She peeled back the cloth that had protected her hands from the handles of the water buckets. Thin red welts ran across her palms, making it hard to straighten her fingers. There was a metallic tang to the air. At first, she couldn't place it. And then she knew—it was the smell of blood. Injured animals were being slaughtered in a not very distant field, as quickly as possible.

Yara lay back and closed her eyes. Haya's daughters and daughters-in-law had served simple food: hummus, bread, pickles. Exhausted and hungry, Yara had wolfed it down, and now the food churned in her stomach.

The room that just yesterday was filled with so much happiness was now packed with children who would not sleep alone. They sniffed and sobbed to the hum of mothers whispering, "Hush, hush" and "It's over now." She was feeling worse. She might be sick.

Yara inched away from the sleeping Saad, crawled past the women and children, past Nana and Shireen, stood, and pressed a hand against the wall. Inch by inch she felt her way to the door. The evening air felt cool after the heat of the room. A gas generator hummed in the distance. She loved the sound. Mama and Baba had used generators in their bakery.

A lantern, sitting on the bench under the olive tree, was the only light in the compound. Yara staggered to the well, lifted the bucket, and splashed water over her face, her neck, her back. The cuts on her hand sent a jolt of pain up her arm. "Uncle Sami," Yara called to the stars, "we need your help."

"Yara?" Yara stood still. "Yara, is that you?"

Yara turned to see Ali standing in the lamplight. They looked at each other for long moments, neither knowing what to say or do. His face was smeared with dust and cinders. She almost laughed; he looked like a little boy who had been playing in the mud. He stepped closer. She could smell his sweat mingled with ash. His eyes seemed to stare deep into her soul. He was almost close enough to touch.

Ali slumped down on a long, rough bench propped against the side of the house. Without saying a word, Yara perched on the bench an arm's length away. She took a long, cooling breath and glanced sideways. It was like being on the sofa again, when the bombs had fallen, when they were searching for Nana. The tip of his shoe had touched her shoe and she'd felt instantly alive and unafraid. She wanted him to . . . to what? There were eyes everywhere: people lying on cots, up on the walls, in the shadows, on the roof. This was not a strict house, but surely a boy and a girl sitting in the dark would not be acceptable.

His hand fell over hers. She flinched.

"What is wrong with your hand?" he asked.

How could he see the welts in this light? She grimaced. "It's nothing." It was a pathetic injury compared to what was all around them. He touched her hand again, a light, feathery touch. There it was again, an electric shock that ran up her spine. She peered down at her feet. Why was it that whenever he was this close her heart pounded, her throat constricted, and her tongue stuck to the roof of her mouth?

"Do you see it?"

Ali looked up at the night sky. All her life she had looked up to these same stars, but tonight they appeared like sparks that flared just for them.

"That one." He pointed. "The North Star, the guiding star. I look up at it every night. It is there, always."

Tears pricked Yara's eyes. Why could she not think of a thing to say? Why couldn't she tell him how she felt?

"You should sleep. The truck will be ready soon." He stood up suddenly.

Truck? What truck? "But Rifa'at's van is still not ready," she said. She stood then, confused and fearful. What if he chose to stay here? They needed fighters, but did he know that they needed him, too?

"They have limited supplies here now. Another truck will take us to Damascus at daybreak," he answered simply.

Tomorrow!

"Ali?" She tried to keep her voice low, but really she wanted to say, "Speak to me. Say something." Without saying anything more, he drifted across the courtyard.

But one word came back to her, one tiny word. He had said "us." He was coming with them.

CHAPTER 17

"Why didn't they give us more warning?" Shireen muttered while slipping her velvet-covered Quran into her string bag. It was just past dawn. Haya's daughters were already up and out tending to the sick, making food, hauling water. "We should stay and help!"

"We are just more mouths to feed," said Nana. "The store-houses were bombed. The food they have must now go a long way. It will have to feed half this village. Yara, stop staring off into space." Nana handed Yara a water bottle.

"But what about Rifa'at?" Oddly Yara was growing attached to the old man with the hairbrush-bristle beard.

"Haya has it all arranged," replied Nana, and that was that. Anyway, all Yara could really think about was Ali.

Yara shoved the bottle in her backpack and looked down at Saad. He was so quiet, it was possible to forget that he was listening, watching, and always ready to run or hide. "Come on, little one. Soon all this will be over and we will see Uncle Sami." She gave him an encouraging smile as she tucked Baba's tobacco pouch back into the pocket of her jeans.

A few minutes later, Nana, Shireen, and Yara were wearing their *abayas* and standing out in the courtyard.

"Hurry, hurry!" A man waved them towards the back of a pickup truck. Men, standing impatiently on the flatbed of the truck, lowered the tailgate. It thumped on the ground, kicking up a puff of dust. Yara peered into the back. Wooden guard-rails ran along the sides. The flatbed part of the truck had been swept out, but sheep or maybe goat dung was caught between the wooden slats. She could smell it. Were they to travel like animals?

Haya and Nana walked arm in arm towards the truck, Nana dragging her tattered suitcase behind her. Haya had filled it with what food they could spare and bottles of water.

"Your daughters are beautiful," said Nana.

Haya smiled. "They are the future of Syria. They will rebuild our country," she said proudly. The two older women stopped and turned to each other.

"I ask Allah, glory be to Him, to protect you. I surround you with Allah's name," said Nana, with a smile that Yara, standing by the truck, had not seen in a long time.

"And I ask Allah, glory be to Him, the same for you, my friend. Blessings on you and your family," Haya replied, and the women kissed each other on the cheek. Haya pointed to a very pale man with a long, sharp nose that hung down over a pencil-thin mustache. "This driver is one of our best," she said.

The driver's mustache twitched as he beckoned to Yara with a long, curled fingernail. Yara recoiled.

"Hurry, Shireen!"

Shireen skipped up the tailgate and stood on the flatbed of the truck. "Here." She held her hand out to Yara. What choice did she have? Yara took a deep breath, grabbed Shireen's hand, and scrambled up, pulling Saad along with her.

"Nana?" Yara called out, but Nana was already sitting in the front seat of the truck.

Ali emerged from a distant building and strode across the compound. Yara's heart skipped as she watched him out of the corner of her eye. He did not look up, or even acknowledge her existence. She felt her breath catch. If only he would nod in her direction. Something!

Meeh, meeh. Yara turned, eyes wide. Trotting across the courtyard were dozens of goats! "Saad, come!" She pulled him against her and pressed her back against the cab of the truck. The men put down a wooden plank to make a ramp for the goats and they clomped up into the back of the truck. Dung dropped on Saad's toes. He howled, and Yara pushed the goats back with both arms, then covered her nose. The stink of them! They could drown in goats! The goats twitched their ears, drew back their hairy lips, and made their *meeh, meeh* sound. "Back, back!" She waved her hands. Stupid, awful goats. *Meeh, meeh,* the goats protested.

Shireen seemed to find it funny. "They are so cute," she hollered over the goats' bleating. *Cute?*

There were more goodbyes and distant voices calling out blessings as the tailgate was locked into place. The engine growled like a Syrian bear. Ali climbed into the cab beside Nana. He was with them—that was all that mattered. The doors to the compound rumbled open.

Rahaf came running alongside the truck. "Yara! Go to the West and teach those boys how to behave!"

"We will come back!" Yara yelled over the bleating. Never mind the stinky goats.

"We will meet again." Rahaf waved. "Go, God be with you."

⸎

They hadn't gone more than a few miles before they were pulled over at a checkpoint. Angry voices demanded papers. The peace of Haya's home vanished as Yara's insides squeezed as tight as a fist.

"It's all right, Saad," Yara hollered over the goats' clamor. "Soon we will be back on the main highway." Already Yara smelled like a goat.

They were waved on and resumed the journey. In the heat, and surrounded by the stink, Saad vomited over the side. She reached into her backpack and pulled out a bottle of water. "Off, off!" She smacked several rumps of several goats. "Here, Saad." She helped him rinse his mouth out. "We will be there soon." They were going to Damascus, but she had no idea how long this journey would take.

A half hour or so later, the driver slammed on the brakes.

Yara bumped into the back of the truck's cab, Saad fell into her, and the goats did a dance on bandy legs as they tried to remain standing. "Back, back!" Yara shoved the goats. Why had they stopped now?

"What's wrong?" Shireen called out.

Yara peered over the side. "I don't know," she yelled back over the goats' *meeh, meeh* noise.

There were no soldiers surrounding them, no trucks blocking their way, no helicopters overhead, just open road in front and behind, and the babble of the driver yelling into his cellphone. The goats settled. Yara listened carefully, and then she heard a long, soulful moan.

"Nana, Ali, what's happening? Stupid goats, get back!" Yara gave the goats a mighty thump. Ali leapt out of the truck's cab, ran around to the tailgate, and slid open its bolts. With a resounding *thunk* the tailgate hit the ground. "Out, OUT!" Ali shrieked at the goats.

Meeh, meeh, the goats squealed as they stampeded off the truck, jumping to the ground.

"Get down. Hurry." Ali waved his arms.

"What is it?" Shireen cried. Ali turned away.

"Come, Saad," said Yara as she crimped her *abaya* in both fists and, following the goats, jumped to the ground.

"Yara, hurry," said Nana. She looked gray.

"What's wrong?" asked Yara, her own voice shaking. They were beside a grove of olive trees. The land up higher was hilly, stark, and bleak. There was nothing around—no cars, no houses, nothing. Haya had described the driver as one of their best. Was he just going to leave them here?

Nana, holding on to the side of the truck, wobbled like a baby goat. Ali threw their bags onto the ground. His jaw was clenched and his brow furrowed.

"Let us come back with you. We can help," Nana was pleading with the driver.

Go back? Go back where? To Haya's? To Aleppo?

"No!" The driver's reply was as sharp as a knife. Yara was shocked. How dare he speak to Nana that way!

The driver's pained look turned to fury as he hustled the goats back onto the truck, slammed the tailgate shut, and slid the bolts back into place. "Someone will come for you," he said, and then he climbed back into the driver's seat, spun the truck around, and was gone.

Yara looked from her grandmother to Ali. Shireen was saying something to her brother. Shoulders slumped, Ali turned his back on them and walked off into the olive grove. Shireen watched her brother walk away, then reached for Saad and held him close.

"Nana, what's happening?" Yara reached out to her grandmother.

Nana staggered over to the olive tree, slowly lowered herself to the ground, and cupped her head with her hands.

"Nana?" Yara, on her knees, leaned in.

"Missiles hit the house." Nana's voice wavered.

Yara sat back and stared at her grandmother. Words rose up in her throat and burst into the air. "Nana, what do you mean?"

Nana let out a long, slow moan. "The driver's call was from a neighbor. A direct hit."

"Where? Haya? Are you talking about Haya and her family?" Yara couldn't take it in. Direct hit? *You are safe here. My sons will protect you.* Haya had said that, exactly that. *Nothing will happen to you here.* She heard Shireen cry out. It was a wrenching scream that came from deep inside.

"How many are . . . ?" Yara, still trying to grasp what she had just been told, couldn't bring herself to say "dead." How many young women and children lived in the house? Their faces floated around her like clouds. How many boys and men? She had no idea. It was like being underground again. Breathing was impossible. She tried to sip air and press down on the panic that was rising up in her body. She felt numb.

Nana shook her head. "We have to wait." She turned her face away and leaned against the knobby tree trunk. Once, there would have been cries, sobs, hands lifted to God, a pummeling of the legs with fists. Now there was only stunned silence.

Bending forward, Yara held on to her middle and folded in half. Slowly she fell to the ground. It would never end . . . never, ever, ever.

⌒•

Cars and trucks and vans passed occasionally. They slowed to a crawl, looked, and drove away. Why should they help? Yara scowled. She knew what they saw—a ragged child, three grief-stricken women, and a boy old enough to be a soldier sitting by the side of the road. They were nothing, nobodies.

One family stopped and offered them water. Nana shook her head. They had water. It was from Haya's well.

There were others, too. Fierce-looking men with long beards glared at them from huge trucks. Who were they? Extremists, certainly, but which ones? Yara and even Shireen adjusted their headscarves. The men looked them up and down as though they were animals in a pen, then drove off, their tires kicking up dust.

"Nana, it is too dangerous here," said Yara slowly. Nana agreed. They dragged themselves deeper into the olive grove.

"Dig here," said Nana. Ali dug a hole with his bare hands, and together they buried the red tin box.

Later, sitting on the ground, with tears catching in her throat, Yara looked up to the sky and thought of Rahaf, her beautiful hair and her night-black eyes. She wasn't dead. She couldn't be dead. Shireen sat down beside her and rested her head on Yara's shoulder. Saad, too, cuddled in close. Ali sat at a distance as always, on guard.

The day passed. No one spoke. The sun dropped like a stone beneath the horizon, and the desert wind whistled tunes through the sparse branches. Yara passed Saad some bread.

"Look, Saad!" Yara twisted him towards her, shielding him from the cool night air. The sky was alive with millions and billions of small flames. "Can you see the moon? It's always with us, no matter where we go. And see that star? It's called the North Star." Nodding, Saad rested his head in her lap and closed his eyes.

Yara looked over at Ali. Did he hear her mention the North Star? Did he know that when she looked up at the stars she thought of him?

Another night passed, and still the truck did not come back for them. Morning sun filtered through the limbs of the crooked olive trees.

A Bedouin boy came down from the hills and approached them. Like all the young shepherds, he had darting black eyes, sunken cheeks, a sharp nose, and brown skin touched with gold by the sun. Two dead hares dangled from his hand.

"*As-salaamu 'alaykum*," said the boy as he came closer.

"*Wa 'alaykum as-salaam*." Ali pressed coins into the boy's hand. He seemed pleased with the price and did not haggle. Ali, holding the hares, assured him that they were just travelers passing through; they would not stay on his family's land. The boy slipped away again.

Yara wasn't looking at Ali or at the hares. She was staring opened-mouthed at the male figure walking up behind him. "Rifa'at!" she whispered. "RIFA'AT!" she called out. She sprang to her feet so quickly that she almost toppled over. Seeing him there, disheveled, clearly exhausted, was like looking at a beloved grandfather. Nana, dozing beside a tree, sat up and cried out, too. Ali dropped the hares and hugged the old man.

"We thought . . . Ohhh, it is good to see that you are safe, my friend!" Nana, even leaning on her cane, flew towards him.

"I was in Homs buying an engine part. I drove back just after . . ." He shook his head.

"Haya . . . the house . . . Did any survive?" It was Shireen who stepped forward with the courage to ask. Her nostrils flared. They all held their breath.

Rifa'at's head slumped down, his dark beard, flecked with white, grazing his chest. He seemed to have aged in the short time they had known him. "The house was deliberately targeted. They were a strong and powerful family, and very wealthy." No one spoke. Rifa'at had used the past tense to speak of them. But they couldn't all be dead. Not all of them. That would be impossible.

"Come, Maha, let us talk." Without waiting for a reply, Rifa'at walked deeper into the olive tree grove. Nana followed slowly, her limp oddly more pronounced.

"Wait!" Yara stumbled forward. Whatever he had to say, they all had a right to hear it!

But neither Nana nor Rifa'at turned back. They stood a distance away and talked. Yara watched Nana's shoulders shudder, and for a moment she thought that her grandmother's legs might buckle. They returned and sat by the fire Ali had built to roast the hares. Nana's head was held high, as if to hold back her tears. She said nothing.

They ate and drank the water from Haya's well. Later they dug up the tin box.

"You are survivors," Rifa'at said approvingly.

One by one they climbed into the sweltering van. "The city of An Nabk is about three hours away. We will take side roads before joining up with the main M5 highway," said Rifa'at as the van roared to life. Nana, Shireen, and Yara took their *abayas* out of their bags and pulled them on as Rifa'at slipped the van into gear.

"Nana." Yara leaned over the seat and whispered in her grandmother's ear. "Haya, Rahaf, the children, the wives, their husbands . . . ?" Yara held her breath.

Nana turned her upper body and looked Yara straight in the eyes. "We have been waiting for a call, some good news to tell you. But there is no call. There is no good news."

"All of them?" Yara held her breath. A lifetime could have passed in those seconds between question and answer.

"Yes." Nana turned back and looked out the window.

Shireen, listening, moaned. Ali said nothing. Yara sank down onto the van's hot tin floor. Tears as big as pearls rolled down her face.

CHAPTER 18

B its of thread stuck in her teeth as she chewed the end of her scarf. *It's almost over. We are almost there,* Yara repeated to herself, over and over. They would be in Damascus soon and find Uncle Sami. All she had to do was keep calm and breathe. When memories of Mama, Baba, Haya and Rahaf and their family bubbled up and threatened to overwhelm her, she pushed them down into the pit of her stomach. Her hands and feet were cold. Her legs twitched. Food was hard to swallow, and harder to keep down. *Later, think later.*

Yara closed her eyes. She had drifted off into the place between awake and sleep when a black flag waved the van off the road.

The panic was instant. Yara bolted up and peered over Rifa'at's shoulder. Nana and Ali were both sitting beside him on the front bench seat. A Toyota truck was parked on the side of the road. Rifa'at coasted to a stop behind it. A machine gun, mounted on the flatbed of the truck, was pointed directly at them. This was not a government checkpoint.

The tailgate of the truck dropped with a thud. Four bearded men wearing military camouflage jackets over long, dirty shirts leapt out and surrounded the van. Only their eyes were visible—black, watery eyes glaring out from under black balaclavas—and strands of beard spread across their chests.

Yara's skin prickled. Kalashnikovs, ugly Russian guns, swung off their shoulders like schoolbags. Handguns were pointed at the van. *Why?* thought Yara. *They are Syrians. We are all Syrians. Why do these men hate us so much?*

"Who are they?" Ali whispered.

"Not sure," Rifa'at muttered under his breath. "Farmers, Bedouins, too, join gangs or terrorist groups in their area. They are paid. But most want money, not trouble. Say nothing!"

Yara hugged Saad harder.

"Take cover," Rifa'at whispered to Yara, Shireen, and Nana.

All three sank deep into their *abayas* and pulled scarves over their hair and faces. "Come closer, Saad," Yara whispered. She flung a blanket over him. They burrowed down as if the cloth made them invisible. *If I can't see you, you can't see me. A baby's game.*

The four men casually waved their guns around as if they were toys that had accidentally fallen into their hands. One of the men, as big as a mountain with a head as round as a cannonball, walked slowly over to the driver's side window and burrowed the barrel of a handgun into Rifa'at's chest. Another man, his eyes as hard and small as bullet holes buried deep into his skull, approached the other side of the van and pointed his gun at Nana and Ali. Two other men stood back looking unconcerned, bored even. *Is it boring to frighten people? Is it boring to murder?* Yara began to quiver. Her hands and legs shook uncontrollably as sweat beaded under her headscarf. She held on to Saad tightly, too tightly. He let out a muffled groan. *Breathe,* she thought, *breathe.* Shireen reached out to Yara and the two held hands under the blanket.

Rifa'at offered up their identification. Cannonball Head— what other name was possible?—waved the papers away. He didn't care who or what they were. What did he want? Money?

Despite the balaclava that covered his face, the crinkles around his eyes showed that he was smiling. Up close Yara could see that his eyes were not black but green. Not the glittering emerald green of Shireen's eyes, but the green of pond scum, flat and empty.

He peered into the back of the van, first at Yara and then at Shireen. Cannonball Head made an ugly, guttural sound, as if he was going to spit. Their faces were covered, but still he pointed to Shireen. "You, get out." One of the men opened the side door of the van.

"Leave her alone," Ali shouted. He tried to open the passenger side door. The fourth man, short with black teeth, pressed his hip into the door and pointed his gun at Ali's head.

"Woman, I said get out," Cannonball Head repeated.

Yara squeezed Shireen's hand. Woman? Shireen was just a girl. "No, don't go," Yara whispered to her.

"OUT!" Cannonball Head yelled again.

Yara could hear Ali huffing like a caged bear. The other one, it was hard to keep track, opened the driver's door and pulled Rifa'at out. He threw the old man onto the road. Rifa'at lay there face down, splayed, as though he had jumped out of a plane and crashed to earth.

Ali drew his knees back and with his feet rammed the side door into the gut of the man attempting to block him. The man howled as Ali jumped out. "Leave her! She is my sister!" he shouted.

"Your sister?" Shifting his great bulk from side to side, Cannonball Head moved around the truck, and he pushed his black balaclava up to his forehead, revealing a snake-oil grin and a row of sharp, pointy teeth like a rat's.

"Don't, Ali," Shireen whispered under her breath. Yara tried to hold her hand but Shireen let go and climbed out of the van, head back, green eyes blazing.

The one with the hard bullet eyes pushed Shireen off the road and into the dust.

"Shireen!" Ali lunged towards her but was stopped by the butt of a gun. A rasping sound came out his throat as he clutched his stomach and fell forward.

"Out! All of you," yelled Cannonball Head. Nana, Yara, and Saad climbed out of the van. Yara couldn't breathe, couldn't even whisper to Saad.

"You should be married." Speaking to Shireen, Cannonball Head placed his great body between brother and sister. He reached out and pulled off her headscarf. Yara gasped. Only a truly evil man who respected nothing of their religion or culture would do such a thing. Shireen stood still, head held high, shoulders back. She looked like a warrior.

Nana reached into a deep pocket of her *abaya*. Yara caught a glimpse of a gold necklace intertwined in her fingers. Nana was looking at Rifa'at, who had rolled over painfully to sit. He gave Nana an almost imperceptible shake of his head. They were not interested in gold trinkets. If not that, then what?

"Brothers." Rifa'at, drawing himself up to stand on two shaky legs, began his speech. "This girl is but a child. Look how small she is. And how bony. Hardly bigger than a chicken. Please, my brothers, let us contribute to your cause and be on our way." As he spoke, beads of sweat appeared in the deep lines on his forehead.

Cannonball Head looked amused. "And leave this poor girl without a husband?" He looked Shireen up and down. His chin jutted out and his lip curled into a sneer. He pulled a knife out of his belt and used it to gesture to his comrade, Bullet Eyes, while he faced Shireen. "You see this man? He is a loyal man. He killed his own father and brother after they were found guilty of collaborating with the President's regime."

Yara shuddered, but Shireen stood calm and steady. All of them, Nana, too, watched and listened in disbelief. Ali and Shireen exchanged glances. Yara could see them talking to each other with their eyes, each one pleading with the other to say nothing.

The two men standing near the truck cheered and fired their guns. *Tat-tat-tat.* Shaking, Saad whimpered as Yara pushed him behind her. "Is this girl worthy of our brother?"

Running his eyes up and down Shireen, Cannonball Head used the tip of his knife to scratch deep into his beard. "Do you know the Quran?" he asked her.

Shireen's green eyes blazed. *"God does not love aggressors."* She quoted from the Quran with a voice as clear as morning birdsong, and for a moment there was silence. And then the man roared like a beast.

"Do you mean to criticize Islam?" Spit gathered at the corners of his mouth.

Ali lurched forward. Again, the soldier rammed the butt of the gun into his belly. Again Ali fell to his knees. Shireen opened her mouth to respond but it was Ali who called out, his voice strangled and raspy. *"And know that Allah is Forgiving and Merciful."* What was he doing? Yara looked from Ali to the hideous pig of a man. And then she understood. He was trying to take the attention off Shireen. He would get himself killed!

Cannonball Head cocked his gun.

"Donkey!" Shireen shouted. "Donkey!"

Yara's mouth gaped open. Shireen had called him an idiot. "SHIREEN!" Yara screamed. Shireen was doing the same thing. She was trying to take the attention off Ali. They would both be killed!

Cannonball Head pivoted and raised his gun. What happened next would take months for Yara to sort out, and even then she could not be sure. Was it luck? Did Allah, glory be on Him, intervene?

A government helicopter came swooping over a hill with the speed of a rocket.

The sand on the ground rose up, swirled, and twisted, creating a whirlpool of grit, gravel, and stones. Screams and commands were muffled and lost in the wind. Cannonball Head and his gang leapt into their truck and aimed their weapons at the sky. Then came the *tat-tat-tat* of a machine gun, followed by the deep-throated thud of a rocket launcher. Yara fell over Saad. Nana lunged towards Shireen. Rifa'at and Ali disappeared in the dust. She could hear the wheels of the truck spinning, the helicopter whining. Was it hit? Would it fall on their heads? The sound was deafening. She heard Nana call out to her. "Nana?" she screamed. Sand filled her mouth, her eyes, and ears.

And then, the helicopter was gone. Gone where? Blinking madly, she looked up.

Something glinted on the ground—a handgun! Yara crawled towards it, lifted it, and pointed. She shot blindly, madly, wildly. And then the gun, blisteringly hot in her hand, thumped back down on the ground.

"Saad." Where was he? She listened. "SAAD!" Standing, she screamed. There he was! He lay curled up, burrowed into hard ground, but he was moving. He was alive.

Spinning in circles she cried, "Rifa'at?" The old man was staggering about, one arm reaching for an invisible wall. Blood leaked out between his fingers and dripped down his shirt. Had he been hit by a rock? A bullet?

And then Shireen made a sound that would ring in Yara's ears forever. It was deep and guttural. Yara spun around.

Nana and Shireen, standing stock-still, peered down the road at . . . at what? *What?*

The truck was disappearing into a brown vapor. Yara began to shake—legs, arms, belly. If she was breathing, she couldn't feel the air in her lungs. And then . . . and then . . . Yara leaned forward, clutched her middle, and felt a scream tear out of her body.

They had taken Ali.

CHAPTER 19

Shireen shot down the road like an arrow, her dark-red hair streaming behind her. Arms pumping, head low, she threw her body forward with the same abandon as if she'd been leaping off a mountain.

"Shireen, nooooo!" Yara cried. Shireen was running directly towards the machine gun.

Pitching herself forward, Yara charged down the road after her. Shireen was older but not faster, and Yara was taller, her legs longer. The truck was fading in and out of dust clouds.

Yara's lungs burned—a stitch in her side cut as deep as a dagger. The truck stopped. A man—more monster than man—standing on the flatbed of the truck, arms extended, head hidden behind the eyepiece of a machine gun, took aim.

"Shireen, DOWN! GET DOWN!" Arms outstretched, Yara threw herself forward and sailed through the air. She landed on Shireen with a solid *whump*. Bullets whooshed over her head. Their hearts beat like drums. Shireen squirmed. "Stay . . . down!" Yara pushed, as if trying to bury her friend in the sand. Shireen exhaled and Yara felt her body deflate.

Bullets drilled into the dry soil around them. Yara waited for the shots to pierce her body. The bullets would be hot. They would shatter bone. They would set her insides on fire. She would die. It wouldn't be terrible. It would be a fast death.

An eternity passed, a lifetime in a second. Shireen squirmed under her. Yara spoke into Shireen's ear. "Wait, wait!" There was a rumble and a squeal of tires. Inching up, Yara peered through hair that had fallen like a veil over her eyes. "Rifa'at! Rifa'at!" she screamed.

The van swerved in front of them, becoming a shield. *Tat-tat-tat.* Bullets punctured the steel wall of the van like knives sliding through butter.

"Get in. NOW!" Rifa'at shouted through the back door. Nana was there on her knees, arms wide. Yara scrambled up and lifted Shireen by her clothes. Shireen swayed, her sand-crusted face hanging down. More bullets pierced the van. With more strength than she thought possible, Yara flung Shireen into the van as if she were a sack of grain. Nana pulled Shireen inside. *Tat-tat-tat.* Nana's body curled over Shireen like a shell. Gasping, Yara fell on top of them both.

"SAAD?" Yara shrieked. "He is here? SAAD! SAAD!" Yara, on all fours, crawled across the floor of the van, reached out for his small, quivering body, and wrapped her arms around him. "Hush, hush," she murmured as she rocked him.

The shooting stopped and the silence that followed was ear-splitting. Shireen, still in Nana's grip, coughed, sputtered, and then howled, "Ali, nooooo!"

Yara looked past Rifa'at and out the front window. They were at a standstill, but she could hear the sound of the truck's tires fading away, and she watched it disappear into whirls of kicked-up dust. What now? Would they come back? She could still imagine the gun, heavy and hot, in her hand. What had she done? She had never fired a gun before, and she hadn't aimed, just pointed and pulled the trigger. Had the bullet found its mark? Impossible.

"Go, Rifa'at, drive!" Shireen lifted herself out of her stupor and began to scream.

Nana was shouting, too, but at Shireen. "Get down, get down!" she cried, her hands clutching at Shireen's clothes. Shireen's nose was skinned raw, and blood ran from her forehead, down her cheeks, to her chin.

Shireen shook off Nana, raised herself up, and shrieked, "Rifa'at, go after them!"

"No, Shireen, no," Yara said. If they caught up to the truck, what then? How would they fight armed soldiers? All Yara could think was, *Ali, jump out. Ali, jump. Break away, Ali. Leap out!*

They weren't moving. "Rifa'at?" Nana called to him. "RIFA'AT!"

Rifa'at's chin rested on the wheel. Blood gushed down the sides of his face. His prickly beard, his shirt, his hands were scarlet with blood.

"Rifa'at!" Nana crawled on her hands and knees across the

floor of the van. She reached across the seat and touched him. Rifa'at's moan was deep and full of pain.

"He's alive, Allah be praised. Yara, find his phone." Nana crawled into the passenger seat and tipped Rifa'at onto his side until his head rested in her lap. "Yara! *The phone!*"

Yara laid Saad's head on the rough blanket and reached breathlessly under the seats. Her hands fell on an old blue first aid kit. She held it up.

"Open it. Hurry!" Nana yanked off her headscarf and tied it tightly around the wound to Rifa'at's head. Cascades of thick silver and black hair fell over Nana's shoulders.

Yara found tidy rows of white bandages wrapped in thin blue plastic. She opened some with her teeth and passed them to her grandmother. "What is this?" Yara held up a brown bottle.

"Iodine, antiseptic. Open it."

Yara twisted the cap and passed it to Nana, who poured it on Rifa'at's wound. It mixed with his blood, creating a black, sticky mess.

"The phone, Yara, find his cell!" Nana's voice shook with frustration.

Yara dropped to the floor. Searching under the seat again with flat palms, she felt her way past forgotten tools, empty pop cans, lost coins, oil tins, rags, candy wrappers, plastic bags, and . . . there! She pulled out a small silver object.

"Now push redial and give it to me." Nana kept one hand on Rifa'at and reached out for the phone with the other. "See to Shireen. Get her and Saad out of the van." Then she lowered her voice and spoke into the phone.

"Shireen?" Yara crawled to Shireen and touched her shoulder. It was like touching frost-covered stone. The heat in the van was stifling, and yet Shireen's teeth were chattering. "Shireen, Ali is strong and he's smart. He will escape." Yara folded her arms around her friend. There was no time for grief or sorrow, or mourning, or even fear—there was nothing but survival. Anyone could come along next—gangs, soldiers, anyone.

"We must get out of here. Come." She pulled Shireen up onto shaky legs. They stumbled out of the van towards a tree. "Sit here, wait." Yara lowered Shireen to the ground carefully, as if she might break. She went back for Saad.

Nana, still in the front seat, looked down at Rifa'at, and snapped the flip-phone shut. "Someone is coming to get him. Help me get him out of here. Bring the blanket."

Coming? Who was coming? Yara didn't ask, she just helped her grandmother drag him out of the van and lay him on the side of the road.

"Rifa'at, my friend, you will be taken care of." Nana fell to her knees. Her face looked as ancient as the buildings of Aleppo.

"Oh, Rifa'at." Yara, too slumped down beside the old man. He had been kind and brave, and she had never said thank you or even given him the respect he deserved. She whispered softly into his ear, "Please don't die. Your grandson and daughter-in-law need you." And then she added, "We need you."

"His pulse is fast," said Nana as she grasped Rifa'at's wrist. Not for the first time, Yara was amazed at the depth of Nana's knowledge.

"Who is coming?" Yara searched her grandmother's face for answers.

"The last call Rifa'at made was to one of Haya's neighbors. I spoke to him. He is a friend of Rifa'at's. I told him Rifa'at would die without medical attention. He will come." Nana's head slumped down on her chest.

"Nana, sit with Shireen and Saad under the tree. I will stay with Rifa'at," said Yara.

Nana shook her head. She would not leave Rifa'at, and Yara would not leave Nana.

Yara made a small tent of sticks and rags to shade him from the sun. They both collapsed beside the dying man under a blistering-hot sun.

An hour passed, maybe more. Saad's eyes were closed but his long, dark lashes fluttered. Shireen remained lifeless, listless, and unreachable.

Yara bit down hard on her lip. She tried not to think of Ali. She took shallow breaths and squeezed her eyes shut. It was as if a great hand had reached down from the sky and scooped him up, flinging him into the far mountains. He was gone. How could someone just be gone?

And then she thought of the gun. She had fired a gun at a man, or at least at a truck carrying men. Her chest contracted. She might have hit a tire, the truck itself, even Ali, but what if the bullet had found a target? What if she had killed a man?

A thought came to her, suddenly and coldly. Rifa'at had a map. It was an odd thing for a Syrian to carry a map and yet Rifa'at did, thanks be to God.

"Nana, I'm sorry." With Nana's eyes drilling into her, Yara patted Rifa'at's body and gently tugged the worn, soft map from his pocket. If she could figure out where they were, she might be able to figure out where to go.

A small car pulled up. A teenaged boy sat behind the wheel; he couldn't have been more than fourteen. "My father sent me," he said, without even looking at them. Hollow-eyed, hollow-cheeked, he looked as though he hadn't slept for days. He said that there was a doctor in Haya's house, or what was left of it. Yara drew in a hopeful breath. He would take Rifa'at to the doctor, but his father said there was no room, no food, for anyone else. Nana understood and asked for nothing.

They wrapped the blanket around Rifa'at and laid him in the back of the car, bending his knees to fit the cramped seat. "Maha," he moaned. Rifa'at's hand shot out from under the blanket.

"Rifa'at, oh, my friend, I am glad to hear your voice." Nana, her face suddenly bright, grabbed his hand and held on to it.

Rifa'at's voice was cracked and garbled. "Do you think I can be killed so easily?" He gave her a tired smile.

"We have to go." The boy, suddenly nervous as a wild hare, looked up and down the road.

"What is your name?" Nana asked the boy.

"Azzam," he replied.

"Thank you for taking care of our friend, Azzam." And to Rifa'at, Nana said, "I am better for knowing you, my friend. *Salamtak,* God be with you." With a deep breath Nana let go of Rifa'at's hand and closed the car door.

"Here." The boy passed three bottles of water through an open window. "From my father." He drove away in a hail of stones.

Nana staggered over to a tree and crumpled like a stuffed doll. Blank-eyed, Shireen lay nearby, frozen in shock. Yara, scrambling over to Saad, held a water bottle up to his chapped lips. He drank like a greedy lamb. Crawling over to Shireen, Yara used some of the water to clean her scraped and bloodied face with a damp rag, then she carefully dribbled water, drop by drop, into her mouth. Shireen sputtered but didn't come out of her daze.

Yara walked back to Rifa'at's damaged van. Its tires were shot out. Gas and oil leaked and seeped into the ground. On the front seat she saw Rifa'at's phone where Nana had dropped it.

"Nana," she called out, "we forgot to give Rifa'at his cell." She held it up.

"Bring it to me," said Nana. Yara placed it in her grandmother's open palm. "It needs to be charged," Nana said as she slipped the phone deep into a hidden pocket in her *abaya*. She grimaced.

"Let me see," Yara ordered. She lifted Nana's gown, exposing her calf, and tried not to look horrified. The stitches from her wound had opened. Nana looked away as though ignoring it, as though she wasn't in great pain.

Yara went back to the van for the first aid kit and found nothing there that would help except a bit of gauze. There had to be something! She reached under the seat, flinging empty bottles, bits of paper, and debris in all directions. Another small bottle of iodine rolled into the palm of her hand—it must have fallen out when she opened the first aid kit. Without waiting for Nana's approval Yara poured the dark-red fluid on her grandmother's leg, then wrapped the wound with the last bit of gauze and tied it with torn fabric. Neither spoke.

⌣•

The sun sank like a stone as the cool night air rolled in. With her back against a gnarled tree trunk, Yara gazed up. The sky was alive with stars.

"Look up, Ali, look up," she whispered. "Look up. Please, look up." She held her breath.

A sob cracked the silence. "Shireen, is that you?" Yara whispered. Crawling towards her, Yara spoke softly into her ear. "Don't cry. Ali is alive." She wasn't just saying it, she believed it.

"But for how long?" Shireen lifted her damp, pale face to the night sky. "And what about Mama? She sacrificed everything for us. How will I tell her? And Father in prison! He will go mad." Shireen curled up into a ball.

Yara couldn't think of anything to say. She especially did not want to think of Roja alone in the house in Aleppo.

"You know those nature shows on television where a lion catches a smaller animal, shakes its head, and rips it apart with its giant teeth?" Shireen whispered. Yara nodded. "I'm the animal," Shireen continued. "I have been ripped into bits. I want it to stop. I don't want to go on."

Yara's head snapped up. Go on? Had Shireen forgotten that Yara's own parents were dead? She didn't want to be unkind, but they were all suffering. Shireen's parents may not be here to protect her but at least they were alive! *It is easy to be killed*, she thought, *but it isn't easy to just die!* Yara was so tired, so hurt, so scared. "It will get better," she told Shireen, hoping that she would be believed.

Shireen bolted up, suddenly defiant. "No. It will get worse. It will *all* get worse." Her nostrils flared as she clenched her fists. "Enough. I have had enough. They have taken my father, my home, my mother is alone, and now my brother is gone. ENOUGH!" She was screaming.

Yara listened, open-mouthed, and then took a deep breath. Up until this very minute Shireen had always been the calm one, the older one, the wiser one. Now it was her turn.

"Maybe it will get worse and maybe it will get better, but we know that tomorrow will be different, because yesterday was different. Next year will be different, because last year was different." Yara, calmer now, brushed Shireen's hair with her hand, leaned down, and kissed her cheek. "It will not end like this." Her words had become whispers. Who was she trying to convince?

CHAPTER 20

Yara held the map. "See? The Qalamoun Mountains." She pointed to a ridge of hills that glowed like bronze pots in the early-morning light.

They were walking on ancient paths. The ground underfoot was uneven and stony. Pebbles crept into their shoes and sandals, and dried up plants crackled under their feet.

Shireen's dark-red hair dribbled down her back in a limp clump. Her *abaya* had been discarded along the path, along with Nana's roller bag.

Nana wore Shireen's headscarf. The red tin box was wrapped in Yara's *abaya* and shoved into her backpack. The bundle of jewels and bits of money were still secreted deep in Nana's *abaya* and scattered in the lining of all their clothes. No one spoke about the night before. What was there to say?

Tearless, blank-faced, Nana stopped and breathed heavily. "Nana?" Yara, in the lead, turned back. "Nana, what's wrong?"

Nana was scanning the horizon, taking in each distant mountain range, the plains, the rolling hills. Her bone-white knuckles were wrapped around her cane. Suddenly she lifted it and stabbed the air in every direction. "For as far as you can see, these are the lands Abraham, Moses, Jesus, and Muhammad walked on." Nana's eyes crinkled against the sun as she rocked on her feet.

"Nana, careful." Yara reached out to touch her grandmother's arm. Nana wrenched her arm away and jabbed her cane into the hard ground.

"Jews, Christians, and Muslims call all these territories sacred, and yet this is the land the world has turned its back on. This is the land they attack and kill on, this is the land they bomb! What does God think?" She shook her head in disgust, then staggered on, weaving back and forth, too stubborn to admit that her body was failing her and her leg was causing her excruciating pain.

On and on they climbed. Saad's little legs seemed too thin and small to hold him up. "Saad." Yara reached out and took his hand. *"One more hill and then we will rest, one more hill and then we will rest,"* she sang, but her voice was ragged and dry. She coughed, but it was as if small pebbles had collected at the back of her throat.

Another hour passed. One bottle of water was left.

Shireen's face was pinched and drawn. She would be sixteen years old soon, but at that moment she could have passed for thirty. She hung her string bag around her neck, letting it hang like a necklace, and lifted Saad onto her back. Yara draped Nana's arm over her own shoulder.

"Shireen?" Yara croaked. Shireen turned back. "We should find a road." Yara pointed to the land below. They were safer in the hills, but Nana was too wobbly on the uneven terrain.

As Shireen opened her mouth to reply, Nana cried out, her arms thrashing the air.

"Nana, nooo!" Yara lurched towards her grandmother, grabbed her arm, and then her sleeve. The material slipped through Yara's hands like silk. "NANA!" Yara leapt ahead of her and tried to break her fall. Both tumbled down the hill. Stones, pebbles, twigs, and thorns pierced Yara's skin. Shireen screamed and Saad howled as Yara and Nana rolled like dustballs before settling in a small gully, breathless and dazed.

"Lie still." Shireen skidded and slipped down the hill with Saad behind her. She bent over Yara. "Is anything broken?" She ran her hands down Yara's arms and legs.

"No, no, I'm fine, I think. What about Nana?" Yara lay still and waited for the sky to stop spinning.

"She's in pain, but awake," said Shireen now a few feet away.

Yara reached out for Saad. "Come, come. I'm not hurt. Are you?" He shook his head but quaked like a frightened bird in her arms. She held him and waited until his trembling stopped.

They had landed in a protected spot, cradled on each side by rolling hills.

With one arm around her little brother Yara propped herself up on her elbow and tried to focus. Crouched like a child with her legs folded under her, Shireen twisted her hair into a knot and bent over Nana. "It's all right. By the grace of God, you are all right," Shireen whispered into Nana's ear. "But you need to move a little. It's your leg . . ." Shireen continued her soft murmurings.

"Let me help." Yara wobbled to her feet. Twigs, tiny stones, and sand were embedded in her clothes. Brushing back her own hair, Yara helped Shireen try to lift Nana. Her grandmother let out a small involuntary cry. "Nana, I'm sorry." Yara propped up her grandmother's head on a backpack. It was Shireen who gingerly exposed Nana's lower leg. Both girls gasped. Mean red streaks shot up her leg. In just a few short hours Nana's leg had become so swollen it looked like the trunk of a small tree. "Oh, Nana." Yara put her hand on Nana's forehead. Worse, she was burning up.

"I'll get the water bottle." Shireen scrambled back up the hill.

Saad stood beside Yara and peered down at his grandmother's leg. His face contorted and drained of color. He swayed as if ready to faint.

"Sit, Saad. Nana will be fine, I promise." Yara propped the boy up beside a rock and thought that she had no right to make such a promise.

In minutes Shireen was back with her string bag and water bottle. Yara slowly dripped water into her grandmother's mouth.

"We must rest," said Shireen as she slumped down and hung her head. The burst of energy had left her drained. Yara closed her eyes. There was nothing left to do.

An hour passed, maybe two. The sun was hard and high. The sky was clear blue and cloudless. Shireen and Saad lay side by side, their eyes closed.

Propping the water bottle beside Shireen and holding Rifa'at's tattered map, Yara climbed out of the small gully up onto a rock. She shaded her eyes with her hand and peered off into the distance.

"Shireen, wake up." Yara ran back and gave Shireen a shake. Shireen's eyes were glassy and distant. "Listen. I think we are near Mar Musa. Look, it's on the map. It's the monastery. Up in the mountains." Yara tapped Rifa'at's map with her finger. Shireen nodded but said nothing.

"See, the note at the bottom? It says that monks live there. And it says that travelers are welcome. Get up. Please, Shireen, help me with Saad and Nana." Yara wrapped her arms around her friend. "Please, please," Yara begged. Shireen's head rocked on her shoulders. "Shireen, I love you. Can you hear me?" Shireen lay motionless on the ground.

Yara scrambled over to Nana. "Nana, can you get up? Drink," she coaxed, as she dribbled water into her grandmother's mouth.

"The tin box," Nana croaked. "Take it and go. Take Saad and Shireen. Don't come back." Gasping, she reached into her clothes and ripped out what was left of the jewels. A small bundle of cash fell out of a pocket. "It's yours now, everything is yours." Her head fell back against the backpack.

Yara stared open-mouthed at her grandmother as Nana closed her eyes. "Nana. *Nana!*" Her grandmother didn't move.

Yara found sticks, rammed them into the hard sand, and draped bits of cloth over the wood, creating a canopy against a blazing sun.

"I'm going to get help. Shireen, can you understand me? I am going for help." Yara gave her a gentle shake.

Shireen nodded dumbly, then opened her eyes and pulled Yara's sleeve. "Take these." With a deep groan Shireen yanked at the bottom of her skirt. The seam split and out spilled the necklaces and two small rings that Nana and Roja had sewn in.

"Nana wanted you to have them," Yara whispered.

"Take them. We will be robbed. Please, Yara," she whispered.

Yara collected the jewelry. One pink opal ring lay in the palm of her hand. Yara slipped it on Shireen's finger, twisted it around so the stone faced her palm, then folded her friend's fingers into a fist. "I will find help, I promise," said Yara.

Shireen nodded and closed her eyes.

Yara crawled over to her grandmother. "I remember the names of your sons, Nana. Aziz, Kareem, and Anas. I will remember their names forever, I promise." Yara kissed her grandmother's cheek. It was as soft as cotton.

Saad lay on the ground like a fallen baby bird, his arms folded under him like clipped wings. "Saad, wake up. *Saad.*" She stroked his hair. He opened his eyes. They were dim and vague. He took in a deep breath and reached for Yara, his fingers clawing at the air.

"Hush, I will be back. I promise." Again she ran her hand over his thick, black-as-coal hair, and then she stood up. If she didn't leave now, she would never leave. She would just curl her arms around the three people she loved and fall asleep with them. They were so small, so thin, that they almost disappeared into the ground. She had wanted to tell Shireen that it wasn't easy to just die, but that was wrong. It *was* easy to die here, in this place, in a war. They could just sink into the earth. No one would even know how hard they had tried to stay alive.

She picked up her backpack and pulled out her *abaya*. It was the only protection she had. The *abaya* swept the ground, catching on twigs and plants as she walked.

I promise. I promise. Yara beat the words into the ground with every step. The red tin box and the small bag of jewels rattled in her backpack.

The sign for the monastery should be straight ahead. Mar Musa was a Catholic place. Would they help her? They accepted travelers—the little box at the bottom of the map had said so. Was she a traveler? Yes, she must be. *I promise. I promise.*

But who was to say that the monastery was still standing, or that anyone still lived there? Maybe the place had been bombed. Questions. Questions.

I promise. I promise. Her tongue was sticky. Sweat collected at the back of her neck, coated her chest, and pooled at the base of her spine. She stopped thinking of her promise and started thinking about water.

The pounding heat had turned the air into rolling waves. Was that the road? She cupped a hand over her eyes and blinked. Riding a wave of air was a car, or maybe it was a truck.

Yara slid down a rocky slope, her backpack slapping against her back. Turning to the sound of the oncoming vehicle, she waved. *Let them be kind. Let them be good.* She swayed on rubbery legs. "Stop, please!" she shouted. The two small words scraped her throat like a knife. The truck swerved around her.

Why didn't they stop? Why? It was so hard to think. And then she remembered. *Show them your hand and arms. They want to make sure you are not holding a detonator.* Rifa'at's words were like a whisper in her ear.

The road rumbled under her feet. She turned. A large vehicle barreled towards her. Yara tossed aside her backpack, pulled the sweat-soaked *abaya* over her head, took off her jeans, and threw everything into a heap on the ground. Removing her clothes was like peeling away skin. There was nothing between her and the wind and blazing sun. She was a bone-thin girl, standing in the middle of the road in a damp T-shirt and underpants.

Her legs wobbled. Her bones dissolved into milk. She bit down on her cracked lip, lifted her rock-heavy arms in the air, and waited to be mowed down. "I'm sorry. Forgive me," she whispered as her arms fell, her eyes closed, and she sank to the ground.

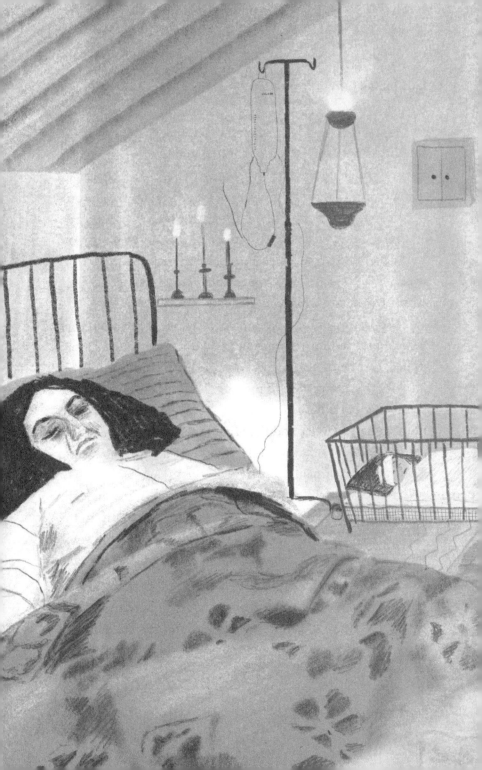

PART 3
Sanctuary: Mar Musa

CHAPTER 21

"Sip slowly." It was a woman's voice. Not Nana's. Not Shireen's. The rim of a cup was pressed against Yara's lips. Cool water. Water!

Yara bolted up, gasped, and spewed back the water. Her gummed-up eyes flew open and darted around as she gulped air. "Where . . . ?" She tried to form a question with blistered lips and a swollen tongue.

"Hush. Breathe. You are in a monastery. One of our delivery trucks found you on the road. Rest now. Lie back." The woman holding the cup knelt beside her. She wore white. Was that a cross around her neck? Panic rose up in Yara's throat. She jerked around, suddenly, quickly, her neck nearly wrenching out of her shoulders. A plastic bag hung from a pole over her head. The liquid was clear, like water. Yara's eyes trailed from the bag down a thin plastic line that led to a needle in her arm. "*Nooooo,*" she cried, waving her arms while gasping for air.

"Hush. No one will hurt you. Lie back down . . . there, dear girl." The nurse's voice was soothing, almost musical. Yara's head fell back on a hard pillow. She was lying on a mat on the floor. A wet towel swept across her face. She couldn't fight. She didn't have the strength. *Think, think.* She desperately needed to remember something, something important.

"The needle in your arm is saline solution, just salt and water. You are badly dehydrated." Dehydrated? What did that mean?

Yara's thoughts began to gather like beads on a string. She had been walking. A truck? She remembered a voice asking, *What is your name?* But it was a man who asked the question, not this woman in white. She was sure of it . . . almost sure. She remembered more questions. *Why are you on the road alone?* Alone? Blue eyes had looked down at her. Blue, like pictures of the sea, like the sky on a cool day.

And then, her memory returned with the speed of an arrow. She reached for the woman in white. "NANA, SAAD, SHIREEN!" she cried. Yara bolted upright, her arms thrashing the air.

The woman placed her hands on Yara's shoulders and restrained her. "Stop! Listen. Just listen!"

But Yara couldn't listen, wouldn't listen. She pushed the woman away. "I must . . . I must . . ." How long had she been here? Could they still be alive? She had left them to die. She was alive and they were dead! It hurt to breathe.

"Listen." Now the woman used all her weight to pin Yara to the mat. "*Your family is here.* There was a monk in the truck. You were delirious but you told him about them. You had a map. We sent out a search party. They are in the infirmary right now. Your grandmother—she is your grandmother, yes? She needed to have her leg wound irrigated and stitched. And the boy, your little brother. He would not leave her side. They are safe. Say it." The sweet voice was now firm and insistent.

"Safe . . . *safe,*" Yara repeated as her blistered lips split open. She sank back down on the bed.

"Sleep now." The woman coated Yara's lips with something cool and soft.

Yara repeated the words in her head: *family, safe.* And then, "Shireen!" she screamed.

"Yes," the woman answered. "Yes, the girl is here, too. Stop now. You must stop."

~•

Darkness was everywhere. Climbing out of sleep was like climbing up an endless ladder. Everything hurt, her legs, her back, her head. She moaned. Her head might split in two. Slowly, she remembered the last word she'd said: *safe.* Nana, Saad, and Shireen were here, alive. But someone was missing. She couldn't quite . . . And then the answer slammed into her like a rock to the chest. *Ali.* Breathless, she lay still and let the pain wash through her as tears leaked from her closed eyes and fell into her hair.

~•

Daybreak, almost. She gazed around, more alert this time. The room had tall windows on all sides. A morning breeze blew in as the sky lightened. A candle flickered, and a lantern, hanging from a hook, cast a yellow hue. The ceiling was made of wood, shaped like the upside-down hull of a ship and stained the color of burnt sugar. She remembered—a woman, a needle, a monastery. Remembering was like capturing clouds.

There was a bandage on her arm. Biting her lower lip, she peeled it away and stared at a red dot as small as a pinprick.

Tossing back the flowered blanket, Yara slowly staggered to her feet and waited for the dizziness to pass. Trembling, she ran her hands down her sides. The shift she wore—it could hardly be called a dress—was the shade of sand. The sleeves reached her elbows, and as she stood, the gown reached to the floor.

Her jeans, T-shirt, underwear, and long black *abaya* lay folded on a wooden chair near her mat. She ran her hands over her hair. It had been washed and combed. Wait. The red tin box! Her eyes darted around. There, under the chair, was her backpack. Yara reached into the pack and pulled out the box. Identification papers and passports—all there. She let out a breath, then tucked them away. Wait, the jewels! She touched the small bundle under her clean clothes. Judging by the weight of it, they, too, had not been touched. Finally, she rested her hand on Baba's tobacco pouch. Her fingers felt thick and clumsy as she fumbled with the string, lifted the pouch to her nose, and breathed in the apple spiced tobacco scent. Warmth spread up and down her spine and left her head spinning. "Baba, stay with me," she whispered.

212 • JAMAL SAEED AND SHARON E. McKAY

Wobbly but standing, Yara reached for a clay cup beside a jug of water. Her hands shook as she tried to swallow. She vomited. Dabbing her chin with a towel she tried again, but more slowly this time. Water trickled down her raw throat. She finished the cup and filled it once more. Finally, she let the cup rest in her hand. Had the woman actually used Shireen's name? She tried to sort dream from reality. It was impossible.

A long line of mats, each one covered with a sheet and topped with a square, floral pillow, stretched the length of the room. How many? Ten? Twelve mats? Who would sleep here? Blankets were folded neatly at the bottom. The long room looked like a dormitory, a place for travelers maybe. There was no sign of Shireen, no sign that any of the other mats had been slept in. But she had heard Shireen's voice, hadn't she? Had she dreamed it? Nana, Saad, how to find them?

"*Marhaba!*" she called out. "Hello?" Her words echoed off the walls.

Plastic sandals had been placed beside her mat. Slipping them on, she shuffled past the row of mats towards a doorway. A Christian cross was nailed above the arch. The flame of the candle cast shadows up to the vaulted ceiling. The sweet smell of paraffin was a guide through small doorways and along cramped passageways. Which way to go? It was a maze of mysterious indoor alleyways.

Leaning against a wall, she waited for the queasiness in her belly to pass. Slowly, her slippers scuffing against the tiled floor, Yara inched towards the entrance to a small stone chamber. She heard a muffled voice murmuring in prayer.

"*Subhana Rabbya Al a'la.* Glory be to my Lord, the Most High." She stepped closer. It was like listening to a voice through fog.

Faded rugs hung over the tiny entrance. Yara parted the rugs and stepped inside. The candles in the room were burned down to their wicks. Wax pooled at the base and glowed gold in the flickering light. As Yara's eyes adjusted to the soft light she saw a mihrab. It was a niche in the wall showing the direction of Mecca, the direction in which Muslims kneel to pray. But this was a Christian place! She looked around, confused. And then . . . Yara fell on her knees. "Shireen," she whispered.

"You are awake!" Shireen bounced up and flung her arms around Yara. Yara could feel Shireen's head nudge deep into the crook of her neck, feel her small, suddenly powerful arms hold her tight, and feel her warmth pass into her. "You were asleep for two days. You had nightmares." Shireen sat back on her heels. Dark smudges, like black crescent moons, lay under her eyes. "I prayed. I have done nothing but pray," she said.

To Yara, she looked so frail and tired. "Oh, Shireen!" Yara trailed her hand over Shireen's cheek. "Have you seen my grandmother? My brother?"

"Yes, yes," said Shireen. A smile spread across her face and suddenly Shireen was a beautiful girl again.

Yara cupped her head in her hands. Saad and Nana were alive. Alive! She took deep breaths. It was a miracle.

"How did it happen?" Yara could barely form the words. She remembered the road and the truck that came hurtling towards her. She remembered the moment when she thought she would die. There were other memories, too, but they were out of reach, at least for now. Tears streamed down Yara's face.

"There is time to talk, to explain," Shireen stroked her friend's hair.

"Nana, Saad . . . I thought . . ."

"Don't cry Yara. It doesn't help. It won't make it all better," Shireen whispered.

At that moment Yara knew that they were both thinking of Ali, and that their prayers would now be for him.

CHAPTER 22

"My grandmother and brother, I have to see them." Yara stared up at a man who stood in the archway gazing down at the two girls sitting on prayer mats. He wore a close-cropped beard, a wooden cross on a leather thong around his neck, and a long gown that reached the floor. "Please," she added. Yara recognized him somehow. She had never met a man with such blue eyes before. How could she recognize someone and not know him?

Shireen, sitting beside her on the floor, reached out for her hand and gave it a gentle squeeze. "It's all right, Yara. He will help." She spoke in a feathery, soft voice.

Yara glanced back at Shireen. She trusted this man. Why? Was he a monk? A priest? He was not the Pope. The Pope wore a tall hat. She had seen him on television. "Who are you?" she asked. Her voice was raspy; her throat was still dry and sore.

He smiled. He seemed to welcome the question. "I am the abbot, the head of the monastery. You may call me Father Ricardo. Your grandmother is in the infirmary." His voice was low and oddly musical.

Yara tried to make sense of it all. "And my brother . . . ?" she asked.

"Yes, he is with your grandmother. We did not want to separate them. I will take you to them. Come."

Yara glanced back at Shireen, who nodded. "Go, it is all right." Shireen's mouth slowly turned into a sweetly sad smile.

Yara, wiping her forehead with the sleeve of her shift, followed.

They went down one passage, then another, and another. Light poured in through windows on her right. She caught glimpses of the outside world—patches of sloping green hills and bald mountains glossy with morning dew. And then she stopped and stood at one of the long windows, mesmerized by the beauty, the peaceful hills, sheep in the distance, flowers creating a carpet of colors. Yara had never been higher than the roof of their house, and here she was close enough to touch clouds.

"Why haven't ISIS or al-Nusra or any of the gangs destroyed this place?" She surprised herself by asking such a bold question. Outside these walls people were killing each other, bombs were being dropped on homes, hospitals, schools. Why not this place? Had this man, this "Father," made a bargain with the President, or with one gang or another?

"God has protected us through the centuries," said Father Ricardo. "We are a sign of hope for the world."

Yara didn't trust "hope," not anymore.

"Come." Father Ricardo led her down another passageway, and at last Yara turned a corner and saw a small room with beds and cots.

"Nana!"

Yara saw them both immediately. She fell to her knees beside her grandmother's bed and brushed her hand over thick hair that lay across the pillow in waves of black and silver. Nana's face was as waxy as the unlit tallow candles.

"Nana, it's me. Nana, I am here," Yara whispered, but her grandmother did not stir. "Wake up, Nana," Yara cried.

"She is fine." A small young woman stood over her. She was wearing a shift much like the one Yara had on but it was belted, and there was something around her neck, like a collar. She wore a cross on a long rope and a dark blue scarf over her hair, tied not under her chin but at the back of her neck. But it was her large round glasses that Yara noticed the most. "Your grandmother has been given a sedative. She arrived in great pain but she's sleeping now."

Yara turned to a much smaller cot beside her grandmother's bed. "Saad, can you hear me?" She put a hand on his narrow chest. His skin was dry and his arms were as thin as twigs.

"He is asleep, too. Give them time," said the woman.

"Thank you." Yara nodded. Would she ever stop crying? Maybe Shireen was right, tears didn't help, but she just couldn't make them stop! Her grandmother and brother were alive. Shireen was alive. Ali was, too, she was sure of it. They were in this strange castle high in the sky, away from soldiers and gangs and guns. How could she not be grateful?

Yara perched like a sparrow on a rickety wooden chair between Saad's cot and Nana's bed. She leaned forward and watched the small vein in Saad's neck pulse. He was so beautiful, so like Baba.

The legs of her chair scraped against the stone floor. Startled, Saad awoke and looked up at her, his eyes wide with surprise.

"It's all right. I'm here." Yara smiled, trying her best to be calm. "How do you feel?" she asked, hoping that he would instinctively blurt out "Good" or "Bad." Just one word would be enough. But he clamped his lips shut and looked away.

"Are you mad at me? I didn't leave you, Saad. I went for help." She threaded her fingers through his coal-black hair and caught a whiff of sweet laurel soap. "Saad, look at me." Yara picked up a small wooden truck that sat on a tiny table beside his bed. "Someone has given you a toy, see? The wheels move and the little doors open. It's not exactly like the one Ali fixed for you but . . ." She stopped. Saad pulled his knees to his chest and curled into a ball. Ali—she should not have mentioned his name. "Here, I'll put it here." She placed the toy within his reach.

A cool breeze wafted into the room. She looked around. Everything was neat and carefully laid out. There were four beds, Saad's cot, chairs, a round wooden table, a desk, cabinets, and a metal cart with needles and mysterious brown bottles lined up on a pristine white cloth. She looked back at her little brother. Saad's eyes were closed, but that didn't mean he was sleeping.

Father Ricardo touched Yara's elbow. Yara was a little startled. She had forgotten about him. Had he been watching her the whole time?

"Come and sit." He motioned to the table by an open window, where a tray of food had been set. He ushered her to a chair and then sat opposite her. "Eat, please." There was soup, bread, a bowl of olives, and a dish of hummus. The small woman returned to her desk and bent over a book.

"Shireen has told me of your parents, your journey here, and of her brother, Ali. Tell me, how can I help you?" Father Ricardo did not reach out but sat patiently, his large hands folded on his lap.

Yara lifted a spoonful of soup to her mouth and then stopped. The aroma of it . . .

"What is it?" Are you alright?" he asked, leaning forward.

"It is . . . delicious." Yara sipped politely, then rested the spoon on the side of the plate.

"Beans and spinach. Did your mother make that soup?" Father Ricardo asked.

Yara, blinking back tears, nodded.

"All Syrians are raised on this soup. Come now, try again. You need to eat." He motioned to the bowl.

Yara's hand shook as she again lifted the spoon to her mouth.

"You are welcome to stay here for as long as it takes to heal. We celebrate one God but all religions, do you understand?"

All religions? Yara looked into his blue eyes and bit her blistered lips. "Why?" she asked quietly.

"We may be Jews, Christians, or Muslims, but we are all descendants of Abraham, and for as long as we live in God's light, we offer you safety." He spoke with such conviction that Yara almost believed him. Almost. She tipped her head. Shireen trusted him. They had gone out and searched for Saad, Shireen, and Nana. How many would have done that? It was a miracle—all of it. But offer protection? Safety? No one could promise that. Not anymore.

The little woman rose from her desk, stood by Yara's side, and waited.

"I must go. Sister would like to talk to you, but not . . ." Father Ricardo paused ". . . until you have finished your soup." His eyes twinkled like Baba's, she thought. Yara wanted to trust him, she needed to trust him. There was nowhere else to go! He said goodbye and the little woman with the big glasses took his place. Sister? Was she his sister?

"Who are you?" Yara asked, and she coughed.

"My name is Sister Mary. I am a nun, but I also have medical training. And your name is Yara, isn't it? Your grandmother has asked for you. Your grandmother was badly dehydrated when she arrived, which made the infection in her leg difficult to treat, even with antibiotics." The nun gazed into Yara's eyes. "Do you understand, Yara? The infection could travel up to her heart. She may be called to God sooner than we would like."

"Called to God," that was probably a Christian expression, but it was easy to understand. It meant that Nana might die. Yara's stomach felt as if it were filled with shards of glass. She couldn't take a proper breath, couldn't stop her heart from hammering, or her fingers from pleating and unpleating her shift.

"Where there is life, there is hope," the nun said with a reassuring smile.

Yara looked over at her grandmother. Lying there, eyes closed, her face might have been carved by a great artist. She was beautiful. How old was she? Fifty? Seventy? Yara had no idea. Weren't all grandparents old? And then Yara remembered Rifa'at's words: *You are very like your grandmother. You are both stubborn as rocks.* She felt a little better. Nana was too stubborn to die.

CHAPTER 23

As Nana slept, Saad played, and Shireen prayed, Yara fell into the gentle rhythm of the monastery. She still wore the shift that had been lent to her. It was cool, and without the leggings she always wore under a dress, she felt comfortable, free.

In the early morning she weeded the rooftop gardens and swept stone floors. Later she peeled vegetables and worked in the kitchen. They ate their meals on a terrace under a tarp. She did everything but think and remember. Hour by hour, and then day by day, she began to settle.

It was late afternoon on the fifth day when Yara, on her way to the kitchen with a basket of eggplants, spotted Shireen. She was across the terrace sitting on a tall stone wall, facing out. Wait, her feet had to be dangling over a forty-foot gorge! *No, no, Shireen. Please, God.* Should she go for help?

"Shireen?" Gently, in a singsong voice, Yara called out to Shireen the way her mama had called to her when she was little and too close to the road.

"Hello!" Shireen twisted around.

"Come down," said Yara, in the most pleasant voice she could manage.

"No, you come up." She smiled. "Go over there, there is a ladder." Shireen lifted a hand off the wall to point.

Yara whirled around. Sure enough, a rickety wooden ladder leaned against the wall a bit farther away. Dropping her basket, and ignoring the eggplants that rolled out of it and across the terrace, Yara climbed hand over hand. The ladder groaned with each step.

"Please, Shireen, come down," said Yara as she reached the ledge. A pebble fell from the wall. It fell so far that they could not even hear the ping when it hit bottom.

"You will be fine, Yara. Sit first, then swing your legs around and inch over like this." Shireen wiggled her bottom to show Yara exactly what she meant. "Don't look down!"

Too late! The distance gaping below made her dizzy. Biting down hard on her lip, she gripped the ledge of craggy rocks and chipped bricks and moved across, inch by inch. When she reached Shireen, she sat stiff as a plank, her legs dangling over the edge.

"Are you scared?" Shireen asked.

"A little." Yara let out a nervous giggle. "When I saw you up here I was worried . . ." Yara didn't know how to finish that thought.

The confused look on Shireen's face suddenly brightened with understanding. "You thought that I might . . . ?" She didn't say the word "jump." She just laughed.

Yara felt foolish. How could she even have thought such a thing?

"I am not going anywhere. Look and see all the colors of the world." Shireen lifted a hand and waved it across the horizon. Yara planted her own hands firmly on the wall.

The air was as thin as an eggshell. The distant mountains shone azure blue, and the valley below was layered in clouds, each layer a different color: scarlet, rose, pink, and a shocking orange that set the world aglow. Below, as far as the eye could see, were yellow plains of wheat and green groves of grapes and olives. Yara let out a breath. Syria was dressed like a queen.

Shireen slapped the wall beneath them with a flat palm. "Do you know how old this wall is?" she asked. Yara wrinkled her nose and shook her head. "The Romans built this place almost two thousand years ago. A monk told me. Think of it, short little Romans running around in tin helmets carrying pointy sticks. I suppose they had metal tips. Then Christian hermits turned the building into the first religious house." Shireen spoke with authority.

"What is a 'hermit'?" asked Yara.

"Someone who lives alone and doesn't bathe," Shireen said in her most matter-of-fact voice.

"Maybe if he bathed, he wouldn't be alone," Yara added. Shireen's laugh seemed to drift up into the sky.

"'Maybe it will get worse and maybe it will get better, but we know that tomorrow will be different, because yesterday was different. Next year will be different, because last year was different.'" Shireen was mimicking Yara's singsong voice. "You told me that, remember?" Yara nodded. "What I am trying to say is, I am sorry," said Shireen.

"Sorry? What are you sorry about?" Yara was shocked.

"I'm sorry that I gave up, that I left you alone. When they took Ali, I lost hope. It's not that I wanted to die, it's just that I didn't want to live. Do you understand?" Shireen looked over at Yara, who dutifully nodded. But she didn't understand, not really.

"You never lost hope, even after your parents were killed." Shireen turned back to gaze at the distant hills.

Yara swallowed hard. What about the ball of fire that smoldered in her belly, that even now threatened to burst into flames and consume her? What about the wall she had built inside her to hold the pain down? She closed her eyes and swayed back and forth.

"Yara, what are you doing? *Yara, be careful!*" Shireen reached out and slapped her hand down hard on Yara's shoulder. "What is wrong?" Shireen asked.

Yara shook her head. What was wrong? What was right? Steady now, she wiped her face with her sleeve. "I have something to tell you, too. I think I might have killed someone." She didn't want to see the look on her friend's face. No matter what, murder was against God's law.

"How? When?" There was a hint of something in Shireen's voice. What was it? Laughter?

"When they took Ali, I found ... I think ..." Her face grew hot. "There was a gun. It was just there, on the ground. I didn't even realize it was a gun until I picked it up. What else do you do with a gun but fire it? So, I did! Shireen . . . what if I killed someone?"

"I hope you did. I hope you killed at least one of them." Shireen did laugh, but it wasn't a nice laugh. It didn't even sound like her.

Yara turned and stared. "It is a life. They kill us. We kill them. They kill us. How do we stop?"

"We are at war, Yara. War." Shireen shrugged. "Likely you did not kill anyone. How could you? It was so hard to see anything that day. And if you did, it was luck!" added Shireen.

Luck?

They sat for a long time and watched the sun slowly sail across the sky, turning the far mountain range blue.

"Ali is alive, and one day we will be together. I know it, I feel it!" said Shireen, bobbing her head. Yara wanted to believe it, too. They would leave Syria, and one day Ali would join them. The question was, when?

"I must get to the kitchen," said Yara. Carefully, inching along, she moved across the wall back towards the ladder.

"Wait, Yara." Shireen reached out. "I said I was sorry, but I never said thank you." She gave Yara a half-smile.

"For what?" Yara swung her legs back over the wall and climbed onto the ladder.

"When they took Ali, you came after me. You tried to protect me. Thank you."

Yara gripped the ladder and turned. The two girls gazed at each other. "But I love you," Yara said simply.

The tears in Shireen's eyes were sudden. "I love you, too."

An hour later, Yara stood at the entrance of the infirmary, holding Nana's dinner on a tray. Nana sat in a chair, her leg extended, looking out a window. A man Yara had never seen before stood beside her. He was a small, stooped man, older than Nana, and older than Rifa'at, too. Yara heard the words, "We leave tonight."

Without looking at Yara, without even saying goodbye to Nana, the man shuffled past Yara and out the door and was quickly out of sight. He disappeared like a ghost.

"I see you, Yara." Nana rearranged herself in the chair. "Before you ask, that man's name is Emad, and he will take us to Sami." Nana again looked out the tall window.

"Nana, this is what we wanted!" She knelt down beside her grandmother and took her hand. Their prayers had been answered, so why were Nana's hands trembling? "Nana, who is he?" Every wish that came true came at a price. Yara knew that now. What was Emad's price?

Sighing deeply, Nana peered over her shoulder, then whispered in Yara's ear, "He works for your uncle."

He worked for Uncle Sami? How? Doing what? Uncle Sami was a teacher. Or maybe now he was head of the whole school?

"But are you well enough to leave?" asked Yara. Nana still wasn't strong, and she had gained very little weight.

Nana nodded. "I don't feel too much like *dancing . . .*" she said, eyes twinkling.

"How did you find him? Emad, I mean," Yara asked, trying not to sound too suspicious.

"I used Rifa'at's phone. Sami gave me a number for emergencies. I tried calling many times and there was never an answer, but then, thanks be to God, someone picked up! I could hear breathing. I said that I was Umm Aziz and I was looking for my son." Nana paused. "Only someone very close to Sami would know that name, only someone he trusted. And if he had not known who I was talking about"—Nana shrugged—"I would have said that I had the wrong number."

"But how . . . ?" Yara had a hundred questions.

"Enough," Nana said. "He is taking us to your uncle, that is all you need to know. Too much information is dangerous." Nana gazed out the window again. "Sadness and secrets are in every Syrian home, Yara. They are as common as spice. Our resistance is silence."

"But Nana, didn't you say that secrets always come out?" Yara sat back on her heels.

Nana nodded. "Eventually, but now we have to outrun them. We will leave when the monks are at their evening prayers. The monastery must not be involved in anything political."

Political? What did that mean? Why was meeting her uncle "political"?

"Tonight?" Yara's eyes widened.

Nana nodded. "At sunset."

━ •

Hours later, all four stood in the infirmary. Everyone—the nuns, the monks, even the cooks—were in the chapel.

Saad's Woody Woodpecker bag, containing only the small bear and a change of clothes, was again bouncing on his back. The red tin box was safely tucked away in Yara's backpack and Baba's tobacco pouch was in the pocket of her jeans. The bag of jewels had been returned to Nana. "You can hide them better than I," Yara had said. Shireen had attempted to return the pretty pink opal ring, but Nana had refused it. "Hide it. It is yours." As usual, Nana had spoken with the finality of a slammed door.

"Nana, we can't just . . . disappear!" Yara felt light-headed with excitement, but to sneak away when the people who had saved them were at prayer made her heartsick.

"I will leave this." Shireen placed her father's Quran high on a shelf. "It will be safe here with the monks," she said, without even a tear.

"We will come back for it one day, after the war," Yara whispered. A kind of shadow passed over Shireen's face and then, as if taken by a light breeze, the look was gone. She squeezed Yara's hand and nodded.

Nana placed a gold chain beside the holy book. It was one of her best and most treasured—Yara could tell by the way Nana held it, the way her eyes trailed over every link. Had it been a gift from her first husband? Her mother or father? "It may help with the repairs of the building," Nana said, then turned away.

Saad, silent but ever listening, took his toy cars from his pockets and lined them up in a row on the little nun's desk. He had collected a half dozen since their arrival. "I think you can keep them. They were meant as presents," said Yara, as she ran her hand over his silky black hair.

Saad shook his head. His face was damp with tears. He and the small nun had become friends, and here he was losing yet another special person in this life.

"Then she will know that you left them for her, as a gift," Yara said softly. "But me, I have nothing to leave to say thank you."

"Yara, you worked from dawn to dusk. I think you have given a great deal," said Nana, just a little tartly.

Yara gave her a long look. To her very soul, Yara felt thankful. "They saved our lives. How can anything be enough?" she asked.

"And now we are trying to protect them. We don't want anyone to have to lie about us. This is best," Nana said firmly. Yara nodded, but no matter what, she felt ungrateful.

The narrow steps out of the monastery and down to the parking lot were rough and uneven. It would take them half an hour to reach the bottom. Yara stopped partway down and looked back up at the monastery.

"Yara, are you all right?" Shireen called over her shoulder. Yara waved and nodded. Clutching Saad's hand, Shireen carried on.

Yara could barely pull her eyes away from the monastery. Built into the mountains and rimming the valley, it rose from the earth as if it had been planted, not built. By day the ancient walls were camel-colored but now, at sunset, they glowed burnt orange.

Yara raised her hand and waved. "Thank you," she whispered.

Emad, a sour-looking man, stood beside a battered old car in the parking lot. He flicked a finger and ground his cigarette butt under his heel. "We have to take back roads," he mumbled.

Their reprieve was over.

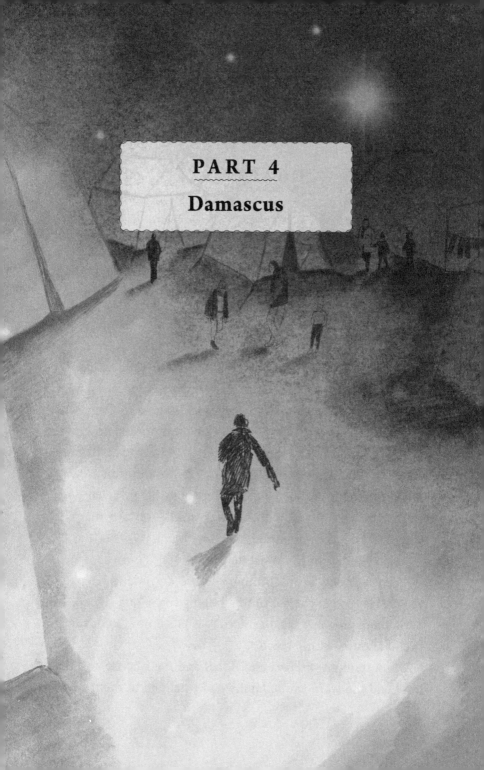

PART 4

Damascus

CHAPTER 24

Nana sat in the front seat next to Emad; Yara, Saad, and Shireen were in the back. They drove in silence. An hour was what it would normally have taken to drive to Damascus from the monastery. Normally. Nothing was normal now.

Emad mumbled into his phone then snapped it shut. "Electric power is out in Damascus. We do not want to wait at a checkpoint." If they had any questions—like, "What does electricity have to do with a checkpoint?"—Emad made it clear that he was in no mood to answer them.

Nana said, calmly, "What do you suggest?"

"We will stay at my brother's house until dawn," replied Emad. He turned the car onto a bumpy road. Yara sighed. In Syria there was always a brother or sister's home, a cousin or friend's house, within reach.

Yara thought of Haya and Rahaf and their house and the food and the warmth the family had extended to them. How could she not? Fear rushed in then, just like before, making it hard to breathe. Yara tried to catch Nana's attention, but her grandmother, maybe deliberately, just squared her shoulders and stared ahead at the setting sun.

Emad pulled into a driveway and drove around to the back of the house. They heard the *meeh, meeh,* as the goats in their pen settled for the night.

Saad pulled his legs up until his knees touched his forehead. He did not have to speak to show her how scared he was. "It will be okay," Yara whispered to him, while trying to stop herself from trembling. Fear was contagious. Shireen squeezed her hand.

Emad turned off the car. They sat.

"You will be welcomed in this house," said Emad, without asking what they thought of the plan.

Nana smiled the sweet smile she so seldom used. "My grandson is very nervous. Would you extend my sincere thanks to your family and ask if they would find it acceptable if we slept in the car?" Again, Nana smiled.

Emad shrugged. And so they slept in the car, cuddling together like kittens.

Dawn came, and after tea with Emad's brother's family they set out again, groggy and stiff.

There was no getting around the government checkpoints that surrounded Damascus like a belt. Bribes changed hands at each one. It was light when at last they drove into a city parking lot.

"Now, we walk. Remember, this area is under government control. Say nothing, pay attention, and don't look around like tourists," Emad grunted as they scrambled out of his car. Beads of sweat collected on his forehead and trickled down the sides of his face. The day had hardly started and already the heat was draining.

Emad led the way, with Nana behind him. *Tap, tap, tap.* They followed the sound of Nana's cane on the cobbles. Emad wove silently through winding, shadowy side streets keeping to the narrow sidewalks.

"Look at the walls!" Yara whispered to Shireen. It was hard not to gawk. Even in the dim light they could make out anti-government graffiti under coats of black and gray paint. Above, on billboards, were smiling pictures of President al-Assad wearing American-style sunglasses.

They walked past the Umayyad Mosque. Men hurried to be in time for *Salat al Fajr*, the dawn prayer. Street markers announced a Greek Orthodox church in one direction and the Jewish Quarter in another. The sign said "Straight Street," but to Yara, Straight Street didn't seem so straight. Sandbags surrounded official-looking buildings but the shops and apartment buildings looked untouched by bombs or shrapnel. Where was the war?

They turned a corner. They stopped. Only Emad carried on.

Yara and Shireen had seen pictures of the beautiful parks of Damascus, but what was this place? It was a park—that was plain to see—but it was filled with tents and plastic tarps. Laundry lines stretched from tree to tree. Small fires smoldered in metal drums. People milled around aimlessly. A great garbage bin sat close to the road. Children scrambled up its sides and tossed watermelon rinds down to the tallest boys below. Was this breakfast?

"Who are they?" Yara whispered.

A frustrated Emad turned back and stomped up beside them. "They came from the countryside and other Syrian cities hoping that President al-Assad would protect them," he said. "Now come. You are not sightseers." Emad waved them on, his arms spinning like windmills. Yara pressed her lips tight. It seemed that he was the one more likely to draw attention!

"Is my son near?" Nana asked Emad. It was plain that her leg was causing her pain.

"Yes." Emad paused, then muttered, "But he is in great danger. He lives in a secret location. He should not have come." He looked past them as if checking to see if they were being followed.

Not come? Secret location? But didn't he live in Damascus? Yara was stunned. A son would always come if his mother called. And why was he in great danger?

Emad took a sharp turn and plunged into an apartment building; he beckoned to them to come along in a hurry. Gripping Saad's hand, Yara followed Shireen and Nana into the building and they climbed slowly up a winding staircase to the third floor.

A man with a clean-shaven face, wearing casual pants and a white button-up shirt, stood in the doorway of an apartment. He was tall and thin, with broad shoulders, high cheekbones, and wide brown eyes. He looked as though he could be walking the streets of Paris or London. But his hair was white, and the creases in his face were as deep as if carved by a knife.

"Uncle Sami?" Yara breathed out his name while Nana let out a small cry.

"Mama?" In one swift movement Uncle Sami pulled his mother into his arms. Nana, so tiny and thin, looked even smaller in his hug. When Nana pulled back, his shoulder was wet with her tears.

"Come, come. We must not stand out here." Laughing, he nodded to Emad as he steered them into the apartment. The old man grunted and charged back down the steps.

Uncle Sami reached for Yara and enveloped her with a warmth she had not felt since Mama and Baba died.

"And this is Saad!" Uncle Sami dropped to one knee. "You have grown, my nephew," he said, kindly and gently. Saad, wary as ever, ducked behind Yara. "I know you don't recognize me, but you are my favorite nephew!" He grinned, and so did Yara. Saad was his *only* nephew.

"He doesn't . . ." Yara paused and looked over at Nana.

"Saad doesn't talk," Nana said, finishing Yara's sentence.

Uncle Sami nodded. "I know many children who do not talk." He turned to Saad and whispered, "I have something for you." He pulled two little toy cars out of his pocket. "I had lots of cars when I was a boy. Remember, Mama?" He didn't see Nana flinch but Yara did.

Uncle Sami looked up at Shireen, who stood back, awkward and embarrassed.

"Do you remember Shireen?" asked Nana. "She is the daughter of Roja, who lived across the road from us in Aleppo." She didn't mention Ali. Shireen just nodded. Funny, thought Yara, Shireen was not usually shy.

"Welcome," said Uncle Sami.

They followed Nana and Uncle Sami down the hall, passed an alcove that might once have been a closet, and landed in a bright living room. The only signs of comfort were an old sofa, mats on the floor, and a pot of water on a low boil on a hot plate.

"Do not stand near a window." Uncle Sami motioned for them to sit. Shireen and Yara slid down a wall and sat on their haunches. Saad was already on his knees, examining the cars.

Uncle Sami propped a cushion behind Nana's back and the two sat on mats and spoke in whispers. His face, smiling one moment, fell into despair the next. Nana was telling him about Mama and Baba, thought Yara, although at one point she heard the name "Ali," too. She leaned in to listen.

"Sometimes we can make a trade," said Uncle Sami.

Trade what? Yara looked at Shireen to see if she was paying attention, but her friend was lost in thought, or pretending to be.

Emad returned with shawarma, tabouli, and yabrak, all favorites. There were sweets, too. Yara looked up at the man in astonishment. He had hardly said a word to them that wasn't absolutely necessary, and here he was laying out a feast?

"Thank you!" Yara smiled, hoping he might smile back.

Emad shrugged. "Revolution or no revolution, we must eat!"

How would Ali ever find them? Yara's hands and feet went cold, as cold as if she were walking on ice. Shireen sat hugging her knees, her eyes blank, as if trying not to think or see anything.

Uncle Sami pulled out a cellphone, mumbled something, and disappeared into a bedroom. Where was he going? Had he finished?

"Nana? What's happening now?" Yara touched her grandmother's arm. Shaking her head, Nana put a finger to her lips. "Please, Nana, tell me," Yara persisted.

"Come closer. It's about Ali." She glanced at Shireen as she whispered.

Yara could barely hear her grandmother over her thundering heart. "Ali?"

"I described the men who abducted Ali to Sami—the location, how the men dressed, behaved, the truck they were driving, their guns. Sami thinks that Ali was abducted by Jaish al-Islam, the Army of Islam. They were once part of the Free Syrian Army but they broke away years ago. They are extremists," said Nana. Yara listened to Nana but kept an eye on Shireen. She was out of earshot and picking at the food. "If they are holding him for ransom it is likely that he is in the Prison of Repentance." Nana gave a deep sigh.

"What does that mean? Prison? Repent what?" whispered Yara.

Nana just shook her head. "Say nothing to Shireen, not yet. They have many prisons in Ghouta, east of Damascus. Or he may be in one of the rooftop cages." Nana spoke quickly as her eyes darted from Saad to Shireen. Emad's phone rang.

"What rooftop cages?" Yara's eyes searched Nana's face.

"On the tops of buildings. People are put inside huge"— her voice broke—"birdcages."

"Birdcages?" Yara gasped.

"They are used as human shields . . . to prevent bombing," Nana added.

Ali—a human shield? Yara covered her mouth. She might be sick. The room spun around her.

"Control yourself," Nana muttered. Yara bit her lip.

Uncle Sami came out of the bedroom just as Emad finished speaking on his phone. "We must leave," the old man barked. "*Now!*"

Nana looked at her son. "Will you come with us?" she asked.

"Mama . . ." Uncle Sami whispered. His shoulders sagged and his sad eyes said everything. Why had Nana even asked? She knew very well that Sami would never leave Syria.

"There has been a change," said Uncle Sami. He whispered into Nana's ear. Nana nodded. Yara watched the two and thought that she was tired of secrets!

Before she could say anything, Uncle Sami pulled Yara into his arms. "I wish you a good life. Remember, niece, you are loved, always. We can survive many things in this world if we know that one thing." He kissed her on the forehead.

She swallowed. "I'll remember," she whispered.

He turned and swooped Saad up in his arms. "May the eye of Allah protect you." He kissed him, too. Saad, at first shocked, gave his uncle the smallest of smiles.

"And you"—Sami looked hard at Shireen—"you will always find protection with me."

Shireen, unflinching, said nothing, but returned his stare. Yara looked at one and then the other. Uncle Sami and Shireen were speaking with their eyes. What were they saying?

"Go now. I have arranged everything." Uncle Sami slipped Nana a thick envelope. Money. For the first time, Yara thought that it might have been more than just her love for her son that had brought them to Damascus.

"*Tislam, habibi.* Be well, my beloved son . . ." Nana's voice wavered.

Oh, Nana. Yara looked away. Sudden tears circled her eyes. Her grandmother was saying goodbye to her last living child.

Swallowing hard and blinking furiously, Yara followed Emad, Saad, and Shireen down the apartment stairs. After a few moments, the *tap, tap, tap* of Nana's cane trailed after them.

"Nana, what does Uncle Sami do?" Yara whispered as they approached the car. Nana looked over her shoulder. No one was near.

She leaned over her cane. "Your uncle is a leader with the Free Syrian Army in Doma, near Damascus," she huffed.

"The FSA?" Yara's jaw dropped.

"Yes."

"In the monastery, remember? You said that you tried calling Uncle Sami's cell number many times but no one picked up. That wasn't true, was it? You had Uncle Sami's phone number all along, didn't you?"

"Yes."

"Why didn't you tell me?" Should she be angry? Grateful? How many more secrets were there?

"I am trying to keep both you and Sami safe. Now get in the car, and watch what you say. There has been a change in plans. We will go into hiding."

"Hiding?" Her relief was instant, as though bricks had been lifted from her shoulders.

"We wait. Sami will do what he can to help find Ali."

"Can we tell Shireen?" Yara hated keeping secrets, this one most of all. Besides, she was bad at it.

"No, not until we are sure," said Nana.

CHAPTER 25

Yara's heart was racing as they climbed out of the car and stood in front of an ancient wooden door set in a stone wall. Ali was all she could think about. But Nana's words were still ringing in her ears. Uncle Sami was a rebel, a freedom fighter. Rifa'at, long ago, had said the Free Syrian Army were good, but some had broken away to form gangs like Jaish al-Islam, or whatever they were called. What if . . .

"Yara." Nana gave her arm a sharp poke. "Pay attention. You are daydreaming."

Blinking, Yara raised her chin and straightened her shoulders.

Emad tapped at the door. An eye, framed by a peephole, appeared. Murmurs, barely words, were exchanged as the door was flung open.

"Quickly, quickly!" Emad flapped his arms. How could anyone not notice him!

They stepped into a courtyard filled with bougainvillea, lemon, olive, and jasmine trees. It was beautiful, welcoming, and the sweet scent of the plants and flowers was overpowering. Yara felt light-headed. She was faintly aware of a young woman standing nearby. Had she opened the door? Nana was right, she wasn't paying attention.

Yara touched the wall to steady herself. Birdcages. She couldn't stop seeing it—people inside giant birdcages.

"Yara, are you all right?" Shireen reached out to her. Yara nodded and pretended to examine the bougainvillea. Didn't Shireen have a right to know that Uncle Sami was looking for Ali? Wasn't Yara denying Shireen what she needed most: hope? The outside door closed with a pronounced thud.

Even preoccupied, even so worried she thought she might faint or cry, or both, Yara caught the elegance of the place. The courtyard was fit for royalty! It was the most beautiful place she had ever been in. The blue sky above matched the blue tiles under their feet. The furniture was a mixture of wrought iron and wicker. And tucked in a corner, protected from the elements, was a sweet gazebo filled with big pillows! She wanted to crawl into them right now and sleep.

At the end of the courtyard were great wooden doors carved with swirling, graceful script.

"Look, Saad." Yara nudged him. "A fountain!" Jets of water spouted from a rocky fountain right in the middle of the courtyard. Saad's grin went from ear to ear. Yara gave him a weak smile, glad that he was happily distracted, if only for a little while.

The young woman stepped forward now. "My name is Yasmin. I take care of this building for the owner. It's an old house that has been converted to apartments. The owners live in America, but they will return." Her voice was soft and welcoming. She was perhaps eighteen, and dressed in jeans and a T-shirt. Earbuds, attached to her phone, dangled around her neck, the cord lost in her long black hair. She gave a respectful nod to Nana, then exchanged hushed words with Emad. And then he was gone.

Saad dipped both hands in the fountain and Yara did nothing to stop him. She wanted to do the same, and then splash cool water on her face. If . . .

The door banged open. They jumped.

"*Marhaba,* hello." An older woman, perhaps a little younger than Nana, dropped two bulging shopping bags at her feet. She looked very Western in a blouse and skirt, with her gray-streaked black hair pinned into a bun. Arching one dark, painted eyebrow, she gave Yasmin a disdainful look and waited for an introduction.

Yasmin returned the woman's greeting with welcoming words, "*Ahlan wa Sahlan,*" before introducing her. "This is Umm Fadi. She lives upstairs," said Yasmin politely. She pointed to a circular stone staircase that led to a second floor. It was stunning, the sort of staircase a queen might descend.

"I live in apartment number two. Number one is empty. They left in a hurry. Who can tell where people go anymore?" Umm Fadi smiled. She had a terrifying smile.

"I am Umm Aziz," said Nana, quickly and politely. "And these are my grandchildren." Clearly, Nana did not want this woman to know who they were.

"Umm Aziz and her grandchildren will be staying in the downstairs apartment for a few days, possibly a week," Yasmin explained.

Umm Fadi ignored Yasmin completely. "Oh, a little boy," she crooned. "I do so love little boys. Perhaps you will come up to my apartment and visit me?" She reached out a hand to Saad, who jumped behind Yara.

"He is very shy." Yara reached her arm back around Saad protectively.

"Well, come anytime. I have lots of toys." She smiled again, but it wasn't really a smile at all, it was a sneer. The woman picked up her bags and climbed the steps to the second floor.

Yasmin put a finger to her lips. They understood. *Walls have ears.*

Silently, Yara, Nana, Shireen, and Saad trailed Yasmin through the courtyard, past the cozy gazebo, and into two back rooms filled with dark wooden tables and chairs, and more colorful pillows.

"Beds!" cried Yara. Four small beds were lined up as if it were a school dormitory.

But the best was yet to come. "Showers!" Shireen cheered as she pointed to a doorway.

Yara touched hand-painted, lacquered wood panels on the walls in what was to be their bedroom. This must have once been a reception room. Had Nana once lived amidst such beautiful walls and furniture? She looked at her grandmother. If the beauty and grandeur of the place brought back old memories, Nana showed no sign of noticing or caring.

"You will be safe here. Emad is a loyal friend. But she . . ." Yasmin pointed to the ceiling and the resident of apartment number two. "Be careful. Ask me if you need anything. Please ask." Yasmin spoke in a low, steady voice.

"*Salamtik*, thank you," said Nana. Yasmin gave a slight nod.

At dusk, the call to prayer drifted over the walls and through the windows. Exhausted, clean, they lay in the four beds, inches between them, listening to the sweet, haunting, and calming music. Yara closed her eyes and there he was, waiting for her in her dreams: Ali.

⌣•

Two days passed. Shireen found a friend in Yasmin. The two huddled together for hours, their heads bobbing. Yara kept to herself, grateful that Shireen had found someone to speak with. The last thing Yara wanted to do right now was talk to Shireen. She would say something, blurt out that they were waiting to hear from Uncle Sami. That he would find Ali.

On the third night, Yara and Saad sat out in the court-yard, in the gazebo. Bathed in the soft candlelight from an overhanging lantern, and surrounded by thick cushions, they gazed up into the dark sky.

"Look, Saad, see the moon? It is following us. It goes wherever we go." Yara jostled him and tried to make him smile. "And that"—she pointed to a bright star in the sky—"is the North Star. It is our guiding star." Saad nodded, taking it all in.

"How did you know that?" asked Shireen. She plopped down beside Saad and looked up at the stars.

"Ali told me," she said, and immediately blushed. Could Shireen see her face in the dark?

"Really? When?" asked Shireen.

"At Haya's . . . one night . . . we were alone . . ." Yara wove her fingers through her hair and hoped that no more questions would follow.

Shireen gave Yara a smile. "I know you love him, and I know he loves you, too," she said simply.

"How did you know? About . . . love, I mean," asked Yara. Blood rushed to her face. She glanced over at her little brother. Saad was still staring up at the sky.

"Oh, Yara, how could anyone not know? Your face is as see-through as glass. Everyone can see what you are thinking!" Shireen giggled.

Love, Yara thought. She could almost taste it—sweet and tart at the same time. And saying it—*love*—it felt electric. She bit down on her lower lip.

"One day your lip will fall off, and then what will you kiss with?" Shireen giggled.

Yara pursed her lips. If Yara's face was a window, then Shireen's face was a wall. What was she thinking? Why did she suddenly seem so much happier now?

Later, much later, Yara woke up at the sound of muffled sobs.

"Saad?" She rested her hand on his small body. No, the sound wasn't coming from him. She heard it again. Yara turned. She could see Shireen's face by moonlight. Her eyes were closed, and yet a shimmering stream of silver ran from her eyes into her hair. She was asleep and crying.

CHAPTER 26

"It is our time."

Yara awoke in the gazebo. She was confused, dazed even. Who had said that? Our time for what? Propped up on one elbow, she ran a hand over the space beside her. "Saad?" Yara called out. Where was he? Likely with Nana. Yara flopped back on the pillows. They finally had perfectly good beds and here they were sleeping in a gazebo in the courtyard!

"We must fight. All of us, women, too." That was Yasmin's voice. Yara bolted upright. "Democracy for Syria." Now Shireen was talking, and both voices were coming from the bedroom. Why did Shireen sound like a protester? Yara looked up to the apartments above. Could they be heard upstairs? Likely not. This was an ancient building made of stone, but still . . .

"Shireen?" Yara called out. There was a scramble of footsteps coming from the bedroom.

"Good morning, sleepyhead!" Shireen, eyes wide and bright, opened the bedroom door. "Yasmin brought oranges!" She picked up a glorious, round, glistening orange as Yasmin, trailing behind, went to a tray and poured tea into a glass. "There are olives, too, plus bread and boiled eggs." Shireen sounded almost giddy.

"I must go, I have work to do," said Yasmin. Yara mumbled a thank-you and watched as the two traded knowing looks. Did they think she didn't notice? The door to the street closed softly behind Yasmin.

"Where is Nana?" Yara dropped to the floor and found one sandal.

"Shopping with Emad." Shireen plopped down in the gazebo, picked up a pillow, and hugged it.

"What were you and Yasmin talking about?" Yara tried to sound casual.

"Nothing." Shireen shrugged.

"What do you think about the camps—the ones Uncle Sami spoke about?" asked Yara as Shireen braided her long, dark-red hair.

"I don't think about them at all," she said plainly, without even a hint of fear. "Did you know that Yasmin is joining the SDF?" She flipped the braid over her shoulder.

"Not so loud!" Yara whispered, pointing to the apartment up the staircase. "What is the SDF?"

"It stands for Syrian Democratic Forces. Woman and girls run field hospitals. And they fight, Yara, really fight, with guns and fists." Shireen's green eyes sparkled. She tossed the pillow aside and reached for an orange.

"That's just what we need, more killing. It's wrong. Do you see my other sandal?"

"Doing wrong doesn't mean that *we* are wrong. Want some?" She offered Yara a section of orange.

"We? Who is 'we'?" Yara, on her hands and knees, shook her head. She wanted her other sandal, not an orange.

"What I am saying is that before our country can become democratic and properly elect its own leaders, bad things must happen first. And when we are a free people who can vote, then we will condemn the past." Shireen made it sound simple.

"Here it is." Yara slipped on her sandal. What did she mean, "bad things must happen"? Yara willed Nana to come through the door with news from Uncle Sami. She had that old feeling again—the ants were marching under her skin, in her veins, up and down her spine.

"Saad, come and eat," Yara called. "Saad?" She poked her head into the bedroom. She didn't expect a response, but she did expect to hear his footsteps. "Shireen, did Saad go out with Nana?"

"No, he was here a minute ago . . ." Shireen looked around as if expecting Saad to pop out from behind a plant.

Yara's panic was instant. "SAAD!" she cried, her eyes darting madly around the courtyard. Could he have opened the door to the outside all by himself? After all, he'd run off from Roja's house in Aleppo once. "The door!" Yara pointed.

"I'll check outside," Shireen called over her shoulder.

"Saad!" Her heart began to hammer. "Saad?" she called loudly. She looked up at the steps that led to the apartments on the second floor. A small toy car rested on the second step, another on the fourth step. Yara took the stairs two at a time. Two doors, a fair distance from each other, were along the walkway. Breathing hard, she hammered on the first door calling out Saad's name.

The second door opened. "Have you lost a little boy?" Umm Fadi, the woman Yasmin had warned them about, asked sweetly.

Three long strides and Yara stood in front of Umm Fadi. The woman opened the door wider, revealing Saad sitting like a little prince at a table. Pastry flakes drifted down his shirt. Small cars ran across the table in a line, like soldiers in a parade.

"He doesn't talk. I asked him his name," said Umm Fadi in that same sickly sweet voice.

"*Shukran*, thank you." Yara took a deep breath.

"Join us." Umm Fadi ushered Yara in. She smiled. There it was again, that terrifying smile.

"No . . . we must . . ." Yara looked behind her in the vain hope that Shireen, or Nana, would come charging towards her.

"Come, come. It's nice to have company. Even quiet company, although I do so love the sound of children's laughter." Umm Fadi beamed at Saad. Clearly, she did love children.

Yara removed her sandals and stepped inside the apartment. A newscaster chatted from a television. She couldn't remember the last time she had watched television.

"He is a lovely child, and such long eyelashes," Umm Fadi continued as she flapped her arms like a large bird, driving

254 • JAMAL SAEED AND SHARON E. McKAY

Yara to the table. Yara sat. If this woman had tied her to the chair with a rope she couldn't have felt more trapped. "Tea?" Without waiting for an answer, Umm Fadi poured Yara a small glass.

The table was beside a lacy-curtained window, and if she glanced through a part in the curtains Yara could see the street below. *"Shukran."* Yara sipped the tea. Where was Shireen?

A speech by President al-Assad was being repeated on the Syrian state television channel. Something the President said made Umm Fadi pause, teapot still in her hand. "The poor man," she said. "What he must be going through." With a deep sigh, Umm Fadi put down the teapot and passed a plate of cookies.

Poor man? Yara chomped hard on the cookie. As far as Yara knew, President al-Assad lived in luxury somewhere in Damascus, with his pretty, British-educated wife, three children, and dozens of servants, not to mention the protection of his entire army! Poor?

"Our President is our captain, our leader. A captain doesn't think of life and death, he thinks of saving his ship. He thinks of us before he thinks of himself," Umm Fadi added, with the satisfied look of a cat lapping cream.

Say nothing, say nothing, Yara repeated to herself.

"The youth of this country—they are out of control," continued Umm Fadi as she poured olive oil onto a plate. *"Za'atar?"* She held a bowl of the spice under Yara's nose.

"Thank you, but . . . but we must go. Our grandmother . . . is waiting for us." She was stammering. Shireen must have come in from the street by now. *Please, please.*

"Then she can join us. You should take your little brother to Up Town, in Dummar. I haven't been in such a long time, but I love amusement parks. Such fun. Do you know it?" She smiled. Yara, caught off guard, couldn't think of what to say. Amusement park? The cookie stuck in her throat.

"My boys went on every ride and ate candyfloss until they were sick." Her eyes drifted to a table near the television. Yara followed her gaze. The photographs of two handsome young soldiers, both in government uniforms, looked back at her. The frames were draped in black ribbons. Yara gulped tea and tried not to cough. Sweat began to gather at the back of her neck.

Umm Fadi pointed to the first photo. "That is Fadi, my firstborn son." Yara nodded. Yes, of course, she had taken the name of her eldest boy.

"Both my sons were killed in the service of our President. My younger boy was in the army only a few weeks before he was martyred. Martyrs are loved by God." Her voice was even and surprisingly calm.

Say nothing, Yara repeated to herself. Did Umm Fadi have daughters? Other sons? There were no other photographs in the room. Yara didn't dare ask. She bit her lip. Umm Fadi had lost two sons fighting for the President. Nana had lost three sons because of the President's father. All that pain, all that loss. None of this was right.

"This revolution—it is a foreign conspiracy!" Umm Fadi's calm voice suddenly spiraled down into a guttural growl. Her nostrils flared, her chin went up, and her eyes narrowed.

Yara swallowed hard and reached under the table for Saad's hand. "We are a great country, and Damascus is a beautiful city," she added. And then words just spilled out of Yara's mouth. "But all those homeless people in the parks, and the bombings in Aleppo . . ." Even if Umm Fadi did support the President, she must be able to see all those people starving right under her nose!

The woman's mouth gaped open in surprise. "The bombings in Aleppo are justified! Those areas harbor extremists. The President is right to root out terrorists! He is right to use any weapons at his disposal to save our country!" Her eyes went wide with alarm.

"But people are dying! Hospitals are bombed. And . . . and the children . . ." Yara stammered.

"The people in those areas are not only hiding terrorists, they are allowing their children to be used as human shields! It is not the President's fault. He is protecting our country!" Her voice rose up like a desert storm. And in that moment Yara understood. Umm Fadi was not only one of the President's loyal followers, she was blindly devoted to him.

Umm Fadi stopped talking, closed her mouth like a steel door, and peered at Yara with something more than curiosity—it was suspicion. "Where do you come from?" she asked.

"Yara, here you are! Come along, Grandmother is waiting." Shireen stood on the threshold of the door smiling as her eyes flew around the room.

Yara bounced up. Her tea splashed onto Umm Fadi's pristine white tablecloth. "I'm so sorry." She reached for Saad's hand. "And, I am sorry about . . . your sons. *Shukran,* thank you . . ."

The woman's forehead wrinkled as her eyes narrowed.

Yara, and silent Saad, followed Shireen out into the hallway. Umm Fadi trailed behind. The woman's eyes beat holes into Yara's back. Yara rammed her feet into her sandals and walked quickly down the hall behind Shireen, pulling Saad behind her.

Umm Fadi gripped the handrail. "President al-Assad is our only hope. We need a hundred more al-Assads," she shouted as the three flew down the stairs.

At the bottom of the stairs Yara looked up to see Umm Fadi stomp purposefully back into her apartment. The sound of the slammed door reverberated down the stairs.

"We have to leave, she will call the Mukhabarat," whispered Shireen as she tore around with the speed of a bee caught in a bottle. The secret police arrested, tortured. What would happen to Saad? Where was Nana? *Mama, Baba, help us.*

Shireen gathered up what she could—Saad's Woody Woodpecker backpack, his teddy bear, a few bits of clothes—and handed everything to Yara. "Go, now," she whispered. "*Now!*"

At that moment, Nana walked through the door with Yasmin on her heels.

"Umm Fadi, the woman upstairs, she knows." Shireen grabbed Yasmin's arm. Instinctively, they all looked up to the apartment door.

Nana fumbled through her shopping bags and threw new running shoes at Yara, Shireen, and Saad. The three scrambled to put them on as Nana limped across the room and snatched the red tin box. Shireen picked up her string bag and together they bolted for the door.

"There is a house, two blocks from here. Turn left. Look for a flowerpot filled with yellow flowers on the doorstep. It's on the right. Knock four times," said Yasmin in mutters and whispers. She threw open the door to the street. Nana grabbed her cane in one hand and Saad's hand in the other.

"*Ma'a as-salaama*." Nana nodded her deep thanks to Yasmin, and she and Saad shot out the door and onto the street.

"Shireen, Yara, hurry," Yasmin called over her shoulder.

Shireen brushed past Yara and stood on the road. Yasmin and Shireen gave each other knowing nods. And then Yasmin stuck in her earbuds, flicked her hair over her shoulders, and sauntered down the road in the opposite direction.

"Yara, come here." Shireen bolted across the street and ducked behind boxes stacked on a two-wheeled cart. Her head turned from side to side watching for suspicious activity and listening for sirens.

"Shireen, what are you doing? We must go!" Yara crouched beside her. They were hidden between the cart and a wall. Yara peered up to Umm Fadi's window. If the woman looked out and down, could she see them? It was hard to tell.

"I need to tell you something," whispered Shireen.

"Now?" Yara was astonished.

The muscles around Shireen's jaw strained but she didn't flinch as she stared deep into Yara's eyes. "I could never have had a kinder or braver sister than you." Shireen's heart-shaped face suddenly softened and she smiled a sweet, rare smile.

Brave? What was she talking about? Yara, forgetting about Umm Fadi, and not caring about the danger, spoke louder than she should have. "I am *not* brave."

"Hush. Yes, you are. You are afraid of dark spaces and yet you charge in." She gripped Yara's arm. There was a siren in the distance. Ears perked, they waited until the sound faded. "Remember, you lived through this, you can take what comes." Shireen, peering around the cart, crouched down.

"What are you doing? Get back!" Yara felt fear start to choke her.

Shireen swiveled, leaned in, and spoke softly into Yara's ear. "I am not going with you. I can't, I won't, leave my country. Not now. Not without my parents and my brother."

"What do you mean? You promised! Your mother . . ." Yara's whole body began to tremble. "You can't stay . . . A girl on her own will be abducted and killed, and worse. Please, Shireen, this war will not last forever. We will come back. We will rebuild." It was Yara's turn to grasp Shireen's arm.

"Come back? When we are married and have children in some foreign land? When we are old? Why would children growing up in Canada, Australia, Britain, Germany, anywhere, return to a country that is no longer their own?" Shireen looked up, her green eyes narrow and wild with anger.

Yara shook her head. How could she answer such a question? What a time to even ask? "Please, Shireen, please, don't do this." The tears were sudden.

Shireen wrapped her arms around her friend. "Do you remember the little boy at Haya's house, the one who said that the sun dies in the West?"

"Boy? What boy?" But she did remember him. He was one of Haya's grandsons, the boy with two missing front teeth. "He was talking nonsense." Yara wiped her eyes with open palms.

"Don't cry. I don't want to make you cry. I do not want to die in the West. This is my land, this is where I will die." Shireen hugged Yara.

Taking a deep breath, Yara said, "If you stay, I will stay, too." Why shouldn't she? Did Shireen think she loved her country any less?

"And what of Saad and your grandmother? What will happen to them alone in a camp? They could wait for years for another country to accept them, for a lifetime!" Shireen kissed Yara's soggy face.

"But you have nothing—no identification, no money." Yara was desperate.

"I have my papers, I have a little money." She stood. Right there, at that moment, Yara realized that this had been planned perhaps from the first moment Shireen and Yasmin met.

"Wait, WAIT!" cried Yara. She caught hold of Shireen's hand. This was her last chance. "Shireen, Uncle Sami is searching for Ali. He will find him. Listen to me, please! Nana said not to tell you in case you would be disappointed. It was wrong . . ." Yara tugged Shireen's arm but she was already poised like a runner at a gate.

"I know, Yara. I have known all along. You have a face like glass—remember? But I am the one who will find Ali. Go, Yara. It will not end like this—you said that. You are different now, stronger. You, too, are a fighter, a warrior. Take this." She pulled at the little pink opal ring that Yara had put on her hand.

"No, it's yours. Nana told you so." Yara pulled away. *Fighter? Warrior?*

"It might get stolen," said Shireen. But the ring was stuck and would not come off.

"See, it is meant for you!" Yara sobbed.

"I love you." Shireen kissed Yara on the cheek. The kiss remained there, stinging. And then she was gone.

"Wait, where are you going? Shireen, WHERE ARE YOU GOING?" Her cries drifted into the air like a piece of silk in the wind. Yara stood on quivering legs and gripped the handle of the cart. "Don't leave me, don't go," she whispered. Then she looked up and saw Umm Fadi's curtains twitch.

CHAPTER 27

Tears turned the street blurry and honey-colored. Ahead, at the corner, the road split into two. Nana and Saad were nowhere in sight.

Two blocks. A flowerpot with yellow flowers. On the right. Or had Yasmin said something about turning left? A speeding car passed her. Inside the car were uniformed men, the Mukhabarat. Yara pitched herself into a passageway.

Rubbing her face with the back of her hand, Yara flipped her bag onto her back and staggered on. Why hadn't she just agreed with that horrible woman? Or just said nothing at all?

Which way? She had to breathe and move forward. Walking too slowly or too fast would attract attention. Looking confused or unsure would attract attention, too.

The roads were tangled, going west, and then turning east, south, west again. The walls on either side closed in; some alleys were so narrow she felt as if the walls were pressing against her. Nana would be so worried.

If she could get to the Umayyad Mosque or Straight Street, perhaps she could work her way back. If the Mukhabarat were at Umm Fadi's apartment, would they be there long? She could hide and wait in the alley, then perhaps, maybe, find Yasmin. Maybe Yasmin and Shireen together. She walked on, eyes forward, shoulders back.

A large-bellied man wearing a blood-stained apron emerged from a doorway and glared at her. Yara let out a small squeak of surprise. The metallic smell of blood and fresh-cut meat wafted out of the shop behind him. A butcher? Her stomach lurched. He arched his thick eyebrows and rammed his two meaty hands against the place where his hips might have been, had he not been so enormous.

A mousy little woman, likely his wife, came up from behind him and poked her twitchy nose around his great bulk. Both husband and wife looked her up and down and frowned in disapproval.

"I have lost my . . . my brother," Yara stammered. Standing tall, throwing back her shoulders, she hoped she sounded calm, but knew she probably didn't. "Could you . . . ?"

They turned their backs on her and slammed the door shut.

Stumbling, using the ancient walls to keep her upright, Yara went on, more slowly now. Occasionally the stink of uncollected garbage made her gag. Head down, she stepped out of the lane and found herself in a large square.

Laughing children strolled, holding stuffed animals and licking ice cream. Women walked beside them, baskets filled with fresh vegetables and fruits dangling from a hand or the crook of an arm. Soldiers casually patrolled the sidewalks, and military trucks inched along the streets beside cars and carts. Where were the homeless people? Where was the revolution? Had she stepped through a mirror? Fallen into a black hole?

The open air, the market, the sight of people going about their business as if there wasn't a war going on felt even worse than the airless, smelly laneways. But it was the behavior of the people that was most astonishing. They didn't rush from place to place. They were not hunched over, running like fugitives, and listening for the *wiss* of a sniper's bullet.

She felt exposed, unsafe. She spun around. It was better to be in the alleyways than out here, visible. "Make your best guess," she murmured to herself. Ten steps forward and she was back in the maze of alleys.

Suddenly, a boy bolted past her, turned, and blocked her path. She pivoted, but another boy was directly behind her, close enough for her to smell him. He stank of dirt, oil, and sweat. Both had cigarettes in their mouths. One laughed.

And then they drew closer. Yara's fingers curled and her fingernails pressed deep into her palms.

"I am looking for my brother," Yara announced coldly. Her shoulders were square and her nostrils flared. She needed a rock or a brick, anything.

"Your brother?" The first boy laughed again, and the other joined him.

"Is he your *little* brother?" The second boy licked his lips.

A door slammed. The butcher, carrying a bloody package, stormed down the alley towards them. He stamped his foot, and the boys scattered like pigeons.

Yara didn't move. "Thank you." The words were no more than a hiss through her teeth.

She turned and walked, and then ran down one lane, then another. Sweat matted her hair to her scalp and dribbled down her back. She stopped and squeezed a stitch in her side. She recognized a door, a bicycle, and a stack of crates. And there it was—the cart she and Shireen had hidden behind. She stepped back and looked up at Umm Fadi's curtained window. Was the woman still there, standing, watching?

"Yara, YARA!"

She turned. The alley was dim. She stood absolutely still, as if one movement, one wisp of air, and the image in front of her would vanish. She felt a cry rise in her throat. She felt every emotion at once—gratitude, relief, joy, fear, love. Ali!

And then she looked up. The curtain moved. Umm Fadi was watching, Yara could feel it. She looked back down the road. Ali lifted his arms and reached out to her.

No. NO! He'd be caught again! She spun around and ran.

CHAPTER 28

Yara turned the corner, darted down one alley, then another, and another. When she could run no farther she stopped and pressed her back against a craggy wall, ignoring the painfully sharp stones. She shouldn't run, mustn't attract attention.

Apartment windows looked down into the alley. It felt as if a million eyes were boring into her from above. They were in government territory. Spies were everywhere. *If walls have ears, then windows have eyes*, she thought.

"Yara!" The sound of feet pounding over stones came towards her. "Yara?" Ali stood right in front of her. Her knees buckled. "Why?" His every breath mingled with the distant voices of children, car horns honking, the cry of a coffee-seller.

She could have reached out and touched him, but instead she gulped back tears, put her hands behind her back, and pressed them hard into the rough stone wall. Ali, red-faced and breathing hard, looking as though he, too, might collapse, placed a hand on the wall above her head. There were marks on his wrists, deep, crimson welts. He leaned into her.

He spoke softly now. "Why did you run away?"

"There was a woman . . . in a window . . ." She tried to look away but his eyes pinned her to the wall. "If she saw us together she would be able to describe you to the Mukhabarat. I couldn't . . ." What she wanted to say was, "I couldn't take the chance of losing you again."

From a distance his eyes were dark green, but up close she could see gold and charcoal flecks, too. His cheeks were hollow, making his cheekbones sharp and defined. When had he last eaten? And those marks on his wrists—was he kept in chains? Was he tortured? She shuddered. "Where were you?"

"Common criminals abduct people and return them for ransom. If the families don't pay, they are killed or sold." Ali's face darkened.

Yara stared at him. Sold?

"I was told that my ransom had been paid. They blind-folded me and I was left on the side of a road."

"But how did you find us?" asked Yara, forgetting for a moment that there was no us, just her, alone and lost.

Ali looked over his shoulder. He cocked his head this way and that, like a bird on a wire. Certain that no one could overhear, he went on. "Emad, do you know him?" he asked. Yara nodded. "He picked me up and brought me to the house you were staying in. We saw the Mukhabarat leave. Emad said that you had to be near, that Shireen was with Saad and your grandmother."

Yara felt her legs buckle. Shireen. She had to tell him, but he kept talking.

"Yara, who arranged my release?" Ali searched her face.

If Emad had not told him about Uncle Sami's involvement, should she? "I'm not sure . . ." Yara was not a good liar. He moved closer still. She felt his breath on her cheeks. He had to be able to see her trembling.

"You two will draw attention to yourselves." Emad, his voice as low and growly as an old dog's, came charging down the alley towards them, his cellphone pressed against his ear. Ali leapt back, Yara stepped aside, both flushed and suddenly as straight and tense as if facing a firing squad.

"Yes, yes," Emad said into his phone before snapping it shut. He looked at Yara for a moment, shook his head, and said, "Stay here." As if to make his point he poked Ali in the shoulder before he turned on his heels and stomped back the way he came. Where was he going? She didn't care. Not now. Not with Ali close enough to touch.

"Come." Ignoring Emad's order, Ali pulled Yara farther down the lane, ducking boxes, garbage, and pushcarts. The alleyway grew dimmer with rows of laundry hanging above and blocking out daylight and lamplight from windows. He stopped in the darkest spot, turned, and stared at her as if she, not he, were the miracle. Cautiously, his eyes trailed from Yara's face up to a thin strip of sky, to the buildings around them, and then down to the alley. He was a soldier, she thought. No, not a soldier, a warrior.

Finally, his eyes returned to her. His finger trailed the length of her face, from the corner of her eye, over her cheekbone, down her jawline, finally resting on her chin. With the tip of his finger he tilted up her chin. She looked into his green-gold eyes and tried, tried so hard, to stop her legs from shaking. His arms went around her. She felt his chest against hers and sensed his heartbeat sounding with her own. And then he pressed his lips on hers, softly at first, and then harder. His arms pinned her close until she could not tell where she ended and he began.

Emad didn't yell or call out, but Yara could feel the vibrations of his feet stomping towards them. They jumped apart. Yara hid her lips behind her hand as if a kiss could be seen. Emad swished aside a damp blanket hanging on a laundry line and held up a headscarf. He shook it under Yara's nose. "Put this on. A car is coming for you," he growled.

"But my grandmother and my brother . . ." Yara fumbled with the scarf. She hadn't added Shireen's name. Had Ali noticed? She gave him a sideways glance but he was looking around again, watching, as poised as a giant cat.

"They are in the car. You will all leave for Dara'a and the Jordanian border now."

Now? She needed to talk to Ali, to explain. Emad stormed ahead. Ali put his arm lightly over her shoulder and steered her forward.

They came to the top of the alley and faced a busy street: cars, pedestrians, soldiers in trucks, police directing traffic, donkeys pulling carts. Soldiers were everywhere, on the sidewalks, in cars and trucks, slumped against walls and smoking. Yara pulled the scarf down until it framed her eyes.

Again, Emad turned and addressed them as though they were small, naughty children. "Wait here. Move quickly when you see your grandmother in the car." He left them there, dodged traffic, and disappeared.

Yara and Ali waited in the shadows, standing side by side, not touching. She needed to tell him about Shireen, to say, "She is gone. She has run off to fight. She has left me." Those were the words she meant to say, but instead what came out her mouth was, "Ali, when you were taken . . . I found a gun. I picked it up . . ." The look on Ali's face stopped her cold. He stared at her in disbelief.

"It was you?" His eyebrows shot up. He smiled, and then his whole body shook with laughter.

She stared back at him, terribly confused.

"You? *You?*" He shook his head. "A man fell on top of me, stone dead, shot in the head." Ali stopped laughing long enough to catch his breath. "The others, the men who abducted me, they were so worried about the helicopter returning, about government soldiers being alerted, that they didn't notice the dead man!" Now he laughed even harder.

She had killed a man. Nothing was funny, nothing! She might have shot Ali instead!

Ali paused. "Why are you so shocked? We are at war, Yara." The laughter faded.

Yara nodded. That was what Shireen had said. He was different now. They were all different now.

A car pulled up. Nana, her face pale as milk, sat in the front seat and looked at her granddaughter with such relief.

Yara flung open the back door. Saad looked up at Yara,

his small face contorted in fear. How much more could he endure? She crawled across the backseat and Saad immediately jumped on her lap, threw his arms around her, and buried his head in her neck. She ran her hands down his spine while whispering in his ear, "Hush, hush."

Ali peered in the car. "Where is she?" He looked at Yara, at the driver. "Where is my sister?"

Nana turned around and stared at Yara.

"She has joined the rebels." The words caught in Yara's throat.

"The rebels?" Ali stared at her uncomprehending, then he doubled over as if he had been kicked in the stomach. Yara sat there, breathless, watching him.

"Get in!" the driver yelled. "GET IN!" Ali got in beside Saad and slammed the car door. The driver stepped on the gas and charged into traffic as if he were on a racetrack.

Yara could see Ali's profile but she could not read his face. Did he think she could have stopped Shireen? Could she have? Why wasn't he asking her a thousand questions?

"Ali," she whispered. "I am sorry."

"You are not responsible." His voice was low and flat.

"It is ninety kilometers between Damascus and Dara'a, and as many as ten checkpoints," the driver muttered. He did not introduce himself, did not turn around. He clutched the wheel and drove.

As the car inched along the crowded highway, Ali sat chewing his knuckles and looking out the car window, and Yara buried her face in Saad's hair.

Things went well at the first checkpoint. "*Allah ma'ak*, God be with you," said the driver with a nod to the government soldier. As he drove away, Nana held up Ali's passport. Wordlessly, Ali reached from the backseat to the front, gently plucked the small blue book from Nana's hand, and tucked it away.

Saad squirmed in the middle seat. Yara took hold of his hand and squeezed it tight. Soon they would cross the border. She looked at the back of the driver's head. She would tell Ali everything as soon as they were out of the driver's hearing.

Yara sat thinking, thinking. Ali would cross over with them, she was sure of it. They could get word to Shireen. If Uncle Sami could find Ali, he could find Shireen. Yes, that was what would happen. Shireen would meet them in Jordan. The more she thought about it, the more realistic the solution seemed.

At the second checkpoint, they were ordered out of the car. Their few belongings were scattered on the road by one young soldier as three more looked on. The young soldier, not much older than Ali, pointed to Yara's pocket. Slowly, her eyes fixed on the soldier, Yara pulled out Baba's tobacco pouch. The soldier grabbed it, sniffed the contents, and, laughing, spilled the remaining threads of tobacco onto the ground. For a brief moment, hardly more than a second, the smell of apple spiced tobacco hung in the air.

"No, NO!" Yara screamed as she lunged after the pouch. The soldier aimed his gun at her head.

"Yara, stop," Ali cried. In one huge leap he stood between the gun and Yara. "Please, she means no harm." Ali flung out his arms.

Nana, fumbling through her *abaya*, passed more money to the driver, who gave it to the soldier.

"Go," snarled the soldier.

Shaking, Yara tucked the pouch into her pocket and crawled back into the car. No one spoke. What a fool. She had put their lives in danger over a tobacco pouch. *Fool. Fool. Fool.*

⌣ •

As they skirted the city of Dara'a, the driver stepped on the gas. It was fifteen kilometers to the Jordanian border, half an hour under normal circumstances.

By midday a beating sun had turned the car into an oven. Sweat dripped down their faces, gluing their clothes to their bodies. It was hard to breathe, and harder to think.

Yara glanced at Ali. He was within an arm's length and as far away as ever. She was sure that once they crossed the border it would get easier for them to talk.

The car slowed until it came to a dead stop. It was sunset. A short drive had taken most of the day. The sky was darkening. Ahead was a line of red brake lights shining and winking like the eyes of a thousand cats.

"We are at the Nasib Border Crossing," said the driver. Yara peered over his shoulder. It was busy, the busiest border crossing in Syria.

Across the border was Jordan, and beyond Jordan was a new life.

Yara looked over at Ali. He didn't seem as nervous as before. In fact, he seemed almost calm. "Ali?" she whispered. He turned, smiled sadly, and looked away again.

It was dark when they inched up to the actual crossing.

"Three hundred American dollars." The soldier leaned down and stuck his head in the window. He studied them for a moment and then he added, "Each."

Each? Nana, Yara, Saad, Ali—that was $1,200! Yara held her breath. Did they have that kind of money?

Nana reached deep into her *abaya*. Calmly, steadily, she passed an envelope over to the driver. It was the envelope Uncle Sami had given her.

"Wait." Ali reached across the seat and snatched the envelope. He took out three hundred dollars, then he gave the envelope back to the driver and the three hundred dollars to Nana.

"What are you doing? Ali?" said Yara. "Nana?" Yara reached over the seat and touched her grandmother's shoulder. "What's happening?" she cried.

Nana calmly handed Ali back the three hundred dollars and said, "This is for you. Go with God's protection."

Yara looked from one to the other. Saad began to whimper.

"Wait." Ali started to fumble with the lining of a torn and dirty jacket. "They never found it," he whispered. There was pride in his voice. Found what? He held up the emerald ring Roja had sewn into his clothes.

"It is yours," said Nana. "Use it well."

"Nana, no! Ali, no! Don't leave! Please. Ali, please!" She couldn't breathe. This could not be happening.

"Blessings upon you." Ali opened the car door and stepped out. Yara reached for the door handle on her side. She heard a click. Locked.

"Let me out," she cried. She yanked the door again and again. Nana and the driver stared ahead. They said nothing. NOTHING!

Yara pushed the button to lower the window. It went down partway but stopped. "ALI, NO!" She curled around and hammered the back window with flat palms. Saad's whimpers turned into howls.

Ali came around to the side of the car and stood by her window. He reached his hand into the car. "Don't do this," she pleaded as she touched his fingers.

"I cannot leave my sister and my mother, you know that," he said softly. All around them drivers yelled at each other, children cried, car horns honked, dogs barked, and still she heard his every word. His eyes burned into hers. The car started to move.

"Ali, please. Let me explain. My uncle . . ." She was shouting in short, breathless spurts. "We can get word to Shireen . . . Please! Nana, stop him!"

"Yara, it is his choice!" Nana's voice reverberated down Yara's spine like a gunshot.

Ahead, fluttering a small flag, the border guard waved them towards the barricade. The car shot forward. Yara peered out the back window as they drove into Jordan.*

---

* *Yara and her family entered Jordan from Syria via the Nasib Border Crossing in March 2015. In April, the crossing was taken over by the Free Syrian Army and al-Nusra Front. The crossing officially reopened on October 15, 2018.*

Lit only by the oncoming car lights, Ali stood on the road as rooted as a rock in a stream. Vehicles funneled around him, honking and yelling, but he did not move. And finally, he was out of sight.

Yara fell back on the seat, her head in her hands. "Nana, we have lost them both!" she whispered.

Just then she felt a touch. It was as soft as a feather on a bird's wing. With tears streaming down her face, Yara turned towards her little brother as he stroked her hair.

THE BEGINNING

AZRAQ REFUGEE CAMP, JORDAN

2016

"Yara?"

It was a man's voice. It sounded as though he was a good way off.

"Yara!"

He was closer this time. Yara opened her eyes and flinched. His face was above her, almost invisible in the dark, but she recognized him all the same. It was Mr. Matthew, the counselor.

"Yes?" she said. And then, "Hello."

Yara had no idea what time it was. She had fallen asleep squashed between two tin shelters, her head on her knees, her arms hugging her legs. She was so stiff.

"We have been turning the camp upside down looking for you." Mr. Matthew didn't sound angry, or even annoyed. He sounded relieved.

"I'm sorry." Yara tried to stand and thumped back down. Her legs were numb. It was almost dark out. Could she have slept all day? "Last night . . . the family that lives with us . . . there is a new baby, and twins . . . None of us slept. I . . ." Her voice trailed off.

Mr. Matthew knelt down beside her, his weight balanced on his toes. His eyes were blue like deep water and he had red hair. Not dark crimson like Shireen's, but red like a flame. He lived in Canada but he said his name came from Scotland. She wasn't sure how that worked. And yet, there was a look of a Syrian about him. It was something about the curve of his mouth and his bushy eyebrows, even if they were red.

He wore a blue and white vest with the initials "UN," United Nations, sewn on one side. He was their caseworker. It had taken Yara a month of living in the camp to figure out that a caseworker was someone who worked on their "file." It had taken another month to understand that a "committee" would eventually judge this "file" and decide if they were to be admitted to a new country, assuming anyone wanted them. Who would want a little boy who didn't talk, a grandmother who walked with a limp, and a girl who hadn't been to a real school in years?

Mr. Matthew stood and offered his hand to help her up.

Yara shook her head, murmuring, "No, thank you," and struggled to her feet on her own. "I came to your office early," she told him. It was dark out. What did "early" mean? "I came to your office this morning." She reached out to the wall to steady herself. The hunk of concrete that she had been holding against her chest fell with a pronounced thud.

Mr. Matthew looked at the concrete on the ground. "I see you came prepared." His lips twitched in what might have been the beginning of a grin. Then he looked towards the front gate. The pack of boys who loitered there thickened at night and buzzed around like flies. Was he surprised that she knew how to protect herself? He had to have figured that out by now.

Something else fell, too, the tobacco pouch. Mr. Matthew bent down and picked it up.

"Are you smoking a pipe now?" he asked with a small smile, knowing very well that the answer was no.

Yara felt her face grow hot. "It was my father's," she said, feeling suddenly shy. She wanted to snatch it out of his hand. She liked him well enough, if it was possible to like someone who held so much power over her, but the pouch was personal, precious.

He sniffed it. "Apple spiced tobacco?"

Yara nodded. "It was once full but it . . ." She shook her head. She had had enough of telling sad stories. "I think the smell is going away," she added.

He handed it back to her, and Yara quickly tucked it back in her pocket.

"Your grandmother is worried," he said gently. "She has been walking the camp for hours."

The guilt was instant, and she lurched forward. "I must—"

"No, come to my office. I'll send word to her," he said.

Silently they passed through the school area and out onto a path, both ignoring the boys at the gate.

Mr. Matthew climbed the three shaky wooden steps that led to his office and banged the door open. "I found her,

Lina," he announced in a voice that boomed through the two sparsely furnished rooms.

Lina, his assistant, looked up from her desk and smiled broadly. She wore jeans and a T-shirt, and her long black hair was held back with a big orange hair clip. "Yara, we were worried," she said, handing Mr. Matthew a large manila envelope.

"I'm sorry." Yara blushed again.

"Thank you, Lina. Call around and see if anyone has laid eyes on Yara's grandmother. If not, run over to their shelter and check. Tell her that Yara is fine and will be along in a half hour or so." He spoke kindly, but it was clear that he was telling, not asking.

Yara followed Mr. Matthew into his office. "Sit," he said. Yara sat. The edges of the plastic chair bit through her thin jeans and scratched the backs of her legs. She gazed around. The posters on Mr. Matthew's office walls were photographs of Syria's most famous buildings. The words "Save Syria's History" were written across the bottom of each one. Yara scowled. It would soon be too late for that. Syria was being bombed to bits. Her stomach made growly noises.

"Tea?" Mr. Matthew put down the file and plugged in the kettle. He didn't wait for an answer. "All I have to eat are cookies. My daughter sends them from Canada. A bit stale, I'm afraid." He shook six maple cookies out of a box and onto a plastic plate. "Please, help yourself."

Yara bit into a cookie and it turned to dust in her mouth. Mr. Matthew dropped tea bags into two mugs, poured boiling water, and mashed the bags with the back of a spoon. "You take creamer and sugar, correct?" He stood with a spoon poised over the horrible white powder that foreigners mixed into their tea and coffee.

"Just sugar." She covered her mouth with her hand to stop the cookie crumbs from flying out.

"Right, then." He perched his reading glasses on his nose, and began to read. The file was huge and filled with letters, documents, passports, identity papers, official forms, some with stamps and seals, and even handwritten letters.

"You arrived in the camp in March 2015? Correct?" Yara nodded. They were lucky. Two weeks later the border crossing had been captured by rebels and the Jordanians had closed it down.

Once in a while, Mr. Matthew made small *ahhh* and *hmm* sounds. It was when he went completely silent that Yara peeked over the rim of her mug.

"Good." He smacked the file with an open palm. "Now, these are the results of the medical exams." Mr. Matthew opened the envelope Lina had given him, sat back, and absentmindedly scratched his chin.

"Saad?" Yara bit down on her lip. "Does it say something about him not speaking?" She held her breath.

"He has selective mutism," he announced plainly, as if saying, "Blessings upon you" or "Please pass the sugar."

Cookie crumbs stopped halfway down Yara's throat. "Mutism?" she repeated, coughing. It sounded fatal, or at least horrible. She gulped the tea.

Mr. Matthew opened his laptop, typed in the words, and began to read aloud. "'It is a social anxiety disorder most commonly found in children and is characterized by a persistent failure to speak.'"

"What does that mean?" Her heart thumped against her ribs. *He can't be sick, he just can't be!*

"When he feels safe, he will speak, and not before." He closed the lid of his computer and went back to the file.

"I have tried to keep him safe," Yara whispered.

"You *have* kept him safe. Physically, he's very healthy. He has gained weight and is the right height for his age. Extraordinary, given what you two have been through." Mr. Matthew looked up.

"Is there nothing to be done? No medicine?" She leaned forward.

Mr. Matthew shook his head. "When things are settled he will talk. Don't think he isn't smart—his intelligence is above average, according to his teacher's comments. He clearly takes after his sister and grandmother." Mr. Matthew smiled. It was an unusual sight.

"The file . . . does it say anything about my grandmother? About her leg?" Yara asked.

Again Mr. Matthew thumbed through the pages. "Pins," he said.

"Pins?"

"She will need an operation on her leg. They will likely put in pins."

Yara thought of Roja and the straight pins sticking out

of her mouth as she sewed *abayas* and headscarves for the neighbors. Roja's beautiful brown eyes were suddenly right there, looking at her. She saw kindness in her eyes. It was as if Yara could reach out and touch her. As if . . .

"Yara, are you all right?" Mr. Matthew peered over the pages in his hand.

"Yes. Sorry." The mug shook in her hand. She set it down. Her legs and arms were trembling. Did he notice? She bit down on her lower lip.

"Don't worry about your grandmother," Mr. Matthew continued. "The operation is a simple one."

Simple? What was simple about an operation in a camp?

"There is also a comment here about you," he continued, his eyes skimming the pages.

"Me?" Yara tensed. She was fine! There was nothing wrong with her.

"You suffer from an anxiety disorder." His voice remained even and unconcerned.

Yara stopped chewing her lip and shook her head. She didn't have it, or them, or whatever it was.

"Do you sometimes have shortness of breath, numbness in your hands and feet, heart palpitations? Maybe you feel sick occasionally? You know, sick, like throwing up?"

Yara said nothing.

"In my experience, it is people who have held out the longest, who have fought the hardest—they are the ones who experience this sort of anxiety." His voice dropped and his chair squeaked as he leaned back. "You have come through a war, Yara. You have seen your parents die, your grandmother injured, friends abducted and become soldiers." Again, he looked down at the words on the page.

"Warriors," she whispered.

"Pardon?"

"My friends—they are warriors, not soldiers." Yara clamped down on her lip.

"Tell me the difference?" he asked quietly.

She looked up, surprised. Didn't he know? "Soldiers are paid. Warriors fight to the end, or . . ." Her stomach hurt, as if she'd been punched. "Or until they die."

"It would seem that you are describing yourself." Mr. Matthew's bushy red brows rose.

Yara, startled, looked at him with astonishment. Warrior? Her?

"You are courageous," said Mr. Matthew. "You told me yourself that your friend . . . what was her name?" He looked down at the file.

"Shireen," said Yara. Had he written everything down?

"Yes, you told me that Shireen said the same thing. I am inclined to agree with her."

Yara looked across the desk in disbelief. What was courageous about hiding out in a camp while her friends fought for their country and their lives?

"You never gave up on your grandmother. When Shireen was in danger you did everything in your power to protect her. When your family was dying in the desert you ran for help. It seems to me that you have been caring for them for a very long time."

There was a soft knock on the door.

"Come in," Mr. Matthew called out.

Lina poked her head around the door. "Your grandmother knows you are safe, Yara," she said with a smile.

Yara nodded, mumbled a thank-you, and felt her shoulders relax. The door closed.

Mr. Matthew studied Yara for a moment and then cleared his throat. "There is an unusual program in Canada, unique to the world, actually. The government has a refugee program, of course, but there is also a way for groups and individuals to sponsor families. Once applicants have cleared security—and as you have experienced, it is a long and difficult task—the sponsor raises money, finds apartments, organizes doctor's appointments, and provides all the necessities of life for one year."

Yara sat back, stunned. "I don't understand."

"Two churches in Kingston, Ontario, have accepted your application. Kingston is a small city, Ontario is a province in Canada." He spoke quietly. "Canada—it is a good fit." Mr. Matthew was all business.

"School?" she whispered.

"Naturally. And since it is Canada, you will have free medical care." He was matter-of-fact about it all. Yara was breathless.

"But there are others in the camp . . . many have waited many years . . ." Her words drifted.

"You have been fast-tracked. Your grandmother's leg needs attention. We will miss your grandmother at the school, though. She is one of the best teachers we have ever had," he added.

Yara wasn't listening. Her hands and feet turned cold. "I really am running away," she whispered. "I am leaving."

"You are not 'leaving,' you are 'going to.' The West is not the fairy-tale land you might imagine. Courage is what you will need now more than ever, a warrior's courage."

Yara bolted forward, startled. "I must fight? There are guns?"

Mr. Matthew looked up. "No, Yara. But it will be hard in other ways. You speak English and French, thanks to your grandmother. And Saad certainly understands English, at least. That is very helpful. But there are still people who will challenge you. There are unkind people in every country."

"No war?" asked Yara.

"No war," said Mr. Matthew.

He went back to reading the giant file. Yara studied his face. Something might still go wrong.

"There is nothing here that would prevent your applications from going forward," he announced. Yara felt a small jolt, like a rush of blood to her head. She pulled in a deep breath as he carried on. "Unless there is something else you want to tell me. You know the rules, you must be completely honest."

There it was. Right now, right here. She could tell the truth. She had picked up a gun and shot a man. She had killed a man who had abducted Ali, who would likely have killed him. Maybe killing was an act of war, but lying about it was a betrayal of her promise to her father.

"I . . ." she began.

There were secrets in every Syrian home. Nana had said that. Saad needed to be in a safe place or he might never talk again. Nana needed an operation. They couldn't stay here forever. *Resistance is silence.*

"Nothing." She looked down and bit her lip. This would be her forever secret.

"You look pale. Do you feel all right?" He studied her from across the desk. If only he would just get this over with!

Mr. Matthew reached into a tiny fridge and pulled out a bottle of orange juice. "Drink this." He pushed it across the desk. "It is not uncommon for refugees to wonder if they really want to leave." His voice was calm, even gentle.

"I want to go to Canada," she lied.

"As hard as this life is, it is the one you know," he continued, as if she hadn't said a word. "You feel guilty."

She bit down hard on her lip and tasted blood.

"Listen carefully." He passed her a box of tissues. "The third-deadliest earthquake in history happened in Aleppo in 1138. The city was almost demolished." Leaning across his desk, he looked into Yara's eyes. "Aleppo has been destroyed, conquered, and rebuilt hundreds of times. Its history begins at the beginning of time and will end at the end of time. The choices of one young girl, a little boy, and a grandmother will not change the course of this war or the destiny of this country." Mr. Matthew shuffled the papers in the file. "Go to Canada and build your life."

A telephone rang in the outside office. Lina, his assistant, answered it.

"How do you know about my country's history?" Yara stood slowly.

"My grandmother was Syrian."

"Shireen, my friend . . . she said that if we left, we would never return."

"I am here," he said with a shrug. "Perhaps your grandchildren will return, too." He closed the brown file and dropped it in a wire basket on the edge of his desk.

Her grandchildren? She almost laughed.

Lina stood at the door. "There is a problem. The director has asked you to come."

Mr. Matthew turned to Yara. "I have to go, but come back tomorrow. We have forms to fill out." And with that he charged out of the office.

Yara left the UN office, too, and stood outside, looking up into a dark sky. She was so tired, even though she'd slept the day away.

"Yara! YARA!"

She turned. Nana was running towards her . . . running! Saad was right behind her.

"Oh, Nana!" Yara reached out and Nana fell into her arms.

"Where were you? We thought . . . I thought . . . It isn't like you to . . ." Nana shuddered, and covered her eyes with her hands. "The boys at the gate, the men who buy brides . . ."

"Nana, I'm sorry. I just fell asleep. I am so sorry. Come, sit." Yara half carried, half dragged her grandmother over to a bench and sat beside her. Nana gave her a weak smile and wiped away streams of tears. "Come, Saad." Yara pulled her brother in close. He was not so little anymore.

"I have news, Nana. It's for you, too, Saad." She picked up his hand and held it tight. "There is a country that wants us." The two stared at Yara. "Canada," she whispered. "Nana, Canada wants us." Even in the moonlight she could see astonishment on her grandmother's face. And other things, too. Fear? Regret? Hesitation?

"Nana?"

Nana seemed far, far away.

"Nana, Uncle Sami would want us to go."

"Yes, I know. You and your brother will have a future," she said softly.

They sat for a while. In the distance there were sounds of laughter, cheers, and the thud of a foot against a soccer ball. A movie played in the community center. Someone had turned on a radio.

"Moon," whispered Saad.

Yara and Nana sat very, very still.

Saad lifted his arm and pointed up into the dark sky. "Moon," he said, a bit louder this time. Nana took in a breath. Yara squeezed her grandmother's hand.

Yara followed her brother's gaze. "That's the North Star," she said. "Can you say it? North Star?" Yara spoke very, very quietly.

"North Star," Saad repeated.

Yara swallowed hard. He had the voice of a boy, not a baby. She could hear Nana's prayers spoken softly into the night. The moon had begun its journey across the sky.

"Come." Nana stood and took Saad's hand. Yara stood up, too, her heart as steady as a drumbeat, her breath even, her hands and feet warm.

"Shireen, I will return," she whispered into the night. "Ali, look up. Look at the star. I will find you. Whatever it takes, I will find you."

AUTHOR'S NOTE

Jamal Saeed

Dear Reader,

The story you have just read is a work of fiction, but the civil war taking place in Syria is very real. I should know.

I was born in Syria, in the beautiful city of Latakia (al-Lādhiqīyah), an ancient city where some of the earliest alphabetic writings were found. Just as Damascus is known as a city enlivened by restaurants, markets, and stores, Latakia is known for its beautiful beaches and its nightlife. Yet so many other cities, including Aleppo, are bombed into oblivion. Syrians suffer the poverty that comes with war, but how can my country be both at war and dancing the night away? How can some people eat their fill while others starve?

The current president, Bashar al-Assad, son of President Hafez al-Assad, is a ruthless man whose ambition knows no bounds. Those who support him, who turn a blind eye to his brutality, will dance at night and swim in the crystal blue sea in the day. The rest will feel his iron grip, his determined ambition to rule and to preserve his father's legacy, enacted with relentless violence. In the end, Syria is a victim of the suppression.

When I was sixteen years old, I became a social activist. My friends and I met a few times a week and discussed wonderous things, including freedom of expression, freedom of the press, women's rights, and parliamentary government. We thought we could change the world. We wrote down our hopes and dreams, printed our small words on flyers, and tucked them in mailboxes, in books, anywhere we could. We called for freedom and the right to vote. In Syria, such activity was, and still is, illegal.

When I was seventeen, the government's secret police (called Mukhabarat) came to my family home to arrest me. By luck, I wasn't there. My mother fought them, but still, they searched our home. They returned again and again, and since they could not find me, they took my younger brother, Kamal. Only after the mayor of our village intervened was he released.

Over the next two and a half years, I hid from the Mukhabarat. I stayed in the homes of friends and sometimes lived on the street. I changed my name, grew a mustache and wore glasses to disguise myself, and took whatever odd jobs I could find. When at last I was caught, I was sent to prison—actually, several prisons—for more than ten years.

Each prison has its own rules. The worst was Tadmor Prison: there, if we lifted our heads, if we met the eyes of another, even a fellow prisoner, we would be beaten. But there is more to being tortured than just physical pain. I was told repeatedly, for weeks, months, and years, that I was useless, that the world did not need me, that I was a dog. Sitting in a cell, always hungry, always dirty, seldom seeing the sun, I thought my life was over. My only wish was that I would die quickly.

Guilt is another form of torture. During my imprisonment, my family was persecuted. My brothers and sisters were harassed and couldn't find employment after they graduated. Most jobs in Syria are under government control.

We were tortured with constant hunger. Most of the food we were allowed was brought by the families of political prisoners on the rare occasions they were allowed to visit. That food was given to an elected committee of three prisoners to distribute so that all was shared equally and even prisoners with no family had a chance to eat.

Loneliness is another form of torture. I did not see my family for two years. I was still not much more than a boy and I missed my family desperately. Eventually, during my six years at Tadmor Prison, I was allowed one visit every three months.

I was never charged with a crime. I had no sentence. So I had no idea when or if I would ever be released.

Finally, I was sent to Sednaya Military Prison near Damascus, where my family was allowed to visit me every month. Amnesty International estimates that between 5,000 and 13,000 people were later executed there, under the rule of Bashar al-Assad.

One day, a guard said, "Get your things." What things? What did I own? I assumed that I was to be transferred again. It was 1991. It turned out that there had been an election, but with only one candidate, Hafez al-Assad, Bashar al-Assad's father. As a show of good faith, some prisoners were to be released. I was one. My family was there waiting for me.

I enrolled at Damascus University and found a job in a publishing house. There I met Rufaida al-Khabbaz, the beautiful poet who would become my wife and the mother of our two sons. I published a short story collection and a few articles, resulting in threats from the Mukhabarat, which denounced my short stories as "poisons." I was arrested twice more because of my writings and my activism. But I did not give up my dreams for my country. How could I when my young friends were suffering, when so many were murdered?

Then came the Arab Spring, when the citizens of Arab countries rose up in protest against their oppressive governments. It began on December 17, 2010, in Tunisia, when a desperate young man named Mohamed Bouazizi set himself on fire in a marketplace. The demand for justice and freedom from tyranny moved like a wave flooding Egypt, Libya, Yemen—and Syria. The peaceful activists who struggled to build the state law and the modern democratic regime were considered traitors by al-Assad regime and atheists by the fanatic militias. Both sides justified destroying the activists." I joined the peaceful activists who were fighting to build the state of law, modernity, democracy, and social justice. The Assad regime considered us traitors, while the fanatic militias considered us atheists. Both groups justified trying to destroy us. The Mukhabarat began phoning our home, threatening whoever answered. My wife and sons were followed by armed men. I had to do something.

ICORN (the International Cities of Refuge Network) helps writers, journalists, and artists at risk of persecution to find a new home—to find safety. I sent them an email asking for their help. I was desperate.

A friend in Dubai helped us get a tourist visa. To escape, we paid a great deal of money to soldiers at twelve checkpoints. I was terrified of what might happen to my wife and sons on that journey; I knew the worst that could happen.

Life in Dubai was difficult. Education for my sons was expensive, and at any moment I could lose what little work I could find. Where would we go? What would happen to us? The ground under my feet felt slippery.

Two years later an email arrived saying that The Kingston Writers' Refugee Committee would sponsor a Syrian writer. Would we like to move to Kingston, Ontario, Canada?

Miracles happen.

We landed at Toronto Pearson International Airport on a snowy night, December 28, 2016. When asked by my family back in Syria what it was like in Canada, I said, "The country is cold, but the people are warm."

In 2018, Canadian writer Sharon McKay asked me if I would like to work with her on a book that would help students understand the kind of life many Syrian children and teens faced before coming to the West. I agreed immediately.

This book is fiction, but in all battles, revolutions, and wars, people experience shattering loss. The fear that Yara experiences is real, as is the longing for safety and the need to connect with family and friends. This fear does not go away the moment a child or teenager arrives in a place of safety. Most war refugees have suffered deeply. The bombs, the threats, the anxiety take a long time to diminish—sometimes a lifetime. To survive, to carry on, is in itself an act of bravery.

I'm still dreaming of a world where there is no war, repression, poverty, or other evils. I believe that the world can be a good homeland for all people.

Blessings upon you all,

—Jamal

ACKNOWLEDGMENTS

I remember my great teacher in narrating: Najeeba Shabow, my mother.

I remember, too, how Rufaida, Ghamr, and Taim shared with me the horrible days in the Qudsaya-Damascus countryside.

Thanks to the International Cities of Refuge Network (ICORN), to PEN Canada, and to the Kingston Writers' Refugee Committee, who helped me to come to Kingston, Ontario.

Deep thanks to Ray Argyle, who helped us start up in Canada. Also to Wayne Myles, Lory Kaufman, Barbara Bell, Larry Scanlan, Joan Hughes, Deborah Windsor, Pamela Paterson, Tarek Hussein.

Thanks to Hussam Shiloki.

Many thanks to Barbara Berson and Catherine Marjoribanks, and to Rick Wilks and the staff at Annick Press, and to artist Nahid Kazemi.

What is to be said to my partner in writing this book, Sharon McKay? She was patient, warm, and very kind during the whole process. She reminds me of mothers and sisters in my faraway Syria, so thanking is not enough.

—Jamal Saeed

My thanks go to—David MacLeod, always. My sons, Joe and Sam MacLeod, who teach me every day.

Editors Barbara Berson and Catherine Marjoribanks, and Rick Wilks and the staff at Annick Press.

Artist Nahid Kazemi, such a talent. We are grateful.

Fares Albonai and Ossaima Sujaa, new Canadians.

Kinda and Fahd Zanadine.

And special thanks to The Gananoque Refugee Settlement Group, Ontario, Canda.

My thanks to the NGOs in Jordan who gave me their time: ARDD–Legal Aid, and Lana Ghawi Zananiri; Queen Rania Teacher Academy, and Taraf Ghanem; Akel Biltaji, Mayor of Amman, who paved the way; the We Love Reading initiative, and Dr. Rana Dajani; Caritas, and Lana Smobar; Discover Jordan, and Laura Rihani along with our driver, Rafat Haddad; Owais Omari with Helping Refugees in Jordan.

To Dr. Susan Hartley, traveler, organizer, and dear friend.

To my amazing, kind, and loving family: Dot and Gus, Val and Bryan, Sam and Mady, Joe and Olivia, Laurel and John, Kai, Lucy, Claire, Ann, Kelly, Shelley, Linda, Patty, Jill—I am blessed.

And most of all, to my writing partner Jamal Saeed and his beautiful wife, Rufaida. What a pleasure! I hope we know each other forever.

—Sharon E. McKay